Whispers of Marriage

G M Terry

Part One

Chapter One

In the first rays of a new dawning day, The Three Ladies of the Vale *look benignly over their domain.*

Having written the opening line to her letter, Anna put down her quill, and gazed out of the window. The three tall spires of Lichfield Cathedral were in her full view as they reached up into the first weak yellow rays of the morning sun. She was nine years old when this house became her home. Since then she had always thought of the spires as three ladies.

It was cold, even though the fire basket was blazing in the grate. It had been for several hours, but her own blue drawing room was large, and it took many hours to warm on a February morning. She pulled her shawl tighter around her shoulders. Her fingers were cold from the grip of the quill. From a desk drawer, she took out her little ivory knife and sharpened the shaft to relieve the numbness in her fingers.

The tallow candle on the desk gave an unpleasant odour. The candle tax made sure she didn't use the expensive, fragrant beeswax light for her early morning writing.

The desk was set in the window with the view over Cathedral Close. She loved the early mornings. There was no one to disturb her. She could think and write. Such precious time was her enjoyment. Later, the business and bustle of the household would absorb her, but for now it was her own thoughts.

She stayed watching the scene from the window as the ornate red brickwork of the cathedral gradually changed hue with the increasing light. Her mind drifted and she wondered what the new day would bring for the three young ladies in the house.

She was the oldest and had recently reached her twenty-first birthday. Then there was Sarah, her younger sister by two years, who was such a delight. The youngest was her parent's ward, Honora, aged fourteen. It was so wonderful that she was part of the family. Her parents treated her as a daughter. To Anna and Sarah, she was a beloved sister.

She looked at the letter she was writing. Her mind had drifted and so the ink was hard on the quill. Emma wouldn't mind waiting for the letter.

Anna felt it was going to be an important day in her life. She sighed at little at the thought of what might happen. Her father, Thomas Seward, a Canon Vicar in the cathedral, had been visiting many of the noble families in the town. He wasn't generally a social visitor, which meant that he had a specific purpose in mind for his trips. Anna feared it was to arrange her betrothal. It was a very solemn thought. Marriage would be good, but what of a loveless marriage? She took a deep breath as she knew of many young women, close to her own age, who were forced into a union. Some were very sad, but many accepted it as their fate and did not complain. Could Anna accept such a fate? She really did not know.

Her mind had been drifting for a while now. She had intended writing a little poetry this morning, but marriage had gripped her thoughts. Everyone told her that she was a sensible and practical young woman. It wasn't the time to drown herself in sorrow, so she would finish her letter to Emma. She would share some of her misgivings. Emma was always a good person to write to.

When Anna was a young girl she had learned that many women secretly kept a daily journal, and had intended to do the same. But her father's words kept ringing in her ears, 'No daughter of mine shall keep a journal. They are the work of the devil!'

She returned her concentration to her letter and she wrote at length about the desire to avoid an unsuitable marriage. Feeling a little better as she finished the letter, she signed the last piece of writing paper.

Anna made sure the ink was dry, by sprinkling pounce sand on it. She re-gathered the sand and tipped it back into the little ornate dish kept at the side of the desk. She carefully picked up the letter and walked across the room to the drawer cabinet, where she kept paper and writing materials. She bent down, opened the very bottom drawer in the corner, and took out a thick pile of letters. She untied the blue ribbon that bound them.

On the top of the pile, she read the letter she had written last week to Emma. There had been no mention of a looming marriage then. The letter was happy and joyous. She carefully placed the letter that she had just written on top of the pile, re-tied the ribbon, and put them all back into the same drawer. They were letters that would never be posted. With a small smile to herself, she went towards her dressing room to get ready for the day.

***

As they walked through the cathedral's nave Abigail whispered in the quietest possible voice, 'Have you heard the news?'

'No,' replied Anna equally quietly.

'The regiment is back in town, they arrived last night,' responded Abigail.

'So Lichfield today will be alive with the red of army uniforms,' answered Anna, and a large smile crossed her face, but her voice reduced to a whisper as she spoke into Abigail's ear, 'I do so much like a soldier!'

'We have already told out fathers that we are walking into town after the service!' replied Abigail. Both of the young ladies gave small and polite giggles to themselves. They chatted quietly about the likelihood of accidentally meeting the soldiers, during their walk.

Abigail, Anna's friend was slim and tall. Her hazel eyes matched her brown hair, which was set high and well powdered. She wore a dark red dress and a pearl necklace. Anna was wearing a long crimson full-following dress. Her long auburn hair, was immaculately presented, and flowed over her shoulders. Her round, well proportioned face showed a healthy glow.

The midday service had just finished in the Lady Chapel of the cathedral, which they left by main doors onto an open apron of ground. The area was enclosed by the majestic houses of Cathedral Close. The sun shone brightly in a clear blue sky, but the chill wind that blew across Stowe Pool, was still vigorous. Snow showers were expected before the end of the day. Anna pulled her bonnet tight and drew her cloak closely around her.

As they were both fine young ladies of the community, they greeted people they knew in a civil and respectful manner. The anticipation on their faces was difficult to suppress for long. Finally, they engaged each other's arm and walked slowly past

Minster Pool, along Dam Street, towards Lichfield Town Centre.

'The street is busy today,' remarked Anna as they walked slowly through the crowds.

'It is now a fine spring day, and the people of Lichfield do like to greet the regiment on their return,' replied Anna.

Anna gave her friend's arm a little tug and a glance was all that was needed. The scarlet uniforms could be seen in the distance near the market. Anna said, 'As we have a visit to make in Market Street, shall we go through the market?'

Abigail replied immediately, 'It would be the quickest way.'

Their eyes darted around. The increase in the number of uniforms that they could see in the distance quickened their pace slightly, but they remained dignified and controlled. The two young ladies turned into Market Square. It was busy and bustling from the day's trading. Anna glanced up at the town's parish church, St Mary's, that dominated the south side of the market, but her interest did not lie in ecclesiastical matters.

Anna started a little as she realised that two officers, in uniform, were standing in their path. They both bowed to the two ladies. Anna gave a small nod, but showed no enthusiasm for the meeting as they had not been introduced.

Then one of the officers said, 'Miss Levitt. Captain Robertson at your service. If I might be permitted to address you in the street as we have been formally introduced when I met your father.'

Abigail replied, 'Yes, of course, Captain.'

'May I introduce my regimental colleague, Captain Temple.' Abigail responded with a nod and then said, 'This is my lifelong friend, Miss Anna Seward.' With the introductions complete Captain Temple said, 'May we walk with you to your destination?'

They immediately agreed and the foursome set their direction along Market Street. The eagerness of the slightly hurried walking before, had now gone. They were content to stroll slowly with the officers of the regiment. It gave Anna a chance to have a good view of Captain Temple, who was walking at her side. He was a tall, slim, able-bodied man, with short blonde hair that could only just be seen under his regimental cap. His eyes were blue and alert, his complexion robust.

He started the conversation by saying, 'I am familiar with the name of Seward. My uncle, who lives in Lichfield, has talked of a man of letters, Thomas Seward, who is a Canon at the cathedral.'

Anna smiled graciously, 'I am proud to say he is my father.'

'Then I hope I may meet him some day soon. Perhaps I might be able to ask Mr Levitt to introduce me.'

'I am sure my father would be proud to invite a member of the local regiment to his house.' They walked a little further and then Anna asked, 'May I ask whether your regiment will be in Lichfield for long.'

'I know nothing for certain, although there are rumours that we will be deployed in the King's name in London fairly soon. Although we do expect to return to our barracks on a regular basis.'

'I have never been to London,' said Anna as the conversation lulled.

Captain Temple replied, 'It is a fine city with many attractions for ladies. It would be my delight to show you some of the more famous aspects of our capital city when you visit.'

'Thank you, Captain, I shall remember that.'

As they had now reached their destination, the officers left them. Anna entered a young curate's house with a present for his wife. It was a knitted bonnet for her new born child.

With their visit complete Anna and Abigail decided to return to Cathedral Close. They had cleared the crowds and were walking along the street to Minster Pool. They could not be overhead as there was no one near them.

Abigail said, 'Captain Temple took a liking to you, as soon as he saw you.'

'He looks a very fine officer to me,' replied Anna with a smile. She then glanced at her friend, 'You seemed to like Captain Robertson.'

Abigail giggled, 'It's the first time I've met him, but he has already promised to call at the house.'

'What will your father say?'

'He always asks me to tell him when a young man might call

and whether I want to see him again. He passes the message on. So I shall tell him Captain Robertson will call, and he will invite him to an evening or other social event.'

'What happens if there is not one planned.'

Abigail laughed, 'He decides, then and there, that we shall have one.'

Anna said with a sigh, 'I wish my father was like that. He tells anyone who calls, that I am not available.'

'Oh! Poor Anna, it must be so difficult for you.'

They walked in silence for a little while, as Anna thought about Captain Temple. Finally Anna said, 'Is you father giving you any hint about marriage?'

'No, all that he has said to me, is that I'm still a young lady and there is no rush to be married.'

'I wish my father would think the same, but he seems intent on finding me a husband.'

'Perhaps nothing will happen quickly.'

Anna was thoughtful for a moment, 'Will you help me?'

'Yes, of course, Anna. What do you want me to do? Find you a husband?' and she laughed.

'Almost!' came Anna's reply. 'Can you get your father to arrange a meeting and introduce the Captain to my father?'

'I see! I see! You are going to try to find a husband before your father does.'

'Well, it is better than letting my father choose, and Captain Temple is very good looking.'

'Do you think it will work?'

'It has a good chance, because father respects Mr Levitt. He wouldn't want to offend him by dismissing an introduction.'

Abigail replied, 'I'll speak to him this evening. He said that he is meeting your father tomorrow about some business.'

Anna was a little more cheerful as they walked around the edge of Minster Pool, to return home. Mr Levitt had left his coach for Abigail. She took her leave of Anna with the promise to do her best with Captain Temple's introduction.

'There you are at last,' said her father as she walked into the hall.

'Good afternoon, father,' Anna replied. She then made a small curtsey and smiled at him, but did not take a great deal of notice of his unusual impatience.

'Come into the drawing room, I need to talk to you,' he said as he led the way. Canon Thomas Seward was a tall, upright man, approaching his mid-fifties, dressed entirely in black, with a small wig on his crown.

'Yes father,' and she followed him into the main drawing room.

'Sit down, sit down!'

She sat on the chaise longue. On the small side table there was a bag that contained her current embroidery. Next to it was a copy of Alexander Pope's, *'Eloisa and Abelard.'* She took up her embroidery bag, and swiftly gathered its contents onto her lap.

'Are you fiddling with that?'

'No, father. You requested that I spend more time on needlework, rather than reading. I can listen to you as I get started.'

'You are at the age...'

Anna said, 'Father, I am twenty-one as you know.'

'Don't interrupt!' he snapped. Anna didn't reply, but looked serious and focused her eyes on her work. 'You are a young woman with a good dowry, as you know.'

'Yes, father.'

'And it is time to find a suitable husband for you.' Anna put down her needlework and looked directly at her father. He had now turned his gaze to the light afternoon snow that was falling outside the window. She waited. His head spun round so that he could see her, 'Why do you not answer me?'

Anna engaged his eyes and replied, 'I'm sorry father, I did not realise you had asked me a question.'

'Pshaw! You always try to be too clever with words.'

Anna continued to catch her father's eyes, 'You speak of marriage, father.'

'Yes, we need to find a suitable husband for you. As you are my eldest daughter, it is right and proper that you are the first to find a husband.'

'Yes, father. Am I allowed an opinion on the matter?'

He looked uncomfortable, but turned to look at the fire. With an intensity that made Anna jump he shouted, 'William!' There was an instant response as the door of the drawing room opened. He snapped, 'The fire needs seeing to.' Anna smiled a little to herself at the distraction to their conversation.

'Yes, sir.' The servant took two logs from the basket at the side of the fireplace and placed them in the centre of the roaring fire. The servant carefully watched his master, who flicked out his hand at him.

'Thank you, sir,' he said as he bowed and withdrew.

'It is important that we make a good match for you. I would want a good family, preferably from our own Lichfield, that can hold its head high, both in the town and in the cathedral.'

'Yes, father that is very important.'

'I'm glad we agree.'

'On very many points, I am sure we totally agree.'

'What do you mean by that?'

'Father, I mean exactly what I say.'

He glared at her, 'Do you think there might be points where you would disagree with my judgement?'

'No father, definitely not.'

'Then what do you mean? You really are the most obtuse girl at times.'

'Do you expect to meet with a suitable family and conclude my marriage with the head of the house.'

'Yes, of course,' he replied.

'Father, the spring in Lichfield is know for its number of balls and other gatherings.'

'Yes, I know,' he replied irritably. 'What has that got to do with the matter in which I am instructing you.'

'What will happen if...'

'Theoretical nonsense Anna! I'm not interested in a young woman's halcyon thoughts.'

'It is possible that at one of these balls, I could meet a man.'

'Anna!' he raised his voice a little.

'The man would have to be from a prestigious family.'

'If they were from Lichfield, I would know them.'

'Yes, father, you would. But what if they were further away in the county. Not too far. Might I suggest Ashbourne.'

'Do you know a family from Ashbourne?'

'No, father.'

'Then stop all this ridiculous conjecturing. You will marry who I determine.'

'Yes, father.' At that point a small knot appeared in Anna's embroidery. She looked down with ardent concentration. Her father stormed out and slammed the door.

Anna listened intently. She heard the second door slam and breathed a sigh of relief. He had gone to his study. That often meant he would not come out for hours. A smile crossed her face, at least he hadn't found a man for her, yet! She would write to Emma to tell her that good news, and all about Captain Temple.

Anna was just tidying her needlework, when the door burst open and in rushed her sister, Sarah, who was with young Honora.

'Well! Well!' Sarah said in excitement. 'Has father told you who you are going to marry?'

'This is so exciting!' added Honora.

Anna laughed because she so much enjoyed their enthusiasm. 'No. Father has only said that he is finding a husband for me.'

'I hope he is handsome,' said Honora.

Anna replied, 'Honora to you, every man has to be handsome or you do not like them. There are many men, who would make excellent husbands, but are not necessarily good looking.'

Honora said indignantly, 'I wouldn't marry anyone who wasn't handsome.'

Sarah said, 'I do hope he finds you a husband soon.'

'Do you want me to leave the house?' said Anna.

'No, of course not, my darling sister. If father finds someone for you, then I will be next. I dream of being married.' Her eyes glazed and she gave a big sigh.

Anna smiled with affection at her sister. Sarah had a much slighter frame than Anna. She wore a dark blue dress and her brown hair was lifted into a small bun, which she had lightly powdered. The beauty with her blue eyes shone in a smooth almost perfect face, but it lacked the healthy complexion of her sister.

Honora's early burst of enthusiasm had now subsided as she sat back in one of the chairs. In complexion and size she could have been Sarah's sister, as they looked so much like each other, despite an age barrier of six or so years. The sharp clear eyes missed nothing that went on around her.

Anna could see both of them were now day dreaming with slightly glazed looks on their faces. Sarah would be thinking about being married, whilst Honora's mind would be drifting in general about handsome men.

Anna said in a quiet voice, 'I've a secret and it's about a man.' The glazed looks had suddenly gone. Both rushed across the room and sat on either side of Anna. They tucked in close to her. 'But can I trust you to keep a secret?'

Both nodded vigorously, but Anna said, 'No one must know.'

There were two eager faces watching her and waiting. Anna teased Honora, 'Did I hear a noise by the door?'

All three listened, but the room was silent. Anna said in a whisper, 'Go and check that William is not listening at the door.'

Honora scampered to the door opened it and peered into the hall. She closed it and rushed back, 'No one there.'

'Very well,' whispered Anna, 'when I was out today, with Abigail, we met two men.'

'Were they handsome?' said Honora in a little hissy whisper.

'Very handsome indeed. They looked perfect officers in their scarlet uniforms.'

'Ooo! They were soldiers as well,' said Sarah quietly, 'how wonderful!'

'What were their names,' asked Honora, looking around to make sure no one was listening.

'Captain Robertson and Captain Temple,' replied Anna.

'Which one is yours?' asked Honora.

'Well, it was Captain Temple, who walked alongside me. Captain Robertson walked with Abigail.'

Sarah sighed, 'Does father know?'

'I'm hoping both of the captains will be introduced by Mr

Levitt. Father will then invite them here, so as not to be impolite to the Levitt family.'

'When are they coming?'

'Shhh! Honora, that's why it's a secret at the moment. I want Mr Levitt to introduce them first.'

'Come on,' said Sarah to Honora, 'let's go up to my bedroom. We can then imagine what Captain Temple is going to look like.'

Anna breathed a sigh of relief. At least there was no man lined up today. Captain Temple she had only met once so there wasn't much hope, but he was going to be better than some aged old man, who had lost his second wife and still wanted an heir.

She was sullen. Even getting to the next meeting with Captain Temple would be difficult. Her father would put a stop to it as soon as he knew. It was time to pack up her needlework, and enquire whether her mother needed any help. The mundane duties of the household were coming to the fore, because she had been busy all day. Anna accepted that she would have to do her duties for the rest of the day and left the drawing room.

William, the butler, was answering the front door and in stepped Mr Levitt. Should she say anything? No course not, because as soon as her father heard Mr Levitt's loud voice, he would come out of his study.

Anna smiled and curtsied. He was a big man, with a large waist, but always had an avuncular smile for Anna. He was dressed in a brown hacking jacket and wore his riding boots. As always he greeted Anna fondly.

'My dear Anna, I heard the weather kept fine for your visit to deliver the baby clothes for the curate.'

'It did, sir,' she replied as she curtsied.

With the hearing of Mr Levitt's voice, her father opened his study door and stepped into the hall. He was a meticulously polite man, so would never consider interrupting his guest, who was speaking.

'I left my coach for Abigail to return.' He glanced at the Canon, and acknowledged him with a nod. 'I am afraid I wasn't as lucky as you to have a walk around Lichfield, I settled down to business.' Anna glanced at her father, who nodded his approval of such a statement. 'But there was one matter, about turnpikes, that I thought I would like to consult with the Canon. So I got into my carriage and came straight back, hoping he would have time to see me.'

'Of course,' said the Canon, 'come into my study.' He turned to lead the way into his room. Mr Levitt followed, but as he went past Anna, he winked and then whispered, 'A Captain!' He immediately changed to a loud voice and said, 'This new turnpike from Sheffield looks very interesting.' He followed the Canon into his study.

Anna went to help her mother with a smile on her face.

Chapter Two

'Amen,' replied the congregation.

Canon Seward, gave the few people sitting before him in the Lady Chapel of the cathedral a perfunctory nod, and retired to the Chapter House, at the side of the nave, to remove his vestments.

There was a deep and serious frown on his face, as he took large strides down the nave to the main doors. His solid boots echoing on the flagstones of the floor. As he left the cathedral his eyes lifted to the sky. The cold winds earlier in the month, which were accompanied by flutterings of snow, had been replaced by a gently warming breeze that was bringing forth the first buds of spring. But the improved weather did nothing to alter his stern face.

He crossed the apron of grass in front of the building and entered a gate between two of the houses opposite. As he walked through the garden, the smell of the herbs caught his nose. It did not distract his intention from the door of the house to which he was going.

Before he could rap on the door, it was opened by a servant, who showed him directly into the drawing room. He then heard the sound of a large man descending the wooden staircase. Soon, the door opened and the man filled the door frame. He stuttered, 'Can.. Can.. Canon Seward. And to what do I owe this pleasure.'

'My wife, Elizabeth, has asked me to call on you, Dr Darwin. She is more concerned than usual about the health of my daughter Sarah, who has developed a persistent cough.' Dr Darwin looked carefully at the Canon. Normally he would have sent a servant. The doctor had no doubt that he was worried about the condition of his daughter.

The doctor was a large corpulent man who, for a gentleman, was careless in his dress. His wig was in need of continual adjustment and, on this day, his waistcoat had been buttoned incorrectly. His pocked marked face, and a lack of teeth on one side, gave him a slightly disproportionate look, which his frequent smiles made worse. He looked much older than his thirty-three years.

'I shall come immediately. I'll collect my bag and join you in the hall.' Canon Seward tapped his foot with impatience as soon as he had stepped into the hall. Dr Darwin did not delay and was soon with him. They left the house and began the short walk, which was the length of Cathedral Close.

'I have not seen you in God's house for many a day, doctor.'

This brought a wry smile from the doctor, but he replied, 'I am finding that an increasing number of people from Lichfield, and the surrounding areas, require my attention.'

'You should not neglect the Lord.'

'It is never my intention to fail in that respect. I see my work, as an instrument of the Almighty's benevolence. So I spend my time helping his flock, so that they may return to church to listen to your sermons.'

The doctor gave a gentle smile to the 'Umpph!' he had received as a reply. The Doctor and the Canon had been neighbours for a long time and knew each other well. The doctor looked straight ahead down the close and asked, 'Have you found a suitor for your daughter Anna?'

The Canon ignored the question and said, 'I believe that Anna is getting too bookish.'

'She is a charming young woman who, thanks to your diligent upbringing of her, is well educated. I would not see that as a barrier to a prestigious marriage.'

'Maybe. Maybe not. But at present there is no one to whom I could present my eldest daughter.'

The doctor replied, 'I have heard that the regiment, after a few short weeks away, have returned to their barracks.'

The Canon said, 'I am saddened by the realisation that a scarlet uniform turns the head and catches the eye of too many young ladies.'

'There are fine gentlemen serving in the regiment.'

'Some are and some aren't,' replied the Canon as he took large strides towards the front steps of his house.

The doctor stopped and said, 'Canon Seward.' This caused him to break his stride and turn to face the doctor, 'As a potential husband for Anna, have you considered one of the merchant families? Many are now well respected in our community, and it is said that some are richer than traditional landowners.'

The frown on the Canon's face deepened. 'I suspect that, as usual, Doctor, you are trying to rile me. But as you know I take a business interest in modern forms such as turnpikes and canals, which means I deal with many of the merchants. It may surprise you to learn that I have met several families of whom I approve. Unfortunately they have no heirs suitable for Anna.' With that he turned and entered his house. The doctor chuckled a little and followed the Canon.

They were greeted immediately by Mrs Seward, 'Doctor so good of you to come. My poor Sarah has this very nasty cough. Will you need to bleed her?'

'Good morning, Mrs Seward. No amount of us talking in this hallway is going to assist your daughter, Sarah. If you take me to her, then I shall be able to give you a diagnosis of her condition.' The Canon took the opportunity to bid the doctor good morning and he retired to his study.

***

Anna scrambled to put her book away as the door of her drawing room opened. She thought it was likely to be her father, who had come to see her about another one of his visits to local families.

Her look of concern was quickly replaced by a smile as she saw that it was the doctor. She relaxed her hold on the book and placed it open on the table in front of her. She rose to her feet and curtsied.

'Good day, Anna.'

'Good morrow, Doctor.'

'What are you reading?'

'Richardson's *Clarissa*.'

The doctor face broke into gentle laughter, which gave way to an uncontrollable stutter. He took sometime to gather himself. Anna had seen him stutter badly before, and on the first occasion it had happened, it caused her distress. When she came to know the doctor on a more regular basis, she could see that it caused him no anxiety. She just waited patiently for it to pass.

Finally he said, 'I thought you only read English classics,

with a preference for poetry. Is not a novel a little common place for you?'

'I certainly do not like that form of writing in general, but there are certain aspects of Richardson's writing, which I admire.'

Anna indicated the chair on the opposite side of the fireplace to where she was sitting. The doctor carefully placed his bag at its side, warmed his hands at the fire, and then took his seat.

She waited for him to settle and, as he showed no signs of going to start the conversation, she said, 'I know you are a very busy man doctor...'

The doctor laughed, 'I am only teasing you. Your poem was very good. A little heavy in places, but overall I was very impressed.'

Anna smiled at the praise she received from the doctor. He went on and explained some of the points he particularly liked and odd parts that he didn't think flowed very well. Finally, his face looked quizzically at her.

'You wish to ask me a question, doctor?'

'From beginning to end I thought the poem very good, but its style is a little deep and perhaps a little morose for a young lady.'

'I assure you that I did write it, doctor. Why would you think otherwise?'

'There will be poems in this house.'

'By my father, I presume you mean.'

'Yes. It would be quite normal to use another's work as a basis for your own thoughts.'

Anna sat up straight in her chair, 'One time in a quiet, jesting moment, you suggested my father's poetry was a little turgid.'

He laughed at her recollection, but said, 'He is a very competent poet, whose style is reflected in his purpose in life, which is dedicated to the wonderful edifice opposite this house. As such I would expect a style in keeping with his outlook and his views of the world.'

Anna was not going to be persuaded to change her claim, 'I can assure you doctor that the poem is entirely my own.'

He smiled, 'I thought you would say that, but so that I may feel totally confident in your abilities, I propose a little test. Just between the two of us.'

The doctor could see the scepticism on her face, but he placed his hand inside a pocket in his jacket and withdrew a piece of paper. He said with a broad grin, 'Are you prepared to take your poetic test?'

A little smile creased Anna face. The doctor was a good man and had become her friend over the years. Although ten years her senior, he moved between age groups very well and always seemed to pitch his conversation at an appropriate level.

'Despite taking offence, because a gentleman did not honour a lady's word, I have decided to forgive you. And to show the sincerity of my forgiveness, I will undertake your test.'

The doctor laughed as he was a man of continual humour. He nodded and passed her the piece of paper. 'On that piece of paper I have started a poem. It is entirely mine, and has never been seen in the light of day by another human being until now.'

'And what shall I do with it?' asked Anna.

'I would wish you to finish it, so that I can appraise your style.'

'How many lines do you expect?'

'You are the poet. You decide.'

The doctor took his leave of Anna, who was not required for any household duties, as young Honora was sitting with Sarah. After a little further reading of her book, she picked up the paper that the doctor had left and it gradually gathered her attention. As father and mother were going to be out visiting that afternoon she had the remainder of her time to do of her own choosing.

***

'I'm feeling very nervous,' said Anna to her music tutor, John Savile, as she moved towards the harpsichord. John Savile was a tall handsome man, with short jet black hair, a few years older than Anna. His height was accentuated by the vicar's cassock that he wore at all times. He had a calm and unflustered manner, which made him very popular as a music teacher. For the evening's entertainment he would sing and be accompanied by Anna on the harpsichord.

John smiled at Anna, 'Just remember to relax and play as well as you did this morning and everything will be fine. I know a great many of the audience. They are always sympathetic to a young lady playing publicly for the first time.'

Anna gave a nervous smile in return, but wasn't convinced by John's words. She knew that many in the audience were fine musicians and singers themselves.

The large music area, which had double doors leading through to the main drawing room, was gradually filling with guests. Mrs Seward considered that the ability to play music to an audience as a very necessary talent for a young lady seeking a husband. She had engaged John Savile, who was the Vicar Choral at the cathedral, to give lessons to Anna.

As Anna and John were briefly discussing the exact nature of the music, so they caught the attention of Dr Darwin, who had recently arrived.

Even in a full room, the doctor's eyes rarely missed what was going on in every corner. As soon as he saw Anna and John talking, he made his way towards them. He studied the pair of them standing next to each other. Directing himself to the music tutor the doctor said, 'How is your wife, vicar?'

John Savile was a serious man, and there was not the slightest change in his expression as he answered the doctor. 'My wife is fully recovered, thanks to your treatment, doctor.'

'I am glad to hear it, Mr Savile. It is a strain on any man when his wife is badly afflicted.'

John Savile declined to reply, but nodded his head to acknowledge. Anna tendered her apologies to the doctor as they needed to prepare. The doctor left the couple with a wry smile, which rather disconcerted Anna. What did he mean by that smile?

As Anna was seating herself at the harpsichord, so a flash of red in the hall caught her attention. Into the back of the room came Captain Robertson. The smile momentarily left her face, but soon returned as Captain Temple followed his colleague. Abigail immediately engaged Captain Robertson and that left his colleague to look around the room at the assembled guests. His keen and quick eyes soon found Anna. He bowed his head to Anna from across the room, and she returned the gesture. It made her forthcoming performance a little more nervous.

The dutiful round of applause after the music, was accompanied by many compliments. Anna was happy to be able to hide behind her indifferent performance by extolling John's excellent singing.

As the invited guests began to take their places at the many card tables that were laid out, Captain Temple took no time in approaching Anna.

Anna then said, 'I believe the regiment returned to Lichfield earlier today.'

'You are generally correct, Miss Seward, but an advance party, which included myself, arrived last week.'

'May I presume that Army matters had prevented you from entering the town and leaving the barracks.'

'It has been a busy time, but I did achieve an introduction to your father, by the kindness of Mr Levitt. I met the Canon a few days ago and he pressed me to attend tonight. It was my pleasure to accept.'

'My father did not mention you had met him, perhaps he expected you to leave a card.'

'Unfortunately you were visiting when I came here, and as I knew I would see you soon, I did not leave a card.' Anna tried not to show disappointment in her face, but he had been in Lichfield for a week and had made no effort to call again and leave a card.

Anna then had to listen while Captain Temple praised both the house, her mother and father and finally her musical entertainments. She tried to deflect his praises to John Savile, but he was unapologetic about insisting his praise was for her.

She was grateful for the relief brought by Mr Levitt as he approached them. 'As I had a little success in some of my business ventures, I propose to hold a celebration ball.' He nodded his head to Anna and said, 'I have already tendered my informal invitation to Canon Seward and his entire family.' Anna acknowledged with a smile. 'I have come over to invite Captain Temple as well.'

'Thank you very much sir, I will most readily accept.' Mr

Levitt took his leave so that he might be able to extend invitations to other people, who were there that evening.

The hopefulness that had been showing on Anna's face as Mr Levitt issued his invitation was not disappointed, when Captain Temple said, 'Provided regimental duties do not cause me to be elsewhere, may I have the honour of your hand for the first dance.'

Anna did not have to delay long before she replied, 'Yes, of course, Captain Temple.'

'Sarah, Honora! What are you doing here I thought you had gone to bed,' said Anna as she walked into her drawing room. She had been helping her father and mother say goodbye to the last of the guests.

Sarah and Honora were both well wrapped in thick dressing gowns and were sitting on either side of the roaring fire.

'It's all too exciting,' said Honora, 'Isn't Captain Temple wonderful?'

Sarah was also full of enthusiasm, 'Is he going to the Levitt's Ball? Has he asked you to dance?'

The expectation of Honora and Sarah was clear to see, but Anna gave them a broad smile and said, 'I'm so excited. He is going to the Levitt's Ball. I'm at the top of his card with the first dance.'

As usual when the three of them were together their attention then changed to what should Anna wear. After much discussion they decided on one dress that they all liked, but it needed new lace trims. Both Sarah and Honora promised all their concentration at making and fitting the trim.

The excitement of the evening prevented any of them feeling tired. Having decided what Anna was going to wear for the ball, they lapsed into a contented silence. After a while it was broken by Honora, who with a serious look on her face said, 'Can we talk about marriage?'

'Of course, we can, Honora,' replied Anna quietly

Anna was so pleased with Honora's interest and passion in so many matters and really had enjoyed teaching her over the past few years. But it was the conversations about life and marriage that she really liked.

She looked at her young friend, who was daydreaming, but Honora then said, 'Oh! It's so exciting. You are going to see Captain Temple again.' Honora pushed herself from the chair, skipped across the room and squeezed in with Anna. 'You are so wonderful to me. It is as though I were your true sister.'

Anna looked at her young friend and said, 'To me you are, as dear as my own Sarah.'

'Of course, you are our sister,' said Sarah.

Anna added, 'Through my eyes I can see nothing but a young sister that I can help guide into the world.'

'What will become of me, Anna?'

'You will grow up to be a very pretty, intelligent and thoughtful woman.'

Honora looked wistful, 'That is not what I meant.'

Anna said indulgently, 'Then ask me clearly, what is it that you wish to know?'

The young girl detached herself from Anna's arm to sit neatly and tidily next to her. 'I know I am a little young for such matters, but in this household I frequently here the word marriage mentioned. Most of the adults change the subject when I appear or send me away.'

'Do not be alarmed at their actions they are not talking of your marriage.'

'No, I didn't think they probably were, as I have not heard my father's name mentioned.'

'Honora, I'm at the age that my father believes it is right for me to marry.'

'That would be so sad.'

'Honora! Remember what I have said to you before, you must think of others before you speak. Otherwise it is easy to give offence.'

She nodded gently, 'I am sorry, what I meant was that I would be sad at losing you.'

'That is better, Honora.'

'Would you be pleased to find a husband, so it would not be

sad for you?'

'Many things in life are fraught with difficulties. I would be very sad to leave my father's house, and especially sad to part with you and Sarah. But I will join a house that is joyful and celebratory, because the son of the house has taken a wife.'

'I think I see,' replied Honora thoughtfully and then added, 'When will you marry?'

Sarah raised her eyebrows, she looked at her sister, and said with a smile, 'What is your answer?'

'It is a particularly worthwhile question, as father is travelling early tomorrow morning in his coach to meet the Rankin family, who live a distance away in the west of Staffordshire.'

Glancing at Honora, Sarah said with wide open eyes, 'Might tomorrow be the very day?'

'Although he only hinted at the intention of going there, he told me to be at dinner tomorrow afternoon, so that he could say what had happened at his meeting with the Rankin family.'

Honora, who had been studying the faces and words of the sisters said, 'Could such a marriage be made without the husband and wife meeting?'

Both turned to look at their young friend. Anna replied calmly, 'Yes, if my father and Mr Rankin were in full agreement over the dowry arrangement, as well as the household, then the betrothal would take place.'

Honora's face gave a slight look of aggrievement. Anna picked it up immediately. 'When you come of age ready for marriage, I am sure your father will only approve a man that he believes is most suitable to you.'

In open honesty Honora said, 'I'm not sure I would like to marry a man that I had never met. It is a long period of one's life that has to be spent with them.'

Anna said, soothingly, 'Our fathers are men who understand the world and the people in it. We see only a small section of it to which we are introduced. It is therefore imperative that we have an implicit trust in their good judgement. There is no reason to move away from the considered views of generations as to the best way to conduct such a relationship.' Anna smiled at Honora, but wondered whether what she had just said, was what she believed.

It was very late before they went to their rooms, but Anna wasn't tired. She only wanted to write to Emma. The letter wasn't going to be about his looks or that he was a soldier. Anna would write about how she could help Captain Temple impress her father.

Chapter Three

Anna walked serenely down the stairs as the gong for the three o'clock dinner sounded. The front door was opened quickly and smoothly by William, the butler, and her father burst into the hall. Anna looked past him and could see the carriage still standing just outside of the gate. She watched her father as he stormed past her into the dining room, where, in a slightly distressed state, he sat in his chair.

She was gratified to see Sarah and Honora appear promptly as well. If their father was in a bad mood, then he would reprimand them for being even a minute late. Her mother was already in her accustomed seat, at the far end of the long table.

She noticed that her father visibly relaxed as he was now in his own home with his family. Anna decided to ask, 'Was it a troublesome journey father?'

He gathered his breath and waited for his soup to be served, before he answered his daughter's question. 'The journey, as it took me close to Birmingham was undesirable, with so many of the roads in that vicinity being in bad repair.'

Anna waited and with a slight nervousness asked, 'Were you well received?'

This time there was no delay, 'I was not well received. They are a household with delusions above their status in society.'

Anna closed her eyes momentarily. She hoped that there was not going to be bad news at the end of her father's account of the visit. But he turned morose during the meal and only spoke further when the mutton was served. 'They offered me no refreshment at all!' He then lapsed into a broody quietness. The rest of the family decided to eat their meal in silence.

Elizabeth Seward watched her husband throughout the meal, but declined to say one word. Anna expected that they would all be left to their own time so that they could get ready for the evening ball at the Levitts. Canon Seward ended the meal by standing and saying, 'Anna, I wish to see you in my study.'

A knot suddenly gripped her stomach. It was going to be bad news. She could feel the tension in her. They might not be a welcoming family in her father's eyes, but perhaps both men wanted to do a deal. Anna had already realised that the Rankin house was very close to one of the proposed new routes for a canal, which might well run through their land. Her father was very keen to invest his money in canal shares. Anna just wondered whether she was part of a deal to gain canal access.

She gathered all the calmness she could and said, 'Yes, father. I shall come with you.' Any delay might exacerbate a bad temper, but there was a surprise in store for the eldest daughter.

'Sit down, Anna. I need to talk to you about marriage.'

'Yes, father,' replied his daughter as she took a seat near to his desk. A worried look crossed her face, this was going to be when she was told the man, who she was going to marry.

Her mind ran through all the questions and queries she wanted to ask. She had sat alone the previous evening thinking of all that she could say if her father had made the decision. But as he was going to talk to her so she would have to wait. For now, she just had to listen.

'I have been trying all spring to find a family that I deem suitable for my eldest daughter, but it has been to no avail.' Anna tried to disguise the gentle breath of relief she let slip from her lips. 'We must bide our time and perhaps search a little wider.' Anna could find no reason to speak, so she sat demurely, waiting for her father. 'You have many attributes Anna, of which I am proud. But there is one that is proving a difficulty in achieving a successful marriage.'

'What is it father? May I assist in removing such a problem.'

He looked a little stern, 'There is nothing that can be done about it Anna. You are known in the town as a very well read young lady. In many evenings we have held in this house, you have composed and read many of your own poems.'

'Is that a problem father?'

'It would be very welcome in many of the traditional families in the town, unfortunately those that have suitable sons come from a merchant background, where such capabilities are not favoured.'

'Yes, father,' but she tried to disguise the relief in her voice.

'All I can say to you at the present time, my daughter, is that your marriage is not likely in the near future.'

'Then I shall do my very best to support my parents in their own home.' With that she sensed the meeting was at an end. Her father did not see the little smile that crossed her lips as she left the room.

She had to admit to herself that her plan was coming together. If only her father could be impressed with Captain Temple. He was a good looking man and she liked him. But she pressed herself to realise it didn't have to be him. It was a matter of choice. She would write to Emma and say that it should be her choice and not her father's.

Having been met by Mr and Mrs Levitt, Anna, with a gleam on her face entered the main ballroom, resplendent in a deep red evening gown that complemented her flowing auburn hair.

'My dear friend,' greeted Abigail, who wore a deep blue dress with her heavily powdered hair piled high on her head. 'I have just glanced out of the door and the two captains are arriving.'

Anna whispered, 'That's good news. You have been such a good friend to me, but I want to make sure Captain Temple talks to my father.'

Abigail looked across the ballroom with little expression in her face, but she whispered, 'Father understands what is going on and he is happy to help. It might seen strange to you and me, but he has worked out that both your father and Captain Temple have an interest in turnpike roads.'

Anna made a slightly strange face, which is all that she could do in such a public company, and said with some disbelief, 'Turnpike roads?'

'Don't look at me like that,' Abigail said, 'I don't know what they would talk about, but father is convinced they will agree about them.'

'Well done, Abigail, you are such a friend. How shall I ever repay you?'

The two women stood close to each other talking as they watched another coach of guests arrive and then Anna said, 'I had rather hoped that Captain Temple might have called at the house, but perhaps he was too busy on army business.'

Abigail was too excited to notice the slight concern in her friend's face, as she said, 'Captain Robertson has called everyday since we last met. Yesterday, he escorted me to my brother's house.'

Anna gave a weak smile to her friend, but on catching sight of Captain Temple entering the room, it changed and her face glowed with anticipation. The evening was arranged so that there would be a period of gentle music before the dancing started, as not all the guests had arrived. There was still a long queue of carriages waiting to set down new arrivals.

Captain Temple was soon by her side, and said, 'It is a pleasant early spring evening. If it is not a little too chill, shall we walk onto the veranda.' Anna nodded. Captain Temple took her arm and they made there way across the ballroom towards the large doors that opened to the outside. She felt proud as the other guests watched her walk on the arm of an officer in his full scarlet dress uniform. Several other young couples were already there. It was a place for a private conversation, but in keeping with the etiquette ascribed by parents, they were in full view of all in the ballroom.

He said to Anna, 'I have received very many invitations to balls and social evenings in Lichfield this season.'

'There are a great many social events of all types,' replied Anna. The Captain frowned a little. 'Is there something that is wrong, Captain?'

'There is some disturbing news that was around the barracks just before we came away tonight. The regiment is likely to be required elsewhere at short notice. We will then have no indication of when we will return.' The same frown crossed Anna's face at the news. The Captain's voice lifted a little as he added, 'Sometimes these rumours do not lead to action, and I hope that these are misplaced.'

'Is there a particular reason you wish to stay in Lichfield?'

'Yes, my dear Miss Seward, it is so that I may be of service to you.'

'You are very kind. It would be my wish that the rumour proved to be false.'

'Once I know of my situation a little better, I should be able to talk to you, about the social events. '

'They need not wait until then.'

'May I take you to the balls for which I have received invitations?'

' I would like that very much, but my father must also agree.'

'I will do that as soon as I can confirm that we will be in town for a while.'

Anna smiled, it was what she wanted, but she also knew her father very well, 'So that you are prepared when you meet him, I would suggest to you that he might ask about your family, as I believe they are not local to Lichfield.'

'You are correct, Miss Seward, my family hails from London. I shall most willingly give your father any particulars that he requires. My father is an honourable and honest merchant in Billingsgate.'

The announcements were made that the dancing was about to commence, so Captain Temple asked, 'May I take you hand?'

'With pleasure, Captain Temple.'

Anna curtsied as the quadrille came to the end. Her partner, who was a cousin of her mother's bowed low, and thanked her for the dance. She glanced around the ballroom, but could not see either the Captain nor Abigail, so she walked through to the verandah to see whether she could find them.

Her heart leapt at the sight. Mr Levitt had engaged both her father and Captain Temple in conversation. Abigail had noticed. Anna walked over to join her.

'They are having and earnest discussion about turnpikes,' said Abigail.

'How is it going? Have they been displeased with each other?'

'No. They all seem to be in agreement. How father managed to achieve it, I do not know.'

'Oh, Abigail, I'm so pleased. I just hope father likes him.' Anna studied their faces carefully. It was a serious discussion, but as there were more nods, than shakes of the head, she concluded that it must be going well.

Finally, Anna heard Mr Levitt say, 'If you come with me Captain Temple I will introduce you.' With that they both formally nodded to the Canon and walked off leaving him standing alone.

Anna was immediately by his side, 'You seemed in earnest conversation father, I didn't like to disturb you when I came on to the veranda.'

He managed a flicker of a smile and said, 'As you know I'm very interested in turnpikes.'

She tried to say as easily as she could, 'Does Captain Temple know about such a topic?'

Her father's rather stern expression didn't change, 'For a young man he has a good understanding, although he is too inexperienced on the financial matters.' Anna didn't see that as a great barrier to stop her going to the balls with the captain.

Anna decided to be brave as she said, 'Captain Temple has asked if he may accompany me to some of the spring balls in Lichfield.'

Her father's face immediately turned towards her, 'And what did you say?'

'That he would have to ask your permission, sir.' He nodded his head, but showed no signs of going to speak. Anna decided to continue, 'Would you consider giving him permission father?'

'He seems a reasonable young man, but he is from London and in the army.'

'His uncle lives in Lichfield, and knows you as a man of letters.'

'I shall consider the matter, Anna. And now it is time for the carriage as we need to go home.'

Anna breathed a small sigh of relief as she went to find her mother. Her father hadn't refused. Tomorrow she would go and see Abigail to ask her to foster an introduction between Captain Temple's uncle and the Canon. She also hoped that the Captain might call tomorrow, so she could speak to him about his uncle.

Chapter Four

'I am so desperate for news of the regiment,' said Anna as she sat with Sarah in the blue drawing room.

'Have you heard from Captain Temple at all?'

'There has been no news since I spoke to him at the Levitt's ball. He was very earnest that night, and intended seeing father so that he could take me to the spring balls. But, here we are, on the brink of summer and there is no word at all.'

'Anna, my dear sister, I do not believe that he would let you down. It was unfortunate that the regiment left the following morning for London. Father said that there were some riots in the capital and they would be using troops to restore order.'

'Oh, if Captain Temple had had only a few days before he went. Then he could have spoken to father and gained permission not only to take me to the balls, but to write to me as well. But it never happened.'

'My poor sister,' said Sarah quietly, as she wrapped her arm around Anna. They stayed in silence for a while. 'Has father seen any more families?'

'Oh, do not torment me so much! I do not want him to find me a husband this summer. When the Captain returns I just hope father takes a liking to him.'

'Come Anna, it is near midday, and the weather is better. Shall we take a walk through town? I feel so much better today.'

'Yes of course. It is good to see a little colour in your cheeks and a willingness to take the air.' Anna stood up with a determined air, 'A good walk with you will lift my spirits.'

The two sisters gathered their cloaks and bonnets from their rooms and went down stairs. The front door was opened by William so they could step out into the warm early summer sun.

'Let us walk to the far side of the town up towards the common.'

'Of course, if you feel up to it,' replied Anna.

'Dr Darwin came yesterday evening and gave me different medication. It seems to have helped greatly.'

'That's wonderful news, Sarah.'

They walked through the town and then Sarah said, 'This way.'

'Sarah this road takes us to the barracks.'

'Yes, I know,' came the reply with a smile, 'there might be someone there who can tell us when the regiment will return.'

'I'm not so sure,' said Anna.

'Come on,' replied Sarah, 'it will do you good to find out.'

Hesitantly Anna was persuaded and they walked up the hill. As they turned the corner, Anna was surprised to see one of the red jackets of the regiment. She looked at the officer's face, 'Captain Robertson!'

'Good afternoon, ladies,' and he bowed.

'It is surprising to see you in Lichfield.'

'Each company in the command is coming back to Lichfield for a short time.'

Anna said, 'May I ask about Captain Temple? When will he be returning?'

Puzzlement and then concern crossed Captain Robertson's face, 'But he was here last week. I have not seen him for at least a month as we have been on different duties. Did he not seek you out?'

'No, Captain he did not.'

'That's very strange,' he said, but Anna could see the concern on his face.

'I'm sorry to be the bearer of bad news.'

Anna did not reply. Sarah glanced at her sister and said to the Captain, 'It is not your fault, Captain.'

He recovered himself a little and said, 'May I walk you back to town, as I am on my way to the Levitt household for dinner.'

Anna nodded. Sarah again glanced at her sister and then positioned herself in the middle of the three and spoke with the Captain as they walked.

After the Captain had left them, Sarah immediately said, 'I'm so sorry, Anna. I know how much you liked him. He seemed very taken with you, but ...' She didn't finish the sentence and they walked up Dam Street and around by the side of Minster Pool in silence.

As the front door opened and they walked in their father was standing in the hall. On seeing his daughters he immediately smiled and said, 'My two delightful daughters.' Both curtsied. 'Sarah, I have some good news for you, come into my study.'

Anna noticed that her father was much happier than normal. His usual serious expression had been replaced by a smile. Anna said, 'I'll wait for Sarah in the drawing room.'

She knew that she had to have a distraction from her sad mood, now that she was aware that Captain Temple had been in Lichfield last week and had not called. Her favourite way of losing herself to the world was in poetry. Despite her upset, Anna soon settled with her book. She did not notice the passing of time, it was only when the clock struck did she realise that Sarah had been with their father for nearly an hour. That was so unusual, whenever one of them spoke to him it was normally about five minutes. He then always wanted to get on with cathedral business.

It was then that the door opened and Sarah walked quietly into the room. She was always gentle in her actions and closed the door without any noise. As she turned into the room, Anna looked at her face and exclaimed, 'Sarah, whatever is the matter? Your face shows surprise and happiness, but you don't say anything.'

Sarah ran across the room and threw her arms around her sister, 'Anna! Anna! My dearest Anna. I am going to be married!'

Anna was quickly caught in her sister's enthusiasm and hugged her back

'Sarah. Who is it? Has father just told you?'

Sarah nodded her head, but for a little while was too overcome to tell Anna the details. Eventually they managed to calm each other sufficiently for Sarah to be able to offer the explanation.

Sarah asked, 'Do you know the Porter family?'

'Yes,' replied Anna, 'they are distant relations of our mother. And I have chatted with Lucy Porter many times.'

'There is a gentleman in that family by the name of Joseph Porter.'

'I have not met him. But is he the man for you?'

Sarah gave a big sigh and her eyes were glazed in happiness. 'Yes, I shall become the wife of Mr Joseph Porter. Father has told me that he has finished all the necessary discussions with old Mr Porter.'

They hugged each other again. Anna was so pleased for her sister, but as she thought about the marriage she realised that it was a great relief for her. There was likely to be only one wedding at the time, although she did start to have a nagging doubt whether her father might try to arrange two on the same day.'

'That's wonderful Sarah, when will the marriage take place.'

'There will be a delay, because it cannot take place quickly.'

A look of concern came over Anna's face, 'Why is there a delay?'

'Don't look so worried Anna, father has explained it all to me. It isn't a problem. Mr Joseph Porter is a merchant, who does a great deal of business in Italy. It means he lives there for a long period of the year.'

Anna said excitedly, 'Are you going to live in Italy?'

'Father thinks that it will be Mr Porter's wish that I travel with him and live in Italy for some part of the year.'

'Oh, that's wonderful. That will be such fun for you.'

Sarah continued, 'Joseph's family wish the marriage to take place in Lichfield. So it must wait for his business commitments to allow him to come home.'

Anna hesitated a moment, 'Do you know the age of your future husband?' It was one of the things that she feared the most about an arranged marriage. Would father want her to marry a much older man. It would be such a horrible thought.

Sarah didn't notice the sudden grim face of her sister and said, 'Yes, father told me that he is much older than me.'

'How old?' asked Anna warily.

'Forty-three,' replied Sarah.

'Oh,' said Anna as she failed to suppress the exclamation.

Sarah looked her sister's face, 'Anna it doesn't matter to me what age he is. It will make no difference, I will just try to be a dutiful wife to him.'

'Of course, you will Sarah, you have always been a loving sister and daughter. I would see no difference in you, when you become Mrs Porter.'

'Thank you so much, Anna.'

With that the door flew open and their mother rushed in followed by Honora. 'My darling! My darling, you are going to be married. Your father has just told me. This is such good news. Now tell me all about it.'

The three women and their ward talked through all the information that Sarah had. There were many questions and answers, as well as talk about dresses and guests. Finally they were all exhausted from the excitement. It was then that Canon Seward came into the drawing room and smiled benevolently at his wife and daughters. His wife turned to him and said, 'We must announce it to our friends and neighbours.'

'In due time, Mrs Seward. There is no urgency as it is not known when Mr Porter will return to England.'

Rather to the surprise of Anna, her mother stood up to talk to her husband. Normally once he had decided on a matter he didn't change his mind.

'Mr Seward. The marriage is arranged. The rumours will be rife. People will think we are ashamed of the match unless we inform people immediately.'

'I'm not ashamed of the match. It is an excellent one,' replied her husband. The Porters are a family with an extremely impressive reputation throughout the whole of Staffordshire.'

'I agree with you. As you already know my relations have some connection with the family, therefore it is essential to show how proud we are of the marriage.'

'My dear wife, you do raise a very good point. Over the next few days, we will make arrangements to tell our friends and other families in Lichfield.'

Anna was even more amazed that her mother had clearly not finished what she was saying. 'Mr Seward, on the day you took me to be your wife, I was in awe of the man of force you were. Your actions were timely and direct.'

He looked a little surprised, but said, 'I hope they still are.'

'In that case, I am sure you will raise no objections to initial announcements being made today.'

'Please father!' pleaded Sarah.

'Very well, it is a day to please the ladies.'

Elizabeth Seward turned to Anna and said, 'Can you write invitations for this evening, and send them to all our near acquaintances.'

'Oh, mama!' exclaimed Sarah.

Her mother replied, 'My daughter is to be married and the world shall know. Now, Sarah will be the centre of attention this evening, so Anna you may play the harpsichord. Perhaps you could ask Mr Savile to join you as before.'

Sarah could only repeat, 'How exciting!' but then had to rest a little as a bad cough gripped her.

Mrs Seward continued in a state of excitement, 'I shall instruct the kitchen, and tell William to summon immediate messengers. Now Mr Seward...'

He looked at his wife and replied, 'I shall be in my study composing a sermon.'

The house was in fervent activity throughout the afternoon. The rooms were prepared, the food cooked and the invitations sent out. There were rapid replies from many of their friends, who were already sending their congratulations.

Anna knocked gently on the door of her father's study. She heard the grunted reply and went in. She was pleased to see that he was still smiling. He immediately said, 'I thought that you might come and see me.'

'I was just wondering...' said Anna, but her voice trailed away and she felt strangely nervous.

Her father studied her for a little while and then said, 'As you know it was my intention that as the eldest daughter you would be the first to marry.' Anna just nodded her head. 'When I first went to the Porters to discuss marriage, it was you that I had in mind.'

'What made you change your mind, father?' Anna said in a very quiet voice.

'The senior Mr Porter knows our family well and so I did

not have to tell him a great deal. He told me that Joseph wished to marry, now that he had established himself in business and owned a fine house and estate. He wanted a home loving wife, who would have children, and would be prepared to put everything else aside.'

'I see father.'

'I have said to you on many occasions Anna, that your wish to dedicate so much time to books and reading would not be liked by some families. I am afraid that it was the case with the Porters. I had no option, but to suggest Sarah. Once they understood it wasn't to be you, then they were all for the agreement.'

Anna left her father's study and as she closed the door she breathed a sigh of relief. She felt sure he would have said if he was thinking about her marriage. Her father seemed very pleased it was going to be Sarah. She walked through the house and found that her mother, Sarah and Honora were all busy, but that she had finished all of her tasks. She had time to write to Emma. With that decision made, she was soon sat at her desk in her drawing room, with her pen and a blank sheet of paper in front of her.

She didn't write, but gazed out at the sunlight falling on the spires of the cathedral. It was then that a sudden thought struck her and she began to cry. There was no one else to tell of her sudden grief, only Emma. No one else would understand.

My dearest Emma

It has always been my belief that I would marry. It was always to be the man of my dreams, not one that father found for me. But now all has changed. Sarah is to marry. In Lichfield, within families there is often one of the daughters, who cannot marry, so that she can look after their parents in old age. Now I will be the only daughter left at home!

Anna looked at the writing paper for a long time. Even if Captain Temple wanted to marry her, then her father might refuse because he wanted Anna to look after him in his old age. She couldn't write anymore to Emma. So she picked up the paper, took it to the fire and watched it burn away.

Her mood was heavy, but she had a duty to her sister. She must be happy and smiling tonight, otherwise everyone would think that she was jealous.

Anna tried to content herself with some reading, but could not concentrate. She walked backwards and forwards in her room. As she was becoming more despondent there was a gentle knock on the door and Honora came in.

'Oh, Anna, I'm so excited for Sarah.'

'It's wonderful news isn't it,' replied Anna and tried not to show her own feelings in her voice.

'But if you get married as well I shall have to leave this house,' and she burst out crying.

'Come, Honora.' Anna sat on the large sofa and wrapped her arms around her young friend. With Sarah leaving home shortly, Honora would become her only companion in the house. She sighed as she looked at her. In just a few years, Honora herself would be ready for marriage, and the Sneyd family, from which she came, had a reputation for marriages at a young age.

After she had calmed Honora she said to her, 'My father has no plans for me at the moment and so we can be together for a long time to come.'

'I do hope so.'

'Now we cannot have tears on such an exciting day, so let us go and put on our best dresses for tonight, so we can show Sarah how very pleased we are.'

Chapter Five

Anna chose her best cream dress for the evening. She checked the mirror and was pleased with the colour as it complemented her long flowing hair. She realised that her healthy appetite meant that she was not as slim as a few years ago. Both Sarah, and her friend Abigail, had very finely drawn waists which, as she looked at her reflection, she could not find in herself. The melancholy thoughts passed from her head as she walked down the stairs to join her father and welcome the guests, who were in an excited mood as they arrived.

The long line of carriages took time to place the guests on the steps of the Seward's house. When all had arrived, Anna walked slowly to the end of the room. Her harpsichord was prepared and John Savile had agreed to sing. She was slightly in her own world as she made passing comments to many of the guests.

A voice behind her, she recognised instantly, and she turned. 'So my poetess is not going to be the first to walk down the aisle.'

'No, doctor, it will be my sister.' The doctor smiled back at Anna and they both cast their eyes on Sarah, who was taking congratulations from everyone around her. As they watched her, she coughed and those nearby waited for her to recover. Anna was struck by the change in the face of the doctor. He had an anguished look as he peered down the room to the future bride. As he turned back to Anna his face changed to its normal happy countenance.

He said, 'Polly told me that you had hopes with a young Captain.'

'Doctor, please keep your voice down. Your wife is a very good friend to me. In a moment of weakness I might have let it slip a little. I did ask her to keep it a secret.'

'There should be no secrets between husband and wife.' Anna knew that she couldn't disagree. 'But your secret is safe with me, as I am sure you know. So do tell me what has happened to the captain?'

Anna's didn't really want to talk to the doctor about the matter, but he was a persistent man, who easily teased her. 'Since his regiment has gone to London I've had no news of him,' she said uneasily. 'There is nothing between us. He wanted to speak to my father, but it never happened.'

'Fine and proper,' said Dr Darwin looking around the room. Both Anna and his eyes caught the same view near the door. Several men in scarlet had arrived.

'Calm yourself, Anna. Captain Temple is not among them.'

Anna felt it no time for joking, but the doctor always enjoyed teasing her. It was also a concern to her that the doctor knew the name of the captain and that he would recognise him.

She replied calmly, 'I can now recognise the insignia and those officers are not from our local regiment.'

'You are a very observant young woman. I agree with you they are not our local soldiers, so our regiment has not returned to the local barracks.'

Within the group of soldiers, one was a little taller than the rest, and he was looking around the room. His face showed recognition as he looked at Anna and the doctor, and he began to make his way towards them. A little surprise registered on Anna's face, but the doctor showed no change in expression.

He stopped just short of them, and bowed low.

Anna was taken by surprise when the doctor said, 'Richard Vyse, it is good to see you again. You look a fine young man in your uniform.'

'Thank you, sir. And it is very good to meet you again, Dr Darwin.'

The doctor said, 'Allow me to introduce one of our host's family, Miss Anna Seward.'

Again the soldier bowed low and said, 'It is an honour to meet you Miss Seward. Cornet Richard Vyse of the King's Dragoon Cavalry at your service.' She studied the man, who was only a few years her senior. He was tall, with brown hair, and had an extremely handsome and well proportioned face. His brown eyes were sparkling and alert.

'Welcome to our house on this happy occasion,' replied Anna without moving her eyes, which were focused on his face. 'Forgive me, but being unaware of military terms, I am not familiar with the title of your rank, although I can see that you are an officer.'

A smile lit his entire face 'I have recently been commissioned into the Dragoons. I am very proud to tell you that as the Cornet, for my company of soldiers, I have the honour of being the mounted standard bearer.'

'A very prestigious honour, Cornet.'

'It is indeed, Miss Seward.'

The doctor was smiling benignly at the exchange between Anna and the soldier. Then to even Anna's surprise, music started and the announcement was made that the evening's entertainment would commence with dancing.

'May I presume that such a beautiful young lady as yourself will already have her dance card full for this evening.' This brought a smile to Anna's lip, and a small smirk from the doctor.

'The evening has been arranged to celebrate a surprise announcement, and so far no one has yet offered me a dance.'

'Then if I may be so bold.'

'Thank you, please lead me to the dance floor.' She turned and said, 'If you will excuse us, Doctor.' He nodded his agreement, but Anna tried not to look at the smile that creased his lips.

It was quiet in the house the following day. Anna had breakfasted alone and helped her father in the morning with some duties in the cathedral. In the afternoon she went down to dinner to find only her father was there. He said as she arrived, 'I suppose I shall have to accept the indisposition of the remainder of my family, due to the exertions of yesterday.'

'I am sure your tolerance is much appreciated.'

'I saw you dancing with Richard Vyse last night, Anna.'

'Yes, father. We danced several times.'

While she took her cup of soup she watched her father who gave a brief smiled, which pleased Anna. She said, 'Do you know Cornet Vyse?'

'I do indeed. I am more familiar with his uncle's family as they hold positions within the diocese, but it is a good and traditional family that sets high standards for its men. With very few exceptions they choose either holy orders or serving his majesty in the cavalry.'

'The doctor also knew him, and it was he who introduced me.' Her father's face showed he didn't like the mention of the doctor's name, but he said, 'The doctor knows a great many people. He treats nearly all of the leading families in the county, and the Vyse household would be one of them.'

They lapsed into silence for a period, but Anna was pleased that her father liked the Vyse family. Her mind drifted as she was eating her food. Her father was not a talkative man, and would often sit through the whole meal without speaking. She kept coming back to her thoughts about looking after him in his old age. But she felt more positive today. She reasoned that she could still get married, but that she would have to take her parents into her house, when they were too old to look after themselves. She had now resolved the matter in her mind and could pay more attention to Richard Vyse.

With no indication that he was going to speak on any subject again Anna chose to remain silent as well. So she was surprised when her father said, 'Richard Vyse called on me late this morning after my cathedral duties.' Anna raised her eyebrows slightly to indicate interest and her face showed hope that her father might continue. 'He first asked me about Sarah and Mrs Seward and as to whether they had enjoyed the evening.' Anna nodded to indicate that is what would be expected of him. 'He then asked about you.'

'I trust you assured him that I very much enjoyed myself.'

'I did.' He paused, 'He also asked if I would give him permission to take you to the Saint's service at St Chad's tomorrow.'

Anna took a deep breath and tried to control her voice, 'How did you reply, father?'

'I thought him a little quick after only meeting you last night. But given that he is from a fine family I gave my agreement.'

'Thank you, father.'

'He said he will come later to see you.'

***

'May I offer you my arm, Anna,' said Richard Vyse as they left the house the following day. As her father had indicated, he came to visit her in the late afternoon and was persuaded by Anna's mother to take a dish of tea with the family. He was relaxed and a perfect gentleman. He attended closely to her father's needs, but he also made time for talking to Sarah and Honora.

When he had arrived to meet her today, he again paid his compliments to her father and as soon as they were alone, lost no time in suggesting that they use first names when on their own. Anna was a little surprised at the haste of such an approach, but readily agreed.

They turned past the cathedral and onto the small path that formed the edge of Stowe Pool.

'May I say what a very civil man your father is. Until the social evening the other night I had never met him, but my family know him well and hold him in high regard.'

Anna nodded her acceptance of the compliment, and said, 'My father holds your family in high esteem.'

'They have long been associated with the cathedral. I chose the cavalry route rather than holy orders.'

'I believe that there have been some riots in London. Are you likely to be moved quickly?'

'I would not think so Anna. It is the foot soldiers, like the local regiment, who go to deal with the matters. It very rarely calls for cavalry.'

They walked and enjoyed the summer's day. They reached St Chad's and joined other people who were entering the old church. Both greeted friends and people they knew. Anna felt proud to be on the arm of such a distinguished looking soldier. They sat next to each other in the square pews for the service, during which Richard sang with a loud and deep voice.

A contented smile came across Anna's face as he walked her home. Her father was not likely to raise objections to Richard Vyse.

When at last she was alone in her room, she spent deep into the night thinking about Richard Vyse. She put all the details in her letter to Emma.

Chapter Six

'You have been with Richard Vyse a great deal over the past few weeks,' said her father.

'Yes, father, he has visited me on most days that his duties would allow. We have most frequently walked in Lichfield, but he did take me to the ball at The Swan, which I believe he asked permission for.'

'He did,' said her father. Anna glanced at his face, but it neither smiled nor showed the stern look when he was about to deliver bad news.

Anna was beginning to get nervous about her father's interest. 'Do you have a reason for mentioning Cornet Vyse's visits father?' She drew in her breath, and her heart beat hard in the tension of the moment.

His facial expression did not change as he said, 'I met Richard Vyse's uncle in the cathedral this morning. I haven't seem him for a long time. We talked about many things, as we always do when we meet. He said that his family approved of Richard visiting you.'

Anna relaxed as her tensions released. There couldn't have been better news. The only sad information was that Richard had said that his military duties would keep him busy for the next few days.

The Seward family was finishing dinner when a messenger arrived with a note for her father. He quickly read it through and then looked at Sarah.

'Yes, sir?' she said enquiringly.

'This message says that your future husband will arrive in Lichfield this afternoon and wishes to come here this evening.'

Mrs Seward said, 'A most thoughtful time to come. We have a few friends in attendance this evening to play a hand of cards, so he will find us pleasantly at home.'

Canon Seward said, 'I will reply immediately.'

After her father had left the dining room, Anna said, 'Mama, I suggest we organise the drawing room with a lot more tables.'

'Only one or two will be necessary. The same as normal.'

Anna replied with a smile, 'It is normal for you to extend open invitation to many family friends for a cards' evening.'

Her mother nodded.

'Under normal circumstances only a few come. It would be my guess that as the news of Mr Porter's arrival in the city is known, we will have very many people, who will be interested to cast their eye over him.'

'I do see what you mean Anna, and we will do as you suggest.'

The household was swiftly made ready, and the ladies retired to their rooms to change into their evening house dresses.

By the time Anna had descended the stairs, various neighbours had begun to arrive. Mr Seward normally stayed in his study when there were card tables, but tonight he waited patiently and personally greeted all those that arrived.

Anna rarely played cards and therefore sat at the harpsichord and played a little music for the entertainment of the players, many tables of which had already started whist. They did not have to wait long and there was the announcement that the Porter's coach had arrived. Anna decided to stay seated at the harpsichord, so that Mr Porter would meet her parents and Sarah first. She called Honora over and explained they must let Sarah meet her future husband first, and that they would be presented to him afterwards.

The general noise in the room quietened considerably as old Mr Porter and Mr Joseph Porter came in. Mr Seward welcomed them to his home. While they were talking it gave Anna a chance to look at Joseph Porter and not to be noticed. He was a small man with a pronounced stoop. His face was irregular and his skin bore the marks of childhood illnesses.

Honora whispered to Anna, 'He looks much older than forty-three.'

'Shh, Honora,' but Anna's face showed that she couldn't disagree with the remark. She continued to watch the man that would be come her brother-in-law. He was very unconventionally dressed. His waistcoat was a very bright shade of blue. His dress jacket was fringed with the silk that was often found on a lady's dress. As he peered around the room, Anna was concerned about his eyesight as he seemed to move his head at a strange angle to look around.

Her father called her over to meet the man, who would marry Sarah. 'Welcome Mr Porter. It is a honour to meet you sir.'

'And you, Miss Seward. You might forgive my rushed appearance, but I was in earnest to meet my future wife at the earliest opportunity.'

'No apology is necessary. I know the urgency to meet was equal with my sister.'

He turned to Mr Seward, and said, 'May I compliment you and Mrs Seward on having such beautiful daughters. One with brown hair and the other with red, I would say a perfect combination.' Mr Seward nodded. Joseph Porter smiled at Sarah, but directed his gaze back at Anna, the discomfort of which showed on her face. He addressed his remarks directly to Anna, 'I would take it as a great honour if you would consent to be a bridesmaid to my future wife at the wedding ceremony.'

Anna went a little red, but replied, 'It would be a great honour, sir.' She curtsied with the intention of withdrawing. Her face was now red with embarrassment and her only wish was to stand behind her sister.

'Before you go Miss Seward.'

'Yes, sir,' Anna replied, but cast her eyes down to the floor.

'It is a long time since I have returned to my home town of Lichfield. Tomorrow I shall propose to my bride that we walk throughout the town so that we may receive congratulations from our friends.'

'That sounds an excellent idea, Mr Porter,' said Anna keeping her eyes firmly downward, but seeing as he did not move or speak again she was forced to glance upwards.

He caught her eye and said, 'When Sarah and I walk in the town, I would be grateful if you would come with us.'

'If that is what you both want, then I shall come.'

Anna was beginning to shake from nervousness, but Mr Porter had not finished, she could sense that, although she could no longer force herself to look at him.

'Miss Seward, or perhaps as we are soon to be brother and sister, may I call you Anna.'

'Of course, brother,' but her concentration on what he was saying was very strained as she was aware her parents and other assembled guests, including Sarah, were watching and listening to them.

'My successful business ventures requires my living in Italy for many months of the year. After Sarah and I are married we will travel to Italy. Shortly after we have arrived and settled in, I will send you an invitation to come for an extended stay with us. Would that suit you?'

Anna was nearly too breathless to answer, but managed to say, 'It is a very kind and generous offer.'

The relief spread over Anna's face as she heard her father say, 'Mr Porter, may I take the opportunity of introducing my ward, Honora Sneyd.'

Mr Porter took his time to respond, but bowed to Anna and then, with an awkward twisted turn, said, 'It will be a pleasure, Canon Seward.'

Anna left the party long before Mr Porter and his family took their leave, so that she avoided any further embarrassment. She had a smile of contentment in the end, because Mr Porter in showing his respect to her father, took a particular interest in his ward. It transpired that Mr Porter knew the Sneyd family well. Therefore he asked Honora many questions. At the end of which he said she was a credit to her father and her guardianship.

Such remarks went down very well with everyone there and Mr Porter and his future wife received a very large number of invitations to visit and to dine. He accepted the kindness of them with dignity and respect, but had to add that he had business to attend to for many of the days he would be in Lichfield.

It was late before Anna had reflected on the rather extraordinary arrival of Mr Porter. Her face, however, had held a stern look since she had entered the realms of her own rooms. She was relieved when she heard the faint knock on the door.

'Come in, Sarah.'

The door slowly opened in the usual manner. Anna smiled kindly at her sister, but she saw the pale drawn face and tired expression. She lost sight of Sarah's face as she closed the door.

'Oh, Anna! Oh Anna!' She struggled to understand her sister's expression as all she could see was the complete tiredness in her face. She waited for just a second. Sarah ran across to her and they embraced. As they moved apart from her, she heard Sarah whisper in her ear, 'He is the most wonderful man on earth.'

Relief swept through Anna as again she drew her sister close. It took a while for the sisters to calm themselves down.

'I know you are so dreadfully tired, Sarah, but please do tell me all, and I do mean all, that you think of Mr Porter.'

Sarah, despite her exhaustion, caught Anna eyes and said in a clear strong tone, 'He is to be your brother and insists that you call him Joseph'

'And I shall be very pleased to call him, Joseph, my brother.'

'He is evidently kind and it gave me great pride in the attention he showed to you, Honora, mother and father.'

Anna replied, 'He speaks very well. I would rejoice in a long conversation with him on any other occasion, but it was your day and did not wish to take too much of his time.'

'That is very kind of you Anna, but we three are altogther, are we not? And it is so good that he invited you to walk with us to town tomorrow. I hope you can come and that it does not disrupt you seeing Cornet Vyse.'

'Whatever you think is the best shall happen, my dear Sarah.' Anna's smiling face hid the concern that lay behind it.

Sarah stepped away from her. Anna eyes followed her as she walked across the room. 'I am so very tired and must go to bed. We'll talk about him tomorrow, when we are both refreshed.'

'That is very wise, Sarah. And do tend that cough of yours. You should ask Dr Darwin for more of his medicine, I believe it has done you good.'

'It has dear Anna. I shall follow your advice. But there is another matter I would like to tell you of my opinion before I go to bed.'

Anna's expression was a little surprised as her younger sister very rarely made such a direct statement.

'Please do.'

'Anna you are a truly beautiful sister. The men who court you must always be described as extremely handsome. Captain Temple and Cornet Vyse are two such men.'

A quizzical expression crossed Anna's face. For once, she could not anticipate what her sister was going to say.

'Joseph has admitted to me that he has a number of physical impediments that do not make him attractive in his appearance.'

Anna's quick intake of breath couldn't be controlled and her sister noticed.

'Anna, I told him, as far as I was concerned. He was the most handsome man in the world and that I never wanted the matter mentioned again.'

She then left her elder sister. As the door closed behind her she did not see the complete look of amazement on Anna's face.

Chapter Seven

Honora tapped lightly on the door of the blue drawing room and rushed in. Anna was seated by the fire, reading a book.

'Anna! Anna! I'm frightened. There is a strange man down stairs and I don't like him.'

The surprise, and then the tension, made Anna suddenly drop her book, 'Honora! Please settle yourself.'

'But he is big and very peculiar.'

'Honora, listen to me,' Anna grabbed the young girls hands, which were waving around and drew her to the front of her so they were face to face. 'Is William there?'

Honora settled a little as her hands were caught. She could see the comfort of Anna's reassuring face.

'Yes, and Mr Seward.'

Anna immediately strained her listening to hear whether there was any unusual sounds coming from downstairs. The noises she heard were the normal everyday matters for the household.

'You have calmed a little Honora, and now I want you to tell me why you think this man seems strange to you.'

'He is very large, has his head on one side, and his waistcoat was twisted around at the wrong angle.'

'It might have been Dr Darwin.'

Honora protested, 'I have seen Dr Darwin many times before, he comes to give Sarah medicines. He is not strange looking.' Then Anna had to wait as Honora's mind passed through her image of Dr Darwin. 'He is not s..' but this time she didn't finish the sentence.

Anna interrupted the girl's thoughts and said, 'If it was not Dr Darwin, then I need you to tell me more.'

Honora thought for a little time and replied, 'He was wearing slippers, but he had come visiting and all men then wear boots or shoes.'

'Go on,' said Anna with a little smile, that she tried not to make evident to her young friend.

Honora was eager to relate her story, 'I went down the stairs just as William opened the front door.' The man stared at me intently and then seemed to do a little dance before he would come in. I was frightened because he was such as big man, so I turned and ran back up the stairs.'

'Is that your story, Honora?'

'No! No! It was the next bit that really frightened me.'

'What did he do?'

'He called out my name, I was so frightened. Anna, how did he know my name?'

'What else did he say?'

'I couldn't understand it. His voice slurred a little.'

'Go on,' said Anna, 'did anything else worry you?'

Honora nodded her head and said, 'Yes. His mouth seemed to keep making twitching noises, but I don't think he was trying to say anything then.' She stopped her rapid talking to think a little more and then added, 'His shoulder seemed to jump each time he moved.'

Anna gave Honora a little time to compose herself, which she did.

'You are growing up now, Honora, and there are times as a young woman in society you might become worried or frightened. You must always take your lead from the men you know and trust. If William and Mr Seward were calm then so should you be. They were there and they would protect you. Do you understand?'

'Yes, I do, but I was frightened.'

'Yes, I can understand that, but look to Mr Seward for reassurance. The gentleman concerned has been known to our family for many years, so there was no need whatsoever to be frightened.'

'I'm sorry, Anna.'

'I can see why you were, Honora, but now I want you to be the bravest young lady in the world. Will you do it if I ask you?'

Anna hid any little smile that might have crossed her face as she looked directly at her young friend.'

'If you ask me Anna, I will do my best.'

'Well done, Honora. There are a number of people in life who are not blessed with perfect health or bodies. We must never shun people for what God has given them.'

'Yes, Anna. What must I do?'

'I want you, completely on your own, to go and introduce yourself to the gentleman. You will find him a kind man and he will ask you many questions. They will be difficult, so remember your schooling and do your very best to answer them.'

'Yes, Anna.'

'Also Honora you will need to speak loudly and clearly as the gentleman is a little deaf.'

Anna could see the tension in Honora's face, but she was a very obedient girl and would do as she was asked. Anna walked her to the door of her room, gave her reassurance, and asked her to go and greet him.

It was sometime later that she realised she had become engrossed in her book and that Honora had not returned. She read on for a further few minutes, until the door opened and Honora came in.

'Did you do as I asked?' enquired Anna.

'Yes, I did Anna.'

'What do you now think of the gentleman?'

'He was very kind to me. He did ask me a lot of questions, but he didn't tell me off when I didn't know the answers.'

'Would you be happy to meet him again?'

'Yes, he was very friendly and as I talked to him, I forgot about him being strange.'

'You have done well, Honora. I shall tell Mr Seward how good you have been to our guest, and now I shall go to the gentleman to give him my good wishes.'

Anna descended the stairs and William told her, that the gentleman was in the drawing room. He had hoped that she would be able to come and talk to him.

She quietly entered the room. His large bulk meant that he struggled to get to his feet.

'Please stay seated.'

As he continued with his struggle he replied, 'A man should always stand when a lady enters the room. Especially if that lady is *The Poetess of Lichfield.*'

Anna stopped in the middle of the room and turned to face him. 'Samuel Johnson the first words you manage to speak to me after a period of over a year, are those of teasing, almost lowering to sarcasm. You know such low humour annoys me so why do you persist?'

He slumped back into his chair as Anna sat opposite him. 'Anna, do you not consider yourself a poetess in this fair city?'

'I know from your previous comments that you think very little of my works, so shall we move on to another topic?'

'Of course, dear lady, and from the range of subjects that the world can supply us with, what would be your choice?'

Anna started to reply and said, 'Sam....' but halted herself. She started again, but on a different tack. 'When, as a young girl, I used to come to visit you in the bookshop in Market Square, we would read together.'

He smiled and said, 'They were precious moments. I remember them well.'

Anna continued, 'Although you were three decades older than me you insisted that I call you Sam.'

'It is my name. Do you not like it?'

Anna said with a serious look on her face, 'You are now a famous man in this country, and throughout Europe. News has reached here that you are in receipt of a King's pension. I would wish to know from you, what you want me to call you.'

He looked serious in return, 'You are perfectly correct, from my former anonymity in Lichfield, I am now invited to the tables of many famous houses in the country. I talk regularly with aristocracy.' He paused, his mouth twitched a little, 'But as far as I know my name is still Sam!' Anna nodded her head in acknowledgement.

A smile contorted Sam's face as he said, 'Are you not a little excited that we will be related by law? I would agree a distant relation, but nevertheless related.'

'Sam, you are a good man, and I know have a very good and benevolent heart, but you do always seem to be able to stretch the veracity of what you say to suit your means.'

He made a mock face of being hurt and replied, 'Joseph Porter is my stepson. There is no dispute about that. He is the son of my poor wife Hetty, may God rest soul.'

'Amen to that Sam, she was a fine woman.'

He continued, 'When Joseph and your charming sister, Sarah, get married then he will become your brother.' Anna nodded her head, before Sam added with a smile, 'but there is no need to call me uncle.'

Anna could not fail to laugh.

He hauled himself to his feet, 'I have passed my blessings to the fine couple.' His eyes focused on the book that lay on top of the needle bag by Anna's seat. He shuffled over and picked it up. He held it so close to his face, it was difficult for him to turn the pages. Anna could only hear the clicking of his mouth. Finally he said, 'It is an epistolary novel, you surprise me!'

Anna put her head a little on one side to acknowledge his surprise. 'It is not my normal fare, but it does have some prowess.'

'Humphh!' came the strong reply. 'But you have never studied the classics.'

'If by that you mean the classics of ancient Greece and Rome, then my answer is no. If you mean the classics of our own fair land then certainly I have.'

'They are not comparable, dear Anna. But we will leave that for another day, otherwise I will be accused of vexing you again.'

'Will you be attending the wedding?'

'God willing, I shall. It is not long to wait, only four days.'

There was a very light tap on the door, Anna called out, 'Come in, Sarah. I'm in here with Sam Johnson.'

Sarah came in. She curtsied, and said, 'Good day, Mr Johnson. I've come to tell Anna, that Joseph will arrive shortly. We are walking into town. Will you join us?'

A look of concern came onto Anna's face, 'Are you sure you are up to it, your face is very pale?'

'I am a little weak, but Dr Darwin has again fortified me. I wish to make the effort to walk with my future husband. And do please join us, Anna. Joseph so enjoys your company.'

Sam was hauling himself out of his chair and when he had managed to stand, Sarah went up to him, curtsied again and said,

'Sir, it would be a great honour, if we may accompany you to the town centre.'

He smiled and replied, 'The honour will be all mine and may God bless you dear Sarah.'

Anna smiled indulgently at her sister and said, 'Let me fetch my bonnet and cape.'

Joseph Porter was waiting patiently at the front door and was ahead of time. After familiar greetings to the two ladies, he was delighted that Mr Johnson would join the walk. The unlikely group of four set off at a slow pace for the town centre. They walked slowly down the tree-lined Cathedral Close. After turning across the grass apron they walked alongside Minster Pool. There they encountered Dr Darwin returning to his house after visiting a patient in town. As he had only been a short distance, the doctor was walking along greeting townsfolk, many of whom he knew well.

As soon as he saw the four walking towards him he stopped and said, 'Now the four of you together is a sight to behold. Good day, ladies.' He bowed low. 'Mr Porter, my congratulations to you.'

'Thank you, sir.'

The two large men eyed each other up. The doctor said, 'It is excellent to meet such a locally famous person.'

Samuel Johnson bowed and said, 'What you have done for this city will be felt through future generations. I cannot possibly equal that as a mere scribe.'

Anna noticed the doctor's eyes focused on Sarah, especially when she gave a little cough. Mr Porter, as was his manner, took the doctor to one side to talk to him about the wedding. Sam wandered off to peer into the water of Minster Pool.

While the two sisters were waiting Sarah said, 'Is Cornet Vyse still busy with Army matters? There has been no news that the Dragoons have left town, has there?'

'Since Joseph has arrived I have seen very little of him, although I have made sure that he knew how to communicate with me. For the past week he has not called once. I just hope that it is army matters that keeps him away.' At that point they bid farewell to the doctor and continued their walk into town.

It was as they turned the corner into Market Street, that Anna noticed Cornet Vyse some distance in front of her, resplendent in his scarlet uniform. She gasped a breath and hoped that neither her sister, nor Joseph, had noticed the Cornet. The soldier had a lady on his arm, he was leaning close and talking intently to her. A visible shiver ran through Anna and she bent down to re-tie her shoelace, which ensured that Sarah and Joseph turned to help her. This allowed the Cornet and the lady on his arm to merge with the crowds as they entered Market Square.

Anna deliberately broke her lace and requested that she must be allowed to return to her house. Sam who hadn't seemed to be paying attention, said, 'My dear Anna. There is my family's bookshop, we can mend the lace there.' There was encouragement from Sarah and Joseph, but Anna wanted to go home.

Sam said, 'You two go and meet the people of Lichfield. The market place is full and many will want to bless you.' They all hesitated, then he added, 'My parlour for mending your lace would be a wise move.' Anna's eyes shot to his face, she looked intently, he smiled gently and said, 'Mending of your lace would be a Vyse move.'

The three were looking at her. She had to react. 'Joseph and Sarah, you go on. Sam will help me mend my lace.'

It was agreed and Sam lead her into the bookshop and straight through to the back parlour.

'Sit yourself down, and compose yourself. It was a nasty shock for you wasn't it?'

'How did you know?' asked Anna quietly.

'People know me here. They always talk to me. I'm not from the big houses. I always find out every thing that is happening in Lichfield from my friends in the market.'

'Thank you, Sam,' said Anna, as she hoped the subject would be dropped.'

'Richard Vyse is a young man full of his own importance.'

'Do you think so, Sam?'

'He walked past me yesterday and totally ignored me.' He chuckled, which made Anna smile. 'A strange looking big man,

55

who shuffles along in his slippers, making peculiar noises is difficult to misplace and not recognise.'

'Oh, Sam, you're none of those things.'

'We all have to look below the surface. Within him its best not to dig too deep. It is best for you. Take my word.'

'I will, Sam.' She looked at him and added, 'Why do you tease me so. I know below your brusque exterior is a heart of gold, but you will never let anyone get close.'

He gave one of his guttural laughs, which turned into a fit of coughing 'You've been reading too many of the those romantic novels.'

Chapter Eight

A sudden noise woke Anna in the middle of the night. Her sleep had been fitful and uneven, as she could not rid her mind of the desperation of seeing Richard Vyse on the previous day. She was preparing herself to return to sleep, believing that it had been the nightmare that had awoken her, when she heard shouting.

There were heavy footsteps as a man ran down the stairs. The noise level increased as more voices could be heard as well as the opening and closing of doors. The household would normally be silent throughout the night, with the few servants, who were at duties, moving without noise. Anna reasoned quickly that something was wrong. She had just dressed in her silk morning chemise, when a gentle knock at the door brought in the maid, who requested that she go to her mother.

Worry was etched on her face as she followed the maid, who turned into Sarah's room.

'Oh! My poor Sarah.' Anna ran to the bed. She went white and began to shake at the sight of her sister, who was propped up on the pillows. She was very pale and drawn. Her delicate face was a ghostly shade. Her mother was already sat on a chair by her youngest daughter holding her hand. Sarah eye's momentarily opened and she caught sight of her sister. A transient smile came onto her lips, before she fell back into sleep.'

Her mother said, 'Dr Darwin has been sent for with urgency. I expect him here within minutes.'

'I shall sit with her mother.'

'No my dear daughter. Please attend to Honora, who must be kept away from such a distressing scene.'

'Of course, mother.'

'And your father is in the library. Will you join him, a man's place is not in a room for the sick.'

Anna went straight to Honora's room. She had been awoken by the noise in the house and was now fully awake. Her eyes looked inquisitively at Anna. She wanted to know what was happening.

'Sarah has been taken ill. The doctor has been called. There is nothing you can do, my angel. So please climb back into bed.' Anna then soothed her as she settled. The young mind cleared quickly in the presence of the calm and serene Anna and before long she had drifted into a peaceful sleep.

Anna gently removed her hand from Honora without disturbing her. Anna whispered to the maid to sit with her throughout the night. Anna slowly and sadly made her way down the stairs to her father's study.

She knocked and without waiting for a reply slipped quietly into the room. Her father was on his knees in the window. He had his hands together and his head raised. If his eyes had been open, he would have seen the three spires of the cathedral reaching into the night sky.

Anna did not hesitate, she knelt by her father and joined his prayers. Her mind never strayed from the picture of poor Sarah in bed. Even the noise of the doctor rushing through the house did not disturb her intense focus of praying for her sister.

Finally her father rose from his kneeling and, in silence, went and sat in one of the chairs on either side of the fireplace. Anna moved slowly to the chair opposite him. The last dying embers of the fire still glowed in the grate, but neither of them moved. Anna shivered uncontrollably. She pulled her chemise around her tight, but she knew that it was not the coldness of the room that was making her shiver.

They spent two hours in the sad silence and neither of them spoke a word during that time. The only sounds that were heard by Anna were the faintest voice of her father as he prayed. The house was silent. No sounds came from outside. The clock was ticking away the seconds.

The twist of the handle on the door, although extremely quiet, made her start, but she did not look in that direction. She focused on her father. The hinge made the slightest of noises as it opened. The heavy footsteps entered the room, and the door closed as quietly as it could.

They arose at the same time. Slowly and deliberately they turned to face the doctor. Both men gave inconspicuous nods acknowledging the other. Anna made no movement at all.

The doctor's eyes darted between them. They then paid full attention to Canon Seward's face and he said in a very low tone, 'Your Anna is in the room, sir.'

He was unflinching as he replied, 'She will be strong.'

The doctor eyes then flashed across them again, and then he dropped his head and said, 'Sarah will go to meet her God before the end of the day.'

Tears streamed down Anna's face. She still made no noise, and stared resolutely at the doctor. Her father lowered his head and said, 'May God rest her soul.'

Anna and the doctor both said, 'Amen.'

In a faltering voice the Canon said, 'Thank you for coming doctor. You have done your best for my poor daughter.'

'As much I would have wished with my whole heart, there is nothing I can do to stop her life ebbing away.'

For the first time the Canon raised his eyes to look at the Doctor.

'Have you suspected for long?'

The doctor looked grave. He did not rush his reply, but in a measured tone he said, 'I have known for about a month, but I suspected for longer.'

'You did not inform me, sir,' said Anna's father in a stronger voice.

'I did not sir. Such news, as I could bear to you, after I was certain of my diagnosis, would not prevent her leaving this world, but would add to the period of grief.'

'I would not have informed my family.'

'Yes, sir, I would be assured of that from my knowledge of you as a man.' They both lapsed into silence, but neither of them moved. The doctor said, in the same measured tone, 'Until the last hours it is a very difficult disease to predict the longevity of the patient. It may be days, week or months, but no longer. In view of the circumstances in this house I decided to spare the head of the household the tragic news.'

'Did you ask for God's help?'

A quivering crossed the Doctor's face, but it was blinked away, 'On becoming a doctor I took the Hippocratic to serve

59

God, and my patients to the best of my ability. And that sir, is exactly what I do.'

Another silence extended between the men, but still neither of them moved. Finally the doctor said, 'I could not alter the outcome of the disease. By being close at hand I could ensure that your daughter did not suffer the same excruciating pain that many young woman have to bear when they succumb to this terrible disease. In the past month, she has been tired, but free from serious pain.'

Canon Seward bowed his head, 'Thank you, doctor. If you will now excuse me. I shall go to take my farewell of my daughter.'

Doctor Darwin lowered his head while the Canon left the room.

***

The slow straggling procession of people in black left the transept door of the cathedral and crossed the Close to the Canon's house. The servants went back to their duties, while Mr Seward and Mr Porter accepted condolences in the study. After the steady queue of people had left, Canon Seward led Mr Porter into the dining room. Mrs Seward was already seated, a slight sob could be heard behind her handkerchief. Honora, dressed in black, had not attended the service, but now sat next to Anna. The ladies rose as the gentlemen arrived.

Canon Seward said grace and then the meal was eaten in silence. Anna was expecting that her father would wish to read from the bible in his study and she would join him there. She waited patiently for her father, who surprised her by speaking.

'I have asked Mr Porter to stay with our family during our period of mourning. He has accepted that offer.' Mr Porter made a solemn bow of the head. 'He will be with us, until the necessities of his business cause his return to Italy.' Anna was a little surprised, but nothing showed on her face, and she listened intently to her father who continued, 'As my family will know, it is my custom to return to our home village of Eyam for two months every summer.' He turned his face towards Mr Porter, 'It is my parish. I was the incumbent there until I was raised to be a

Canon. My curate, administers the parish on my behalf. Among other duties, I have to approve the parish finances for the past year.'

Mr Porter showed great attention to the Canon, but apart from some gentle nods of approval made no effort to speak. The Canon continued. 'I see no reason to change the arrangements. This house will remain in mourning where my wife will receive condolences.' He looked around the table. 'We will all be in mourning, but our location is not important for that process. Therefore I propose that Mr Porter, and my daughter Anna, join me in the trip to my home village.'

'Of course, father,' replied Anna.

The Canon looked at Mr Porter who replied, 'I will do as you suggest, sir.'

He then turned his attention to his wife. 'I shall make the necessary reparation in our home village on behalf of both of us. Peter Cunningham, my curate has insisted he move into a small cottage in the village, which will leave the old Rectory at our disposal.'

Chapter Nine

She stepped out of the Rectory in the bright of the morning after breakfast. In town she would never have walked alone, but in her home village, the custom was very different.

'Good morning, Miss Seward'

'Good morning, Major Wright.'

'Will you be visiting people in the village?'

'Yes, that is my intention,' replied Anna. It gave her the opportunity to look at the Major. She had only recently met him for the first time, although she had been in the village for a month. He had been at Eyam Hall a few days ago when she took a dish of tea there.

The Major was a stout man, with a round face and thinning hair. He rarely wore a wig, because he spent a great deal of the time with his horses. After spending over twenty years in the army, he had recently returned to his home, Eyam Hall, where his elder brother was the owner of the estate.

'I notice that you normally have Mr Porter with you.'

'Yes, he has been very kind in accompanying me around the village, but business matters have taken him to Sheffield for several days.'

'In that case, may I offer to escort you and to carry your basket.'

'That is very kind, I was intending visiting the miner's cottages today.'

Anna didn't think he looked pleased, but he said, 'Of course. Wherever you would like to go. If you need to leave the village for any of the farms, I can have a horse available very quickly.'

'Thank you, Major, but walking in the village is all for today.'

Mr Porter had been her constant companion for the past four weeks. He was a good man, she had no doubt. He was dutiful, diligent in his mourning, and greeted all the people in the village regardless of status. He seemed at ease when they visited the Hall, and equally he was well received, when he went to thank the poor families for their condolences. He was an intense man and talked a lot. In a very short space of time he had become very popular. The Major was a complete contrast to Mr Porter. He passed the time of day with people, but rarely engaged them. That had been evident at the little social meeting Anna had attended a few days previously at Eyam Hall. He did his duties by speaking to everyone, but soon disappeared from the gathering. When Anna had glanced out of one of the windows, she had seen him riding his horse towards Eyam ridge.

As she left the rectory, she turned towards the Hall and then went down the hill towards the miner's cottages. It was a gloriously sunny day. The constant nagging feeling about Sarah was only very slowing lifting, but some of the immediate pain of losing a sister had gone. She believed the long term sadness would last for ever. She was still dressed in black. Her laced trimmed bonnet gave shelter to her in the sun.

She walked along with the Major, who had greeted a few people, but generally stayed quietly at her side. 'Do you know which cottage belongs to whom in this area? The cook at the rectory asked me to go to a few in particular and gave me their names.'

'Unfortunately no. I will be most willing to find out. Who is the first person you want to meet?'

Anna replied, 'It is Dotty Middleton.'

She regretted her action as the Major shouted, 'You lad!' He pointed to a man in his twenties, who was rebuilding a stonewall.

'Which is Dotty's cottage?'

The man fixed the Major without a smile. He carried on working as he replied, 'Third on the right after the bend.'

'Awkward fellows, some of the locals,' said the Major, but he did not seem to care.

It had been the opposite to what she had found when she had walked with Mr Porter. He addressed everyone with the utmost courtesy and there was never any animosity shown to him.

Dotty turned out to be a very old lady, and Anna's suggestion that the Major wait outside the very small cottage seemed to be welcomed by all.

By the time they had left the miner's cottages she was regretting that she was not with Mr Porter, and hoped that the Major would not want to join her again.

'There is one last visit, near Highcliffe.'

'I could get the horses.'

'No that will not be necessary. Thank you for coming with me so far, but please do not feel obliged to come up there. It is a fine day and I am happy to walk.'

'Miss Seward. I am really quite enjoying myself.' His remark took Anna by surprise.

As soon as they were clear of the main road through the village and there was no one around, he seemed to change. He said, 'Eyam village is a delight, and I always welcome returning home, but everyone is in other people's business and I find that very tedious.'

'The history of many of the village families goes back centuries.'

'I know that with a force of certainty.'

Anna thought a change of subject might help the conversation.

'May I presume you do not live in the village permanently.'

'I live in London a lot. Many of my former colleagues from the army are there. We were bound by some of the situations we faced together, so it is always a pleasure to be around them. Also I am a keen horseman, especially hunting. Fortunately, I receive many invitations to indulge my passion in many parts of the country.'

Anna smiled. At least he was now talking, and the edge that had been in his voice, when mentioning the village, had gone.

'Now, what about yourself, Miss Seward. Is Lichfield your permanent home or do you travel a lot as well?'

It was now a relaxed conversation as they slowly headed up the hill. 'I would like to travel a little more. I do receive a good number of invitations, but the demands of family life have to be obeyed.'

'Is yours a large family?'

'No, but my mother is a little ailing. Father has many cathedral duties that require family support.'

'Yes, I do see.'

The conversation lapsed a little, until Anna said, 'It is hot climbing this hill. Shall we rest in the shade of that tree for a few minutes?'

'Of course.' He made sure Anna was comfortable on a nearby fallen log, but he didn't sit himself. 'Rumours in the village are that you are a very well-read poet.'

'I wouldn't say that,' replied Anna softly.

'Modesty becomes you, Miss Seward, but do tell me your favourite poets.'

'Do you have an interest in poetry? I am sure it is not usually a soldier's fare.'

'Surprising as it may seem to you. I very much enjoy poetry, although its composition is beyond me. If you give me a few moments.'

Anna waited and was rewarded by a lengthy quote. She smiled, 'Oh, that is excellent Major. It is Milton's *Paradise Lost* and is one of my favourites.'

She had been completely surprised at the transformation that came over the Major as soon as he was away from the eyes and ears of the village. The day had proved enjoyable for her. He was a very knowledgeable and well read man, that far surpassed her expectations. His interpretation of some of the poetry was extremely good. She had to admit that he showed a far greater understanding than she had.

The next few days proceeded very much the same as the first. He was waiting outside the rectory as her escort. When within the village compounds he was polite and courteous to all, but never more. But once away from the constraint, his whole personality lit up and they had some fascinating discussions. Anna had particularly chosen some farms that were a good walk so that she could engage in conversation with him.

On the fourth day he had said that he had been invited by some friends to spent the day with them in Hathersage. Would she like to ride over there with him? Given that he was from an old family of the village and her father had known them for years, she accepted the invitation. She told her father at dinner where she was planning to go the next day. He merely acknowledged, but made no extra comment.

****

'Good morning, Miss Seward,' said the Major as he waited in the hall of the Rectory for her to descend the stairs, 'I do believe it will be a fine day for a ride. The wind is a little fresh, but the sun is out.' Away from his village duties, she found him to be of the most delightful company. He was witty and his tales from the army were given with genuine modesty, but were very entertaining. She had ridden a lot when she was younger, but in recent years in Lichfield, the coach had become her favourite form of transport, whenever leaving town.

They walked past the church and spent a few minutes talking to the Reverend Cunningham, who both agreed was a fine man, and a very able servant of her father. The stables for the Hall were not far past the church. The groom brought out Anna's mount, which the Major had especially chosen for her. The mare was placid and was regularly ridden by side saddle riders. It was obedient and never lively.

It wasn't long before they were mounted and walked through the village. Their destination was only about five miles away, so they had time to linger along the tracks and grassy stretches. The two riders had now reached the familiarity of first names.

Anna noticed that he was watching her so she turned and smiled. 'I do declare,' said John Wright, 'you are the most beautiful woman that I have ever met. Your hair is exquisite and perfectly matches such an exact face.'

'Thank you, John,' she said as her mind ran through her own thoughts. Although twenty years her senior he was an energetic man, who belied his age. He was not intrinsically handsome, but neither had any serious defaults to either his face or his person.

'I hope we shall be able to enjoy many more rides together.'

Anna replied, 'It is a most refreshing change to being in town, where I now rarely ride. It is most delightful.'

Suddenly he looked a little downcast.

'Is anything the matter, John?'

'Since you have come to this village you have had an escort.'

'I presume you mean, Mr Porter.'

'I would not like to put myself at odds with you, or that gentleman, for any reason at all.'

Anna smiled, 'I now understand your meaning. Mr Porter as you know was to marry poor Sarah. I believe that it would have been as happy a match on earth as is possible. Since then he has shown no lack of duty to both my father and me. I find him a very intense man, but cannot fault his dedication to do what is right in the circumstances.'

John Wright nodded.

'There has been absolutely no indication from Mr Porter of any actions towards me. It is my expectation that when he returns from Sheffield, he will stay only a few days. After that it is father's belief that he will go back to Italy. It is therefore quite likely that we will never meet again.'

A broad smile came across his face, 'Thank you Anna for being so open with me. I feared that because of the mourning, no possible announcement could be made, but that some form of private understanding might be in the offing.'

Anna smiled to herself. There were no men in her life that should restrict John's attention to her. They chatted more amiably and in a much more relaxed way than previously. Anna was sure that at sometime John Wright would ask for her hand, but mourning would prevent such a move at the moment. She had a duty to her sister, so she would place any motive of John Wright at the back of her mind for the time being,

As they were now clear of the village and travelling along a flat and even track, John suggested a canter. Anna willingly agreed and, with the wind flowing through her hair, they set the horses going. John was a regular and extremely experienced rider and so was able to pay constant attention to Anna. Since leaving the village about a mile back they had only passed the time of day with one farmer. Apart from that they were alone as they crossed the moor, which suited both their temperaments on that day.

'Oh! A little too fast for me,' called Anna as she brought her horse back to a trot. John smiled at her and reined his large hunter back as well. As they turned to speak to each other, her mare stumbled slightly. It jolted Anna. John pulled his mount immediately and reached for the reins of the mare to steady her. Whether it was that reach or a further stumble by the mare, it was too difficult to tell from the succeeding events. The mare twisted rapidly and collided with the large hunter. Both horses jumped slightly. John Wright easily stayed steady in his saddle, but the twist of the mare, and Anna's recent lack of experience, meant she could not keep her balance.

'Ahhh!,' was the first part of her scream as she fell between the two horses. More damage would have been done, if both horses had kicked, rather than backing away as they did. Anna's left leg was out and hit the ground first. She then crumpled as her body weight landed, and dashed her head on the ground. The groan was loud as she collapsed into a motionless figure.

John Wright was from his horse in a second and down to the ground to tend to Anna, with a chilling call of, 'Anna!' which she heard in the recesses of her mind as she lost consciousness. With the presence of mind of a soldier, he slapped both horses to remove them from the area. They galloped away into the distance.

John Wright was down close to Anna's face, which had turned white from the shock of the fall. She groaned, which gave John the hope that she was still alive. He caught her hand and watched her face intently, 'Anna! Anna!'

He breathed a silent prayer, as her eyes flickered and she groaned again. He removed his cloak and placed it over her to give her some comfort. His jacket was quickly removed and it made a pillow. Anna was laying on her side so he very gently lifted her head and slipped the jacket under the side of he face.

'John,' came the very shallow voice of Anna.

'Stay still Anna. Do not move, I will need to find assistance,' he said looking around desperately, but he could see no one. They were alone.

'My leg! My leg!' cried Anna and she moved enough to be able to grasp her knee. John Wright feared a broken leg. Again he looked around for any signs of life. But there was no one who could be seen.

'I must go for help, Anna! There is no one else nearby. I must get you to the doctor.'

'Don't leave me! Don't leave me!' Anna twisted a little and then screamed with pain.

'Anna! Anna!' He soothed her hair as best he could to try to calm her.

'Don't move. Don't move it will only increase the pain. Stay steady Anna.' She did her best to adhere to his instructions. A few minutes and she opened her eyes again. She murmured, 'The pain is easier, if I do not move.'

'Then stay still Anna. Rest, please rest.' He studied her and could see the slightest of colour returning to her face. He immediately feared the onset of fever. His hand rested gently on her forehead, but it was cool. He breathed a sigh of relief.

Again he lifted his head and looked around. The mare was nowhere to be seen, and his hunter was eating from a hedgerow over half a mile away. It wasn't a horse that he had had for long so would be unlikely to come to his voice.

A slight murmuring brought his attention back to Anna whom he was kneeling next to, she said, 'The pain is ebbing John.'

'Oh, Anna! I shall need to seek help.'

'No, John just give me a little time.'

'Yes, of course.' Then for the first time he noticed the sound of a nearby spring. 'Anna there is a spring nearby. Let me wet a kerchief for you to wipe your face and lips.'

'Do not leave me.'

'No Anna, I will not. It is just there. You will hear my voice the whole time.'

He made her as comfortable as possible. He was less worried as she had begun to talk a little. But there was still no signs of any other person and both of the horses had now disappeared from view

'I feel a little less in pain, I will sit up.'

He guided her gently, but allowed her to use his steadiness as a support. With the kerchief he bathed the graze on her forehead.

'How is your head?' he asked soothingly.

'The injury does not hurt and my head is now quite clear.'

He instructed her to move her right leg, which she could do freely while sitting on the floor. They gradually established that the pain was in her left knee, and apart from that she was not injured.

She was now able to look around with the sharpness of her eyes returning, she sighed, 'The horses have fled.'

'Yes, they are not in view, and neither is a field worker or a traveller. If I can catch a horse, I can race to the nearest cottage and return in minutes.' They searched the horizon in hope, but the countryside showed no signs of life, except for a few sheep resting in the fields.

Anna had fully recovered her senses by now and some of her colour had returned to her face.

'It's only a mile back to Eyam, isn't it?'

'Yes probably a little less,' he said.

'Then perhaps you will help me stand and lend me your arm.'

He carefully helped her to her feet, but her knee resisted any effort to put that leg to the floor.

'We shall wait in the shade there. I will make you a seat. At some point a traveller or farmer will pass.'

Anna said, 'Let us see if we can make some progress back to the Rectory, but I might need to rest.' Very slowly with a great deal of support from John she made a little progress.

'You are a very brave lady, Anna,' said the Major as they moved very slowly along the track.'

'But I am now so tired.'

'We only need to reach the edge of the moor and then we will be in sight of Eyam. One of the village people will soon spot us, and we can then get you safely home.' He looked at her face and the colour was draining again. She rested for a moment, but then tried to press on, but he felt the strength flow from her. He was holding her firmly so she could not slip to the ground. He put her down on a mossy bank.

'I must rest.'

'Anna we are too close now to stop.'

'But I must rest.'

John feared the worse. She was slipping into sleep.

'Forgive me, Anna, but this is necessary.'

He reached under her body with both of his arms and lifted her. She grimaced a little in pain. He said, 'You will need to lean into me, so that I may carry you.'

Anna felt the strength in his arms and the power of his body. He was a strong man and did not struggle to lift her. As she closed her eyes, her head dropped to his shoulder and she said, 'I will do what you say.'

John was now free to move at his own speed. There was only one thought in his mind and that was to return Anna to the safety of the Rectory and to summon help for treatment. Despite the weight that he was carrying he took large and purposeful strides. It was only a few minutes before he could see the edge of the moor, which would lead down to the village.

Anna opened her eyes slightly and murmured, 'Thank you, John.' No sooner than she had said that, he reached the edge and could look down on his village. Within minutes he saw a horse being ridden fast towards them. He breathed a sigh of relief. They had been spotted. It wasn't long before help reached them. He declined the use of a cart and carried Anna into the village. There were many in attendance, but he did not stop until the Rectory door opened in front of him and the cook, being the most senior woman in the house, instructed him where to place Anna.

Anna's maid appeared, immediately cried out and then began to cry. Anna who had recovered a little as the pain in her leg eased with the carrying, called to the maid, 'Hush, I am not badly hurt, with the exception of my knee.'

Canon Seward, who had been visiting an outlying part of the parish, had been sent a message. He had now come into the room. His presence meant that all others, except the cook and the maid faded away.

He rapidly assessed the situation and only quickly spoke to Anna to assure her of his presence. The local apothecary was sent for and told to come with all speed. The Canon then left the cook and the maid to tend to Anna needs. He stepped from the room, where Anna lay, and asked Major Wright to join him in the study.

Within a few days, Anna had recovered sufficiently to be able to very gingerly descend the stairs with the help of her father. She took a chair in the drawing room with her leg resting on a small stool. Anna received a good number of well wishers, but declined many more due to tiredness.

The evening brought peace and quiet to the household. Anna busied herself with some needlework, which she would later give to some of the younger women in the village. The door opened and her father entered.

'Anna I wish to speak to you.'

'Yes, father' Anna replied looking directly at him

He said in a serious voice, 'I am satisfied that your fall from the horse was an accident.'

Anna's face showed surprise, 'Why did you doubt it, father? I had given you an account of what happened. I believe Major Wright also gave you his version.'

He nodded, 'My concern was that he was not paying attention to you and did not realise that you are an inexperienced horse-woman.'

'I was riding quite within my capabilities, until the horse unfortunately stumbled. As you ride yourself, sir, you know that on most occasions it is easy to regain one's balance. I did not and fell.' She could see from his face that he did not like the direction of this conversation.

'That was not what I came to talk to you about.'

'Very well, father. May I ask what you did want to talk to me about.'

'It is related to Major Wright.' As was usual in most conversations, her father showed no indication in his face of any approval or disapproval. It was necessary to wait to hear his words. 'Since the absence of Mr Porter, he has been meeting with you a great deal.'

'Yes, father. He has accompanied me throughout the village in the visits I have made. The ride to Hathersage was the first time that he wished to go anywhere apart from the village.'

Her father did not move his head, 'Given his position in the village, it would be very difficult for you to stop seeing him at all.'

Anger quickly crossed Anna face, 'Do you wish me to stop meeting him?'

'That is my wish.'

Anna went red as she snapped, 'May I ask why? He appears to me to be the most honourable of men.'

'He has spent a long time in the army.'

Anna was still furious with her father, 'Father, why does that matter. He comes from a prestigious family in the village and you have known the man all your life.'

'I wish that you would make no further arrangements to see him. I have also spoken with him and advised him of my decision.'

'Father! That is outrageous. On what grounds?'

'Do not raise your voice to me! I have made a decision and that is final. Now you will obey me.'

'Please father give me a reason,' she said in a firm voice.

Her father stared at her and, like Anna, was going red with anger. Finally under Anna's stare he relented a little, 'A long life in the army can affect men in different ways. Some remain honourable and others do not.'

Anna snapped, 'Are you saying John Wright is not honourable?'

'I will not argue with you! He has drifted in life and shows no inclination to take on normal gentlemanly duties. Therefore I insist you make no further arrangements to meet him.'

Anna struggled to her feet.

'Where are you going?'

'Father, I might have to obey you. But I do not have to speak to you. Good night.' She was bright red in the face as she limped to the door. She did not look back, nor did she listen to discover whether her father spoke to her again.

Chapter Ten

Anna's sad mood deepened as she awoke the following morning. She was wrong to talk to her father as she did. It would be her duty to make amends later in the day. Her father was already present at breakfast when she arrived. She greeted him with the normal words, but the way they were uttered meant there was no meaning in them. He acknowledged only with a nod of the head. Breakfast was then taken in silence.

With the meal nearly finished, the main door of the room opened and Mr Porter entered. He had travelled early from Sheffield so he could be with them all day. An expanse of the Canon's hand towards the buffet was accepted and he helped himself to food. He also ate his food in silence. At the end of the meal Anna could see Mr Porter's eyes switching between her and her father. The look on his face meant that he was deciding who to speak to.

The Canon asked Mr Porter to join him for a few minutes in his study. That gave Anna a pang of regret, because she knew that it wouldn't be long before she would have Mr Porter's attention. She had no alternative, but to accept that he would take up his position by her side. She had planned to go the very short distance to the Reverend Cunningham's cottage to assist him in some church matters.

She limped badly, but was determined to meet with the curate. Mr Porter was at her side as they took the path through the graveyard. Perhaps because she was moving so much slower than normal, the grave of Mrs Mompesson, the wife of the vicar during the terrible plague, stood out more. She reflected on how a young woman had married and then her life ceased with the dreadful disease that took many villagers.

The curate sent a message to say that he was delayed with a parishioner, but would attend on her shortly. Anna rested on a bench in the small front garden of the cottage. Joseph Porter sat next to her. 'Your father told me of your very bad accident.'

She smiled in reply, 'It was not that bad, Joseph. I shall make a quick recovery. Major Wright was a complete gentleman and tended to my every need,' she said as she hoped the curate would not be long.

'Quite so.'

Anna preferred to lapse into silence and watch the village people passing by, while she waited.

Joseph said, 'My business activities in Italy will force me to return there, but the exact date of my leaving is not yet fixed, but it will be before...'

Anna wasn't sure why he had suddenly stopped. He was normally a very precise man with his speech, and didn't leave sentences unfinished. She inclined her head, and although she feared the answer she said, 'Before what? Joseph.'

'I am in a very difficult position and would wish to cause you no conflict with your duties.'

In a much stronger voice Anna said, 'I would not wish you to put yourself under any pressure.'

He studied her for a few minutes and then said, 'Under every circumstance, except my imminent return to Italy, I would delay this matter, but it cannot be dealt with at a distance.'

Anna looked straight ahead, with an unflinching face.

Joseph continued, 'Since the tragic event I have got to know you much better. You are a very fine and intelligent women, who has impeccable conduct through your performance of the duties to all around you.'

Anna gave a slight nod of the head.

'I would therefore wish to ask you, after the period of mourning is complete, may I have your permission to ask your father to take you to be my wife.'

Anna swallowed deeply. She looked ahead and her eyes glazed. 'Joseph, I feel greatly honoured by your attention and your wish that I would become your wife. You are a fine and honourable man.' She needed to pause, so she could draw a deep breath because her heart was beating fast with nervousness. 'I am afraid your presence at all times reminds me of my poor sister Sarah, and I would not feel at ease to become your wife.'

He took sometime to reply and said, 'Thank you for accepting my request in the manner in which it was intended.'

A sudden thought struck Anna, 'Joseph I would think that my father would also be reluctant to give permission.'

'Yes, I did think about the right of clergy to refuse to marry a man to another sister in the same family after the death of his wife. I concluded that as the marriage had never taken place, he would suspend such judgement.' His eyes looked up and down the street in the front of the cottages and he added, 'I see the Reverend Cunningham is coming, I will take my leave of you.'

Anna rose as he left and waited for the curate to arrive. While Anna's mood had deepened, she was still prepared to assist the curate. They were quickly settled in the cottage. He was a tall man, not many years older than herself, but he looked much more aged. He had little hair which blew around uncontrollably even in the slightest breeze. His head was a little lop-sided and he tended to walk with a slight leaning stoop. His face was marked with the scars of childhood illnesses. When she spoke to him it was necessary to speak loud and clear as he was a little deaf. However, he was very even tempered, and had a smile and a good word for everyone regardless of status.

Once they were seated, Anna said, 'How may I help you Reverend?'

He chuckled a little and smiled at her, 'I have been your father's curate for only a few years, but I have got to know you well. Perhaps I might be so bold as to suggest that you call me Peter.'

'And therefore we will know each other as Peter and Anna.'

'There are a number of jobs that must be completed with parish documents, but the writing is very small and my eyesight is poor. I wonder if you would be good enough to read some of them to me.'

She looked at the large pile of documents and boxes on the nearby bench and replied, 'It will give me a useful job to do while I need to rest my knee.'

The next week passed in a familiar pattern each day. After breakfast Mr Porter would accompany her as far through the village as her leg would permit and then he would escort her to the curate's house. After she had been there sometime, with her leg getting better each day, she would walk along to the high street and on two occasions was invited into Eyam Hall for a rest. This meant that although the invitation had not come from John Wright, she still met him either in the village or at the hall.

It was her last day assisting on parish business. As he closed the last of the boxes he turned to her and said, 'Thank you so much for your help. Not only are the documents up-to-date, but I cannot think when I have passed a more pleasant week. I really have so much enjoyed your company.'

'Thank you, Peter. The conversations have been extremely agreeable.'

He hesitated drew a deep breath, but then chose not to speak.

Anna said gently, 'Peter there is something on your mind, I can tell.'

'It is not my position to speak. I apologise if I have caused you any concern.'

'Peter, I can tell you are worried about a matter. We are good friends. Position in life does not matter between friends. Now I would like to hear what you have to say.'

'You have many fine men who are no doubt seeking your hand. I could never aspire to be one of them. Your father would expect so much more and so would you. I have a very small stipend and live by the grace of your father in the Rectory during his absence. If he returns, a cottage like this is my life. Also your father would never seriously consider me to be a suitor.'

'Go on,' encouraged Anna, who could sense his embarrassment as he spoke.

'Life throws many difficulties in the way, especially of attractive young women like yourself. If in the future, you are in difficulties and need a haven and a place to called home, a husband who would love you dearly, then please remember that I am here for you.'

'Peter, you are the sweetest and kindest man that I have ever met.'

He straightened his shoulders and said, 'I shall say not one word more and will now walk you back to the rectory.'

As she entered the Rectory so her father was waiting at the door. A look of anxiety came over her face. Mr Porter was just behind her father and it was clear they had just emerged from the study.

She stared at her father, but it was his usual taciturn expression that greeted her. 'I need to speak to you in the study immediately.'

Anna took a deep breath as she followed him. Mr Porter bowed slightly and stood to one side. He then walked towards the front door to greet Reverend Cunningham.

Her father sat behind his desk. He indicated a chair, but only added, 'To take the weight from your knee.'

'My knee feels much stronger, I will stand.'

'Animosity between a father and daughter at this particular time cannot be tolerated,' said her father in a stern voice.

'My apologies father for being rude to you last week, but I thought you were unjustified in your actions.'

'So you do not apologise for what you did.'

'No father I do not. My apology is for losing my temper with you. That is not acceptable. As regard to my conduct I have behaved at all times within the standards that you have rightly set for me.'

'Be that as it may. We will move on to the reason I wanted to talk to you.'

'Yes, father,' replied Anna with a deep frown.

'It has come to my notice that you have disobeyed me.'

Anna could feel her face going red, but knew that this time she would have to control her temper. A deep breath and a glance out of the window tried to balance her mind. 'Father, I know of no instance in which I have disobeyed you.'

'Very well,' he said as he gripped his fists tightly, 'then I must tell you and await your apology.'

Anna was struggling between a mixture of temper and tears.

'I clearly instructed you not to make any liaison with Major Wright.'

She waited to see whether he would add anything else. It also gave her time to compose her thoughts.

'Since you spoke to me. I have met Major Wright on three occasions. The first time on Church Street when he greeted me, enquired about my knee and then passed by.'

'That is not what I meant.'

'On the other two occasions the lady of the Hall invited me to take tea with her, which I did. Major Wright was present in the Hall on both occasions, but apart from a normal greeting we did not speak. So I have not disobeyed you, father.'

Her father thought about matters for a few minutes. Anna tried to calm herself, but desperately wanted to sit down as her knee was now aching.

'There is another matter.'

'Yes, father?' but it was said with a resigned voice.

'It is a delicate matter under the circumstances.'

Anna's stern face did not change and she waited for her father.

'Mr Porter will need to return to his business in Italy. He had indicated that he may well return to England in the autumn, which would be after our period of morning for blessed Sarah.' He then waited and looked at his daughter.

Anna was feeling very nervous, but it was clear her father was not going to add to his statement. She drew in a deep breath and said in a slow and deliberate tone, 'When Mr Porter leaves our family, then I shall wish him Godspeed and sincerely hope that he may have the Lord's blessing.' She paused and then added, 'It would be of no interest to me whether he returned to these shores or not.' The directness of the statement made her father take a deep breath.

He eyed his daughter and then said, 'You may go and rest your knee.'

Anna did not move, but fixed a look on her father and said, 'Given that my presence in Eyam leads to so much discord, I would earnestly ask you to let me return to Lichfield.'

Chapter Eleven

It was a late February morning, when Canon Seward asked to see Anna in his study after breakfast. She went into him as soon as the meal was over.

In recent times when he had asked to see her, he had immediately sat behind his desk and left her the choice of standing or sitting in front of him. But this time he seemed different. He went and sat in his armchair near the fire, and beckoned her to sit opposite.

He smiled gently at her. Whilst her father nearly always had a serious face, in the past he had smiled at her. But since the day she had left Eyam there had been no feeling or tenderness from his side. Her mother would not even discuss the matter, or offer an opinion on even the smallest matter between Anna and her father. She, with a great deal of extra friendliness, only talked to Anna about needlecraft and the household duties of a wife.

So it came as a surprise that her father had suddenly decided to smile on her again. They sat opposite one another and he lapsed into silence for a short while. As such behaviour was normal for him, she took no notice and stared into the fire to watch the burning ember patterns.

'There are two matters that I wish to talk with you about.'

'Yes father.'

'The first is a difficult duty, but it is now past six months since we lost our beloved Sarah and therefore it is time to lift the mourning.' Anna had been proud to wear the black in respect of her sister, but reflected as he spoke that it was the memories that were important, not the way she dressed. 'I propose that later today in a small private ceremony, we will thank the Lord for the life of Sarah and lift the mourning.'

'Of course father.'

'The second matter is something that I have thought long and hard about. It gives me no comfort, but it cannot be avoided.' Anna merely bowed her head and then looked into the fire. 'I am conscious that there has been some serious discord between us over the past months.' Anna chose to make no acknowledgement nor did she show any indication of her thoughts in her face. 'Sometime ago you expressed a wish to visit our capital city. At the time I stated I would only be happy for you to go, if chaperone arrangements, of which I approved, could be made.' Anna began to wonder what her father intended. 'I am now confident such an arrangement may be put into place.'

'Father, how is that possible?' she asked meekly.

'As you know, I have had a long regard for the Levitt family. Mr Levitt's business now means that he and his family spend much of their time in their house in Wimpole Street. I have a great admiration for the family and the principles they hold.'

'It is justified, father, I am sure.'

'As you are a favourite of both Mr and Mrs Levitt and their daughter Abigail, you have been invited to spend the rest of the season with them in London.'

The news was too good for Anna's to be at odds with her father and she said, 'I would only wish to go, if it is with your express agreement.'

'Yes, my daughter I think it might be a period of healing. Therefore I will not only invite you to visit London, but do everything in my power to ensure your needs are met.'

'Then I shall be very pleased to go, sir.'

Her father then detailed the arrangements all of which suited Anna. He closed by saying that as the Levitts were already in London, they would welcome her at any time she was prepared to travel there.'

She thanked her father and left the room in a state of high excitement, and went to seek her mother. Her radiant smile told Anna that she already knew of her husband's decision. There was then several days of shopping, needlecraft and packing to be done.

'My dearest Anna,' called Abigail as she came to greet her friend. They embraced and Anna then stood back and looked at the Levitt House in Wimpole street. Her father had been true to his word. He had despatched his own coach and servants to bring her to London, along with a gentleman and his wife from the cathedral, who were also travelling to the capital city.

Anna stood in awe at the sight of the street. She had been transfixed by the noise and bustle as the coach slowly made its way to the Levitt House. She was full of excitement, and no less so, was her friend, who had greeted her. The servants were left to the luggage and Abigail took Anna to meet her parents.

Anna curtsied low to Mr Levitt, 'It is a great honour to be here sir, I thank you most sincerely.'

'Stand up, dear girl, you are amongst friends now. I think you will find that we have a little less formality than you are used to in Cathedral Close.'

'My father was very earnest that I convey his good wishes to you and your wife.'

'Your father is a very fine man, and I shall write to him with haste to assure him of the safe arrival of his daughter. We will perhaps dwell on our mutual reflections of Lichfield at a later date, for your arrival is a time of celebration.'

'Thank you.' Anna greeted Mrs Levitt, who informed her that she had a room just along from Abigail and she expected they would spend much time in each other's company.

Mr Levitt said, 'This will be our first full season in London. I only purchased and made good this house last year and my whole family is in the expectation of the wonders of this city.'

'Oh father, do let me tell Anna what we shall do tomorrow if she feels recovered from her journey.'

Benevolently Mr Levitt said, 'Anna you can see what excitement you have caused. Go on, tell Anna what you are proposing for tomorrow.'

Abigail was so agitated by excitement she could hardly make clear her words, but managed to say, 'We shall walk to Bond Street, where we can visit some of the finest shops in the land.'

Anna's face showed immediate enjoyment at the idea, but it recomposed with a look of concern.

'What is the matter, dear Anna? What concerns you about Bond Street?' asked Abigail, 'I thought you would like the idea.'

Anna said, 'Very much I do. It would be delightful to see the shops that one only hears about in Lichfield. But this is London. Will it be safe to walk?' She turned to Mr Levitt, 'Unless of course Mr Levitt were with us.'

He gave a great roar of laughter, 'Dearest Anna, because I shall call you Anna under my own roof, and treat you as fair as my daughters. There is nothing I could think of being worse than going with two young ladies to the shops of Bond Street.' Again he roared with laughter. Anna observed a far more jovial and relaxed man than whenever she had seen him in the presence of her father. 'It comes as a great surprise to many that it is perfectly safe for you and my daughter to walk the short distance to Bond Street. I nevertheless understand your apprehension and assure you that either my wife or my servants would be at your command if you so wish.'

'Thank you very much sir, but I will follow your guidance.'

'I will retire to my study shortly, but as this is my Abigail's and your first season in London I shall allow you, in conjunction with my wife, to decide what we will do for entertainment.'

'That is extremely generous of you sir,' replied Anna.

'Your life is one of devotion and duty to your family. It brings the greatest admiration from me, but you are a young woman and a little light entertainment cannot be a bad influence on you.' With that he retired to his study. Abigail and Anna went upstairs to the drawing room, which they would share for the remainder of the season.

As soon as the were behind closed doors Abigail said, 'Anna there are so many soldiers and gentlemen in London. I have only been to a few balls, but I danced every single dance, with fine and honourable men.'

'It sounds very different from Lichfield,' replied Anna warily.

'It's so exciting. I never know what is going to happen next.'

'It will be wonderful to visit Bond street tomorrow with you,' but it was said with a worried voice.

'There is nothing to worry about, you will see how different life is in London.'

Abigail then looked at her friend with a quizzical face.

'What is it, Abigail?'

'In London the fashion is for hair to be worn high and powdered.'

Anna thought for a little time and replied, 'While I might be tempted at sometime in the future during my stay, I would prefer to keep my hair on my shoulders.'

It was with a look of trepidation that Anna descended the stairs the following morning to meet her friend. The nervous look had grown throughout breakfast and although she had great faith in Mr Levitt's judgment, she couldn't help thinking that it wasn't the right thing to do. More importantly she thought that her father would be extremely displeased. But she had a duty to her hosts and chose to raise no objections.

Abigail, came skipping down the stairs with a broad smile. They were both dressed in winter coats, although London was not as cold as Lichfield. The servant opened the door and they left the house.

Anna quivered as soon as she set foot outside of the front door. The street was full of noise, people and carriages. 'Oh, my goodness,' she said to herself.

'Come on, Anna, this way.' Anna was expecting some relief from the number of people and the noise as she turned the corner towards Bond Street, but both increased. She tightly grasped Abigail's arm, who was enjoying her walk along the busy pavements. At times they had to stop to allow other ladies to pass in front of them. Gradually her fear of walking with Abigail began to dissipate as there were very many women of all ages walking without male escorts. And while Anna could see some were from poorer backgrounds, there were very many who were dressed in the best of clothes.

Within minutes Abigail led Anna around another corner and said, 'Anna this is Bond Street and the finest shops in the kingdom.' It took the two women a long time to pass the first few shops. There were carriages lined up along side the pavement. The shop owners insisted on bringing out more and more samples of cloth and dresses to the ladies, so they did not need to get out from their carriages. The shop assistants carrying rolls had to cross an already busy pavement, which meant that progress was very slow. They went into several shops to view materials. Anna had never seen such a range of colours and patterns. In the dress shop there were hundreds of choices. Although one or two caught her eye she never mentioned them because she had heard how much they cost.

After a few hours they were feeling tired and they decided to walk back to Wigmore Street.

Anna was looking very carefully down and in front of her in the attempt to avoid all the people. They tightly held each others arm as many pairs of young ladies were doing. Abigail stopped suddenly, and then said, 'Excuse me, sir, but we have not been introduced. You are deliberately standing in my way.'

A shiver rang through Anna who quickly looked up, her fear changed to a face of surprise, 'Major Wright!' Abigail looked at her friend and breathed a sigh of relief as a gentle smile crossed Anna's face.

'Good day, Miss Seward,' he said with a gracious bow, 'this is a very unexpected pleasure.'

Anna had now recovered herself, 'Major Wright, it is very much a surprise.' She then introduced Abigail.

He said, 'I often come to London for part of the season. Eyam is very quiet and a little dull at this time of year.'

They enquired of each other's families and were just about to take their leave, when Abigail said, 'Major as you clearly come from the Seward's home village and know the family well, may I give you my calling card.' Anna shivered, but there was nothing she could do about it. Abigail continued, 'I am sure that my father would wish you to call upon him as you have a mutual friend in Canon Seward.'

As they took their leave Anna began to worry about how it could all go wrong in London. It was her first day and a very serious problem had now arisen. The walk back to the Levitt house did not take long. Anna immediately suggested she would retire for a short period to write some letters. Abigail agreed to do the same. Anna put her bonnet and coat in her room, checked her dress in the mirror and went downstairs to gently knock on the door of Mr Levitt's study.

A strong voice from inside called, 'Enter!'

Mr Levitt was sat behind his desk. She went up to the front of it, curtsied and said, 'May I speak with you at a time of your convenience, sir?'

He smiled at her benevolently, 'I can see from your face that it is covered in worry, so we will speak now.'

'Thank you, sir.' Anna went to explain why she had come to see him but he put up his hand.

'No, no, Anna. I cannot have you standing, with me behind the desk. We will sit in comfortable chairs by the fire.'

'Thank you, sir.'

Once they were both seated he said, 'Tell me what concerns you.'

Anna explained about the accidental meeting with Major Wright and that Abigail had given him a card and asked him to call on Mr Levitt.

He nodded, 'Both yourself and my daughter behaved exactly as I would have expected, but I can see from your face that there is more to the matter that what I have just heard.'

'Yes sir. While we were in Eyam, Major Wright asked my father for permission to escort me on visits to other houses and to various events. But my father refused.'

Mr Levitt raised his eyebrows, and said, 'But you say he is from the main Hall in the village.'

'Yes, sir.'

'Then I see no problem. Your father has advised you what action he believes necessary, if Major Wright approaches me then I will know what to say.'

Anna gave the faintest of nods.

He studied her for a little while then said, 'Come Anna. There is something else isn't there.'

'It is very difficult to explain sir, without seeming ungrateful to my father.'

'Let me see if I am able to put you at ease. If what we had discussed before was the end of the matter, you would not still be sat there. So I would conclude something else happened.' A little nod from Anna, encouraged Mr Levitt to continue. 'My guess would be that there were further accidental meetings, which your father disapproved of.'

Anna closed her eyes, but gave a gentle nod of her head.

'Your father is a very fine man. There is no doubt, however, he can be a little over possessive of you. You are such a sensible young lady and would never go against his wishes, but I can see the current situation.'

'Thank you, sir. I do not know what is the best approach. Perhaps it may be better for me to return to Lichfield.'

'Absolutely not, Anna. I shall write to your father and explain exactly what has happened, and that you came to tell me immediately after the event. I shall given your father assurances that at anytime Major Wright is in my house, I will be present and fulfil your father's wishes.'

'Thank you, sir. It is a great relief to talk to you.'

As Anna left Mr Levitt's study, the butler handed her a letter that had just been delivered. She looked at the envelope and it was in her father's handwriting. Reflecting on the conversation with Mr Levitt and wondering if it would be better for all if she returned to Lichfield, she went to her room to read the letter.

Even though she had not long left her home city it gave her warmth to hear from her father. She read it with a degree of seriousness following on from her meeting with Major Wright. It was the last paragraph that caused her a great pang of worry.

'My dearest daughter before I bid you adieu it is time to partly fulfil the commitment I made to you, when I entrusted you to the care of the Levitts in London. I stated that I would do everything in my power to assist you in enjoying the experience. As you know before I met your dear mother I lived in London for a number of years and therefore understand what the season means especially to a young woman.

Therefore I have made bankers' communication to Mr Levitt to ensure that you may be equipped with new dresses for the social occasions. You might be surprised at the sum, but I do know that such a sum is necessary in London, whereas in Lichfield it would buy ten times that number...'

'Oh, dearest father, why do you torment me so?'

Chapter Twelve

Several visits to the shops with Abigail and Mrs Levitt had produced a wardrobe for Anna that she could hardly believe. She had again gone to Mr Levitt to ask his advice as to whether she should decline the offer from her father and in his avuncular manner he had given her two options. To accept her father's offer was the first. The second was to return it, whereby Mr Levitt would buy the same wardrobe for her. He insisted that she had new clothes. So as not to be obliged to Mr Levitt, she accepted her father's money.

Anna was now ready and standing in front of the mirror of the private drawing room and looking at one of her new dresses, which she thought was magnificent. Abigail burst into the room in her usual ebullient mood. 'Isn't it exciting, I've never been before.'

'Neither have I,' replied Anna, but she couldn't show such enthusiasm as she was still concerned about what was happening in London.

By the time they went downstairs a large group of about sixteen people had assembled. They were all friends of Mr Levitt and some of them knew Anna. She was complimented very highly on her dress and gradually began to feel a little more at ease with the number of friendly faces. It was the next part of the evening that held trepidation for her. They were all to be part of Mr Levitt's party and were going out for the evening. It seemed very unusual to her to visit a location in early spring, where some of the entertainment would be in a park.

As well as the sixteen guests a good number of servants and footmen would accompany them. By the time they left the house there was a long line of carriages to take them to their destination. It was a journey of a few miles to outside London. The evening would be spent in Ranelagh Gardens.

The Levitt's carriages joined a long line from which many fine ladies and gentleman were disembarking. Finally, Mr Levitt led his group through hundreds of people to a large booth that was equipped with fires, drinks, food and a musical quartet. Ladies and gentleman were walking in the grounds and through walkways in the park, which were lit with many lanterns and fires. Anna was very quiet as she absorbed all of the scene that was in front of her. There were so many different people to watch and all types of music to listen to. Acrobats and dancers mixed with walking musicians. There were a good number of military men, some of very high rank.

Anna was transfixed by watching everything that happened so she did not notice others joining Mr Levitt's booth, until he called her name, and she looked round in his direction.

She immediately rose to her feet, 'Captain Temple.'

'At your service Miss Seward.'

Anna caught sight out of the corner of her eye, Abigail talking to Captain Robertson.

'This is indeed a surprise, Captain Temple.'

'I'm afraid that it was necessary to leave with the regiment early from Lichfield. I did not have opportunity to ask your father for permission to write, I just hoped we would return to our barracks after a short while.'

'So you did not return to Lichfield at all?' asked Anna remembering the conversation she'd had with Captain Robertson.

'I did for a short period accompanied by the most damnable luck.' Anna didn't reply, but waited to see whether he would explain. 'On my journey from London I fell ill, and had to stay in the sick bay of the barracks for the remainder of the week. Even before I was better, the army sent me back to London.'

Anna felt a little relieved, at least he hadn't just ignored her. But she still held a few doubts now that such time had passed since they were last together. He seemed a little lost as to what to say next.

She said, 'I'm afraid I was away for a while, so I do not know whether you were in my home town.'

'Alas no. We were expecting to return when we received the orders of the King. We were despatched to America where we have been until very recently. As a regiment we have only just reformed in London. So it is a wonderful opportunity to meet with you again.'

Anna smiled and looked on the handsome face, who for so long she had sought even the slightest contact.

'Is you father here? So that I may now ask permission to escort you.'

Anna looked around the assembled fashionable elite and quietly replied, 'My father remains in Lichfield with his duties.'

'Yes, of course,' he replied with a nod, 'May I assume that as you are of Mr Levitt's party and he is acting as your guardian while you are in London.'

Anna nodded.

'May I have your permission to ask Mr Levitt if I may attend you.'

Anna wished with all her heart to be able to say yes, but her father's distant presence came to mind, but finally she said, 'Yes, Captain Temple, you may.'

Anna had already guessed that Mr Levitt would agree, which he did.

Captain Temple then said, 'Perhaps we could start your introduction to London by my showing you around the gardens. Unless you have seen them before.'

'I have not, Captain, this is my first visit.'

'Then we shall delay no longer and I propose we visit the magnificent Rotunda and then perhaps the Chinese building.'

Anna had heard of both of these through the newspapers and had a longing to see them. But she was somewhat surprised when Caption Temple led her in one direction, while Captain Robertson went the other way with Abigail.

To be assured that this was intended she glanced back at Mr Levitt, who gave them both a cheery wave.

Anna doubted whether there had been an hour in her life that she had enjoyed more than the walk through the park and buildings with Captain Temple. Finally, as both were getting a little hungry they returned to Mr Levitt, who greeted them both very cordially. As well as friends of Mr Levitt coming to the booth to talk, there were also a number of messengers carrying notes around the garden.

Captain Temple delivered Anna safely back to Mr Levitt and he took his leave to return to his own party.

She was very happy with the evening and marvelled that such entertainment went on so late. The evening was not coming to a close, because several members of the group moved to newly erected card tables to begin playing. Anna declined to play and was content to sit and watch the unfolding scene. It had been quite enough excitement for one day.

She sat back and relaxed. She scarcely noticed a messenger arrive and give a note to Mr Levitt. He read it and raised his eyebrows, and replied, 'Please tell your master it will be an honour to meet him.' The messenger withdrew. Mr Levitt, raised his voice a little to be heard by all who were in the booth. 'Please prepare yourself, we will shortly have an important visitor.' All the group looked a little surprised, but followed his instructions.

Shortly afterwards Anna noticed a man of high rank walking slowly in their direction. He was attended by several footmen. From his manner and his attendees, the crowds sensed a man of importance and cleared the way for him. To her surprise she realised he was walking directly for the Levitt booth. As he arrived a footman stepped to the front and announced, 'Lord Grafton, Privy Councillor.'

The whole group rose to its feet. Mr Levitt and the men all bowed and the ladies curtsied. 'Welcome to my booth, your Lordship. How may I be of service to you?'

'Thank you for your welcome Mr Levitt. Ladies and gentleman, as this is an informal entertainment evening please be seated. It has come to my notice that you have a lady in your group with whom I would wish to speak. Although I cannot say for certain, as my information may be false.'

Anna was watching him with fascination. His name had been in the newspapers recently and it was strongly suggested that he could soon be the next Prime Minister.

'If I could know the name of that lady. I am sure she would be most willing to oblige.'

Lord Grafton looked around the group and then returned his eyes to the host. He said with a smile, 'As I can recognise her face, I now know she is part of your group. It is Miss Seward.'

Anna's eyes opened in amazement, she went a little pale and held the arm of her chair to steady her nerves. She heard an exclamation from Abigail, 'Anna!'

She quickly remembered her manners and rose to her feet and, not being sure what to do next, she curtsied. Mr Levitt said, 'Come dear Anna and pay your respects to Lord Grafton.'

Anna stepped forward, 'Good evening, your Lordship.'

Lord Grafton said, 'Is Thomas Seward your father?'

Anna replied quietly, 'Yes, sir he is.'

'Your face could only be descended from your father.' Anna was too awestruck to reply. Lord Grafton turned to address Mr Levitt, 'May I take the liberty of escorting Miss Seward to join our group, as I have several people with me, who will remember her father.'

If it was possible Anna opened her eyes even wider. She looked at Mr Levitt to say she couldn't possibly go through with such a visit but he said, 'Of course, Lord Grafton. If you would be kind enough to send a servant at the end of her visit, then I will accompany Miss Seward back to our party.'

'No need, Mr Levitt, I will be very happy to personally deliver her to your party. However, I suspect it may take some time as there is a lot to talk about.'

Anna had gone white with nervousness. How could she possibly join such as prestigious party.

'Come my dear, you look a little distressed. Do not fear we will make you very much at home.' With her eyes flashing, a nervous feeling inside, and with very weak legs she walked alongside Lord Grafton.

As she arrived at a magnificent booth she received the kindest of welcomes and was introduced to many who were present. They all seemed to know of her, but there was a great blur of names.

Finally she managed to have enough self-composure to say, 'My lordship, I am honoured that you have chosen to introduce me to such a distinguished company, but I am unable to hold all the names in my head.' This brought a laugh from the assembled company, but also sympathy. 'Also your Lordship I do not know why you have selected me apart from mention of my father.'

'You are quite right young lady, we are the devil trying to confuse you.' Anna then worried whether she had said too much. 'Come sit by me, with a few old friends and we shall explain.' Anna was very reluctant to sit down in such distinguished company, but Lord Grafton insisted she took a seat next to him.

'Let me ask you a question first.'

'Yes, your Lordship.'

'Has your father told you how he spent his time as a young man?'

Anna managed to say in a more confident voice. 'Nothing beyond that he was a tutor and lived in London.' This brought a few smiles from the men, who were sitting near her. 'I think I have the right to increase your knowledge of your father when he was a young man.'

Anna looked in horror at Lord Grafton.

'Do not concern yourself my dear Anna. He has always been, and I am sure still is, a man of impeccable judgement, the highest standard of morality and a servant of God.'

'In that sir, I would fully agree with you.'

'Excellent. Well let me tell you my story. When I was born, I was the third son of my father. My eldest brother died as an infant and so my elder brother, Charles would become Lord Grafton. He had a tutor, who was your father. Anna started to believe she was in a dream. 'Your father accompanied my brother on the Grand Tour.'

Anna was completely overawed by the details she was receiving and said, 'My father did the Grand Tour!'

'He did my child, with my elder brother. Unfortunately my brother succumbed to a fatal disease, before he returned to England. I do believe that at the time the family was in such shock that it did not take kindly to your father, who was with Charles at the time. Both the family's rejection of him and that his master had died, greatly upset your father. It is my belief that is what caused him to take holy orders. To you, Miss Seward, I would offer my families most humble apologies for the way in which we failed to support your father. He had done nothing wrong at all. Later reports showed he had done his utmost to save my brother's life.' Anna bowed her head, as she could not think of one word to say. He smiled and continued. My present information as a Privy Councillor tells me that he is a Canon at that very fine cathedral in Lichfield.'

'That is correct your Lordship, although how he knew all the information was beyond Anna's comprehension.'

'Now my dear Anna make yourself comfortable so you may explain to us the life of your father since you came into the world. We will explain to you what a fine young man he was.'

Anna was proud to explain the current life of her father. The men who had known him asked many questions. They told her many matters of interest about her father, from which she gleaned how much of a poet he was in his younger days.

By the end of the meeting Anna was very tired indeed, but the ordeal had passed in a remarkably amiable manner, considering who was present. As promised Lord Grafton walked her back to Mr Levitt. She was beginning to relax as she arrived when Lord Grafton said, 'Mr Levitt, if I may impose on your hospitality again.'

'Of course, my Lord.'

'I would like to extend my invitation to Miss Anna to join my family for dinner one evening.' Anna couldn't believe what she was hearing. 'We will then have a much more leisurely evening and we can note all the names she needs to write to her father about.'

'My carriage and servants will be at her disposal to fulfil your lordship's wishes.'

As his lordship left Anna slumped with tiredness into a chair. Abigail came to sit next to her and said, 'Anna tell all!'

'Not now dear Abigail, I am too tired.'

Chapter Thirteen

'Good evening, Captain Temple, what a surprise!' said Anna as she entered the main drawing room in Wimpole Street.

'My compliments to you,' he said as he bowed, 'Mr Levitt has been kind enough to include myself and Captain Robertson in his party for the theatre.'

Anna said, 'It will be good to go in a large group. Miss Levitt tells me we are to have a box at Drury Lane.'

'I have seen Mr Levitt and his family before at the theatre, when I have been lucky enough to attend.' As no one else had appeared, and she was alone with Captain Temple, Anna began to feel a little nervous.

Captain Temple said, 'I believe you are somewhat of an expert on Shakespeare.'

'No, no,' protested Anna, 'I merely enjoy reading and there is no better writer than him. It is so refreshing to know that he has grown in reputation in literary circles recently.' She paused and looked steadfastly at Captain Temple, 'Do you read much Shakespeare?'

'Dear Miss Seward, being in the army is more of a life of action, but I do enjoy watching his plays. And I believe, that tonight, we will see the man with the most fulsome skills in the world in delivering such a play. Mr David Garrick is unequalled in most people's eyes.'

'His reputation goes before him, but I have never been privileged to see him perform.'

'He is without doubt magnificent, in which ever Shakespearean role that he plays. Also I'm reliably informed that he is from Lichfield.'

'Yes, his family have been there for generations, although I have only met them in passing.'

'Have you met, David Garrick?'

'No, Captain, it had not been my pleasure. While my father's house is open to the more classical forms of literature, entertaining players tend not to be invited.'

With that the door opened and Mr Levitt came in. He said,

'I heard you mention Mr Garrick. As you will know he is from our city, but little known in Cathedral Close.' He smiled at Anna, 'Miss Seward is a classicist in her reading and so we would not want to spoil her anticipation of the evening, by giving too much away.'

'Quite so,' replied the Captain.

The conversation was relieved by the arrival of many others of the party. Anna was getting more used to the line of coaches to take them on visits. In Lichfield each good family had a coach and went to events and to friends. In London everything seemed on a much larger scale.

Anna had entered the Levitt box in amazement at how many people were crammed into the theatre. There was a sea of people in the pit and they were noisy. Some of her party wanted to talk, even as the play was being performed. Anna was trying to listen and watch without interruption.

Mr Levitt immediately spotted the problem and persuaded Anna to move to the front of the box nearest to the stage, where she would have an uninterrupted view and no distractions as to noise. As she had read the play many times in advance she spoke quietly to herself the lines she knew by heart.

She clapped enthusiastically at the end of the first act. 'Did you enjoy that?' asked the smiling Mr Levitt.

Anna turned and smiled, 'It was a most magnificent experience. Mr David Garrick is the man that Shakespeare would have wished to perform his plays.'

'Praise indeed,' replied Mr Levitt. 'Anna,' he whispered, 'you were spotted from the pit.' Anna shivered at the thought that anyone down there would know her. 'He has asked me if he may pay you his compliments.' Anna wasn't sure of the gentle smile on Mr Levitt's face so she looked around.

'Major Wright.'

They chatted for a little while as he had some news from Eyam. Anna could not resist to ask, 'Mr Levitt says that you were in the pit.'

'Yes, I regularly come here in the season and sometimes have a box and party of my own, but quite often I come with a few friends and then we go to the pit. It is a little raucous at times, but quite safe, you would be surprised the number of real ladies who are there.' Anna did not wish to contradict him, so held back the comment she had formed. He said with a smile, 'The pit will get much livelier later when the farce starts.'

He took his leave and his seat was immediately taken by Captain Temple, who wished to know her opinion on the first act. She was engaged by him and had difficulty in curbing his enthusiasm to talk to her so she could watch the remainder of the play.

Mr Levitt decided that the farce that followed on from the Shakespeare, might be a little too bawdy for some of the ladies of the group and proposed returning to Wimpole Street. To Anna's surprise, although it was quite late, a supper had been set out and there were some musicians and the usual card tables. They were also joined by a party from another box. The buffet was in full swing as well as the music, when Mr Levitt approached Anna.

'Some gentlemen have just arrived that I would like you to meet.'

'Of course, sir, it will be my pleasure.' She followed Mr Levitt to the main double doors of the room. She could see some gentlemen waiting in the hall, but could not see enough of them to discern who they might be. She was a little nervous of new faces after the astounding night she'd had at the Ranelagh, but she prepared herself.

She recognised the man at the front immediately, and it quite took her breath away. Mr Levitt said, 'Miss Seward, please let me introduce, Mr David Garrick.'

She curtsied low, and said, 'It is a great honour to meet you Mr Garrick.' By then several other people in the room had spotted the well known figure and there was a ripple of applause. But, while he waved, he said, 'Miss Seward, from Cathedral Close. I know all about you.' His words were delivered in a strong voice so that many around would hear. He laughed heartily as Anna's face went red with embarrassment.

Mr Levitt said, 'We thought we would keep his visit as a surprise.'

'Thank you, sir, I am quite speechless meeting such a man as Mr Garrick.'

'There is another gentleman, but this time it is one whom you know,' said Mr Levitt, as he stepped into the hall and beckoned to another man.

Shuffling around the corner and into the room came Samuel Johnson, 'Mr Johnson, it is a pleasure to meet you again, sir,' said Anna who had only just recovered from her embarrassment of Mr Garrick's remarks.

Samuel Johnson acknowledged Anna with a gracious rather lop-sided bow, and then called to David Garrick, who was already half way across the room being greeted by other people. 'Hi, Davy, we'd better be on our best behaviour, young Anna here is calling me Mr Johnson and I thought my name was Sam.'

This brought roars of laughter from David Garrick and total embarrassment again for Anna, who found that Sam pleased her and annoyed her in equal measure. There was then a faint cough from behind Samuel Johnson from a man that she did not recognise.

Sam turned and said, 'Anna, let me introduce my very good friend, James Boswell.' The man provided a complete contrast to Sam. He was tall and about the same age as Anna. He was very smartly dressed in a clean, and neat coat. His grey wig was well powered and his boots clean and shiny.

He greeted Anna with a gracious smile, 'Good evening, Miss Seward, it is a pleasure to make your acquaintance. May I escort you back to your seat while Mr Johnson and Mr Garrick talk to the other guests, it will at least free you from their torment for a short period.'

'That is very thoughtful of you,' replied Anna, taking an instant liking to the man.

'I am privileged to say that I have become a friend of Mr Johnson, but suffer an undue amount of his humour as I am Scottish, which is something he will never forgive me for.' He gave Anna a pleasant and gentle smile.

'Does he not like the Scots?'

'They are a constant source of mimicry for him, even in his famous dictionary.'

'What has he written against the Scots?' she said with a puzzled look.

'His definition of "oats", is "a grain, which in England is generally given to horses, but in Scotland supports the people."' Anna tried to withhold the smile as she did not want Mr Boswell to think bad of her. 'You may relax and smile Miss Seward, I am long used to his wit and do not take offence.'

Mr Boswell and her were now sat next to each other and there was a slight pause in the conversation so Anna asked, 'Tell me a little about where you live in Scotland, Mr Boswell.'

'I live on an estate of several thousand acres at Auchinleck, where my father is the Laird. One day it may be supposed that, as I am the oldest son, I shall retire to the moors of that area, but for now I choose to be in Edinburgh and London.'

They were then noisily interrupted by Mr Garrick and Samuel Johnson joining them.

Anna said, 'Mr Garrick may I say how much I enjoyed....'

He waved his arm nonchalantly, 'Enough, enough, otherwise Sam here will be hounding me over the praise I receive. And if you are calling him Sam, then I'm Davy.'

Anna was quite taken aback by their humour and rather flamboyant style. She was now confused as to how to address them, especially when Mr Boswell said, 'And I'm James.'

'Now my dear Anna,' said Davy, 'Sam and I have come to talk to you about your house.'

Anna was trying to think quickly so she did not get caught out by any witty remarks. She couldn't think why they would want to talk to her about where she lived.

Davy said, 'I do not know your father, Anna, but Sam does.'

Sam sat up and said in a slow voice, 'He is a serious man who would not like a player,' and at this point he indicated Davy, 'into his house.'

Davy then said dramatically, 'But we have both been there many times, haven't we Sam?'

'Have you been to where I live many times?' said Anna not

sure whether to believe him or not.

Sam said, 'I have been in more recent times, when reluctantly invited by your father, but we both know he would never invite a player to his table.' Anna nodded because she knew this to be the truth, but Sam went on, 'despite the fact that my good friend here is deemed suitable for his Majesty's table.'

Anna just smiled, she had no answer to offer.

Davy said, 'We will torment you no more, Anna. There was a very fine man named Walmsley, who lived in that very same house before your father. Neither Sam nor I had access to many of the classics and he had a library full of them. He used to allow us to go there to read. He was a very generous man and wrote letters of introduction for us to people in London, when we left our home city to seek our fame and fortune.'

By the end of the evening Anna was very tired, but so exhilarated by the theatre and then meeting with Sam and Davy, who after the early humour, were excellent company. She also spent a little time with a gentleman, who was travelling north and going through Lichfield in a day or so. He kindly said he would pay his respects to her father and pass on her good wishes.

Chapter Fourteen

A few days later, there was a trip planned to go to Covent Garden Opera House to listen to Handel's music. Anna came down to the main drawing room with Abigail. She was a little early and was engaged in a conversation jointly with Major Wright and Captain Temple.

The door opened and the servant announced the next arrival, 'Canon Seward.' As his name was called out, so silence fell on the room.

Anna was first to react, 'Father, what a wonderful surprise!' She went immediately towards him, but his serious frown never lifted as she approached. Both Major Wright and Captain Temple greeted him, but they only received a perfunctory nod. Canon Seward did not go towards either of the two men who offered their hands of welcome.

Her father stood in stony silence.

The atmosphere was only broken by the door opening and Mr Levitt coming in. He was his usual ebullient self, 'Canon Seward, how very good to see you. I'm sorry I didn't greet you personally. My butler has only just told me you had arrived. I wasn't expecting you.' Again the Canon ignored the hand that he was offered. A slightly quizzical look crossed Mr Levitt's face.

'I travelled in haste from Lichfield,' the Canon stated in a clear loud voice. The early evening lightness of conversation and the smiles had all disappeared now. The Canon was the centre of attention and he was in a bad humour, so both Captain Temple and Major Wright remained silent.

'I trust you are not carrying bad news from our home city of Lichfield,' asked Mr Levitt, who had now adopted a serious tone to his voice. The original greeting levity had gone.

The Canon almost snapped his reply in the same loud stern voice, 'There is no current bad news that I know of in Lichfield.' Mr Levitt went to speak but the Canon said, 'May I ask the use of a private room to talk to my daughter?'

Mr Levitt looked rather taken back by such a direct statement, but his gentle nature came through and he said, 'Yes, of course, please use my study. I will show you.'

Canon Seward, turned and with a frown on his face. He snapped, 'Anna! Come with me.' There was a hushed silence in the room. At first all eyes were on the Canon, but after issuing the orders, the attention switched to Anna. The sudden shock of her father and his manner, made her go red with embarrassment. She nodded to the others and followed her father.

As soon as the door was closed and they were alone he snapped, 'You are a disgrace to the family name.'

Anna went white from the sudden shock of the attack of her father. The emotion welled up in her. She had been so pleased to see him when he had walked into the room, but now she felt very hurt by his manner.

Inside her there was a temper lurking, which she had thought was inherited from her father. On most occasions however she controlled the inner feeling and would often choose to be quiet, when she felt the anger rising within her. But the sudden and unjustified attack on her could not be subsumed.

'I beg of you, sir, that I have done no wrong. I have made no injustice to the name of Seward. All my conduct has been beyond reproach. So father I wish you to withdraw your remark.'

'What! What! You have the impertinence to question my judgement!'

'Sir, I do not know how you have come to your conclusions, but they are based on false premises.'

'As you are such a failed daughter, I shall list the conduct that has brought disrepute onto my house,' he said in a loud and projected voice.

Anna's voice was now as loud as her father's. Neither of them would know, but they were speaking so loudly that they could be heard throughout the ground floor of the house. 'Yes, father, do list them. Each and everyone. And then I shall refute them one by one. Again I have done nothing to disobey you. There is nothing in my conduct of which I am ashamed.'

Canon Seward's face was bright red with anger and he was clenching his fists. 'You are walking out with a soldier!'

The fury on her father face would normally mean she would

remain quiet. Often when he lost his temper she could not cope and began to silently cry. But this time was different, her temper had got the better of her although she attempted to control her words carefully, 'You are totally incorrect sir. I have been in the regular company with Captain Temple, only within the confines of Mr Levitt's group. On one occasion he and I walked together to view the Chinese House at the Ranelagh Gardens.'

This threw Mr Seward into a new pitch of anger, 'Ranelagh Gardens! Ranelagh Gardens! A complete den of iniquity!'

'Father at all times I was with a member of Mr Levitt's party and mainly with him. I was escorted to and from his booth when another prestigious party wished to talk to me.'

This seemed to confuse the Canon because he was not expecting it, but his temper had not subsided. 'What party?'

'Lord Grafton's.'

'What! What! Why has he been speaking to you. I totally ban you from his presence.'

This was too much for Anna, 'Father! You have lost your temper and control of your words. I suggest you gather your thoughts before speaking again.'

But the reply was instant, 'No daughter of mind shall tell me what to say!'

Anna managed to clam herself just a little and said in a quieter voice, 'You are embarrassing yourself, father.'

He just glared at her, and shouted, 'I walk into this house, and the first sight is you talking to Major Wright, a man I banned you from seeing.'

While Anna had calmed for a minute or so, the unfairness of her father's criticism hurt her, so her temper rose again. Her voice reached a new piercing level as she said, 'Sir, you did not ban me from seeing him. You said I must refuse his offer of an escort, which I have done consistently both in Eyam and in London.' Anna took a deep breath and fought back the tears.

'When he made my acquaintance in Bond Street. I came back to this very house and related the whole matter to Mr Levitt, who wrote to you. Sir, Mr Levitt is the master of this house and I saw no contradiction between your order and the master being able to add to his own party as he sees fit.' Anna took another deep breath. 'Is that your list, sir or have you more?'

The look on the Canon's face was a mixture of surprise and anger, as his daughter had never spoken to him in this manner before. But the Canon had not finished. 'At a party in this very house your made an exhibition of yourself with a player.'

'Sir, that is totally preposterous. I was speaking to three gentleman who arrived as guests of Mr Levitt. Mr Samuel Johnson was one. You have invited him to your house on many occasions. The second man was a native of Lichfield, Mr David Garrick and the third, Mr James Boswell, was a friend of Mr Johnson and will become the Laird of a large estate in Scotland. I do not see how you can have any objection to me talking to these men in a crowded room.' Anna took a deep breath, and the Canon went to intervene.

She held up her hand and said, 'Sir, please hear me out.' Without waiting for an acknowledgment she continued, 'Mr Garrick and Mr Johnson, talked to me at length about the previous inhabitant of the house in which we live.' It was only a momentary pause before she continued, 'As for your accusation that I made a fool of myself. There was a common humour in the air after the trip to the theatre and my exhibition as you call it, was me being embarrassed by the jokes of the two men until Mr Johnson's friend interceded on my behalf.'

'It is clear that London has affected your good judgement.'

'I beg to differ, sir. I have conducted myself in this house as I would anywhere, and in your absence I consulted with Mr Levitt whenever I needed advice.'

The Canon still with a loud voice only just less than a shout, 'Mr Levitt has disappointed me in the extreme. His standards are far below what I would have expected.'

Anna replied in as strong a voice as her father, 'Sir, yet again I beg to differ. He is an honourable man and this is a honourable house. And I have been treated in an exemplary manner.'

'You disobey me and when I come here to give you a reprimand about your conduct, you answer your own father back. You are a disgrace to my name, and if such behaviour continues

I shall disinherit you.'

Anna opened her mouth and went to speak, but changed her mind and remained silent, waiting for the next part of her father's outburst.

'You will return to Lichfield. That is my final word.'

They stood and looked at each other in a stony silence. The Canon was clearly waiting for his daughter to respond to his order, but she said, 'Do you consider the Reverend Tobias Steven's house to meet your honourable standards?'

'The Reverend Stevens? What has he to do with this?'

'Father I implore you to answer this question.' The tears began to stream down her face, but the seriousness of her face never flickered. Whether it was the tears or the realisation of what he had just said, he replied in a much quieter voice. 'Yes, he is the best of men, and a servant of God. I have known him since I was a boy.' The deflation in his voice was noticed by Anna, but her anger was still in full rage. 'Sir, I shall write to the Revered Stevens and his wife. They have begged me each year to spend spring with them in their remote location. I shall accept and advise them I will arrive within a few days. I shall leave London, sir, as you have ordered, but it will be better for both of us if I do not return to Cathedral Close to allow us both a period of reflection and prayer.'

She gave her father a piercing look. He replied, 'Very well, so be it.'

With that, there was knock on the door of the study, and it burst open immediately as Mr Levitt walked in. Anna looked at his face. There was no smile this time. His face was the sternest and gravest she had ever seen it.

'What is the meaning of this?' shouted the Canon before he realised it was Mr Levitt.

Mr Levitt ignored the Canon's outburst. He walked up to him holding a letter and said, 'This is a letter from Lord Grafton. He has heard you are in London, and has issued myself, yourself and your daughter Anna an invitation to dinner at his house, tomorrow night.' The Canon had already begun to shake his head, but Mr Levitt had not finished, so he raised his hand, and said, 'On my behalf only, I shall decline his invitation, but I shall also add that as Canon Seward is no longer a welcome guest in my house I cannot answer for him. And now sir, if you would be as good as to take your leave at the same speed with which you arrived.'

Part Two

Chapter Fifteen

'Doctor Darwin, this is a surprise, if you have time please do join me for a dish of tea.'

'Thank you, Anna, I am in no hurry at present, so to talk with you will be a pleasure.'

'I do not believe that I have seen you at these baths in Buxton before,' said Anna.

'No, I am not a great frequenter of such spas. Although I do recommend them to many of my patients. Is there a matter which ails you? I have not seen you for a consultation for many years.'

'No, doctor, like you I have a slightly damaged knee from an accident about three years ago and find the waters very healing.'

He nodded, but did not show agreement to what she said. He looked around at the other people who were sat in the assembly rooms, but then changed the subject and said, 'You seem to be absent from Lichfield for long periods. I have been waiting to renew our poetry liaison.'

'I am disappointed at missing that certainly. I have had a large number of invitations pressed on me, and so I have taken them all.'

The doctor smiled knowingly, but only asked, 'Is Honora well? She must have been with you a lot of the time?'

'As you know she is a little weak in constitution, but is growing into a fine woman. I am inclined to think that her father will be seeking a man for her before the year is out.'

'Is she yet seventeen?'

'Very soon.'

Doctor Darwin studied Anna for a little while and then asked, 'Is your father here? As I shall need to pay him my regards.'

'Yes, he is. Buxton is particularly attractive to him. The distance from Lichfield is not great, and he thoroughly enjoys the literary circles that form in the hotels, and here in the assembly room. I tend to stay much longer at the resort than he does, as often there is pressing cathedral business.'

The doctor replied, 'I find such groups a little slow and pedantic.'

They smiled at each other with knowing looks. The doctor removed himself from his seat with difficulty as he struggled with his large girth. He had noticed that they were being approached by Canon Seward.

They greeted each other in their accustomed manner of reserved coolness. They sat together and conversed a little about the events in Lichfield.

The doctor then looked between Anna and her father. He said, 'My medical practice is expanding and takes up a great deal of my time.' His eyes stayed on the Canon, 'Of course, I could decline and refer them to another doctor. But I do like to support the Bishop personally.'

Canon Seward nodded, 'Of course.'

So the doctor continued, 'An unfortunate consequent is that I am away often, which leaves my poor wife, Polly, to dine on her own. Of course, you would be most welcome to dine with her, but I have a request for you.' The Canon nodded his head to indicate the doctor should continue. 'Would you mind Anna dining on a regular basis with Polly.'

'Doctor, I will decline any dinner invitation, that I would feel obliged to accept, as a neighbour, if you were present. I raise no objection to your household extending an invitation for my daughter to dine with your wife.'

Anna gave a little smile to herself and drank from her dish of tea. The conversation was interrupted by a message for the doctor. He excused himself and quickly read the short message.

'Very interesting,' he said as he rejoined the group.

'Good news, I hope,' asked Anna.

'A patient of mine, a Mr Davenport, wishes to see me and asks if I might travel home through Cheadle, so that he is able to have a consultation.'

Canon Seward said, 'To go back to Lichfield, through Cheadle, does not take you far from the direct route.'

'You are correct, Canon, so I shall reply that I will attend on him tomorrow. It is not urgent and I have already agreed to stay tonight.'

Anna assumed that it was the close of the matter, but the doctor studied Anna and then said, 'I believe you have read *Julie, The New Heloise, and Emile*?'

'Yes, I have and they raise some interesting points, but I fear there is a great deal wrong with them. I would not recommend them for young minds.' Anna was intrigued to know why the doctor had suddenly brought up the subject of the book. 'Why do you ask?'

Before answering her, the doctor turned his gaze to the Canon, 'Have you read them, sir?'

'No, I have not, doctor. They are not my type of reading.'

'Quite so. But I thought I would ask. 'The author...?'

'Monsieur Jean-Jacques Rousseau,' replied Anna immediately.

'Do you know anything about the man, Anna? Or you sir?'

'I do not, doctor, except the references in the Gentleman's Magazine.'

'What you both probably do not know is that Monsieur Rousseau is currently staying at Cheadle, with Mr Davenport. I know Mr Davenport well and feel sure that he would introduce me to the reclusive Mr Rousseau. I wanted to ascertain if Miss Anna would like to accompany me.'

Anna already knew the reply that her father would give, 'I would never tolerate a meeting between my daughter and such a scurrilous man.'

Anna said, 'Thank you for the kind thought doctor, but I shall decline the invitation.' Her father stared at her with an intensity she had not seen for a long time.

'In that case Canon, Miss Anna, I shall take my leave of you.'

'Before you go, doctor.'

'Yes, Canon,' replied the doctor as he slumped his frame back into his seat.

'I notice you have a new adornment to the livery on your coach.'

'Yes the carriage has been improved, and as you say aspects of the livery updated.'

Anna was watching her father. It was usual to see him with his stern face in a constant frown, but now he was smiling, or Anna tried to interpret his expression. It was more like a grin.

'The small group I was with this afternoon noticed the new words under your crest and wrote a little poem to celebrate it.'

He then handed the doctor a short poem, which he duly read and then replied, 'A little satirical I think. May I keep it?'

A clear smile was returned by the Canon, who said, 'Yes of course. The meaning is abundantly clear is it not?'

The doctor bowed his head as he stood, 'It is. Good day Canon. Good day, Miss Anna.'

Anna looked between the men and rose from her chair, 'I intend to visit some of the invalid ladies I met in the waters this morning. If you are passing the hotel perhaps you would be good enough to walk with me.'

'Of course, Miss Anna.' She bade her father farewell. The customary scowl had returned by then.

As soon as they were clear of the assembly rooms, Anna said, 'Was it a good poem?'

The doctor did not delay. He handed it to her and so they both stopped, while she read it. She said pensively, 'So my father is threatening to tell your most important patients that you do not believe in God. Is it because of what you have on your new crest?'

'That is correct, Anna.'

'May I ask what is written there?'

'The English equivalent of the Latin is, "Everything from shells.'

Anna raised her eyebrows. Conversation about religion between her and the doctor was generally avoided. As far as she was concerned, he always used clever words when he referred to religion, which left certain ambiguities, which she could not accept.

They parted amicably. She entered the hotel, to seek out the ladies, who she had shared the waters with that morning. They were on the far side of the large seating area. It was good to see them smiling, even though they suffered from constant pain. As she approached them she could see that their source of amusement was a young man. He was of medium height, smartly dressed, with a neat wig, and black dress coat. Anna put his age to be less than twenty.

Anna smiled as she approached the group for she could see that Honora was sat in their midst. As she arrived, so the young gentleman rose to his feet and gave Anna a low bow. 'Forgive me the intrusion, I escorted one of these ladies to her seat, and they have been regaling me with the pleasures of the local area.'

One of ladies, who was held in high repute by all those who visited the spa went to rise to her feet. 'Please remain seated Madam,' said Anna. 'In what way may I be of assistance to you?'

'I wish to introduce this young man to you. He has been most attentive to our care and well-being over the past few days since his arrival.'

'Miss Anna Seward please meet Mr John Andre.'

Again he bowed low. 'At your service, Miss Seward. I recognise the name. You are the guardian of Miss Honora Sneyd, who sits there so regally between the ladies.' It amused Anna that he thought her to be Honora's guardian, but she let the remark pass.

Anna said, 'I came to enquire of the ladies as to whether they required any assistance, but I see you have supplied their needs. Except that,' and she turned to the ladies, 'I intend visiting the shops in the Colonnade. May I be of any service to you?'

They all indicated they had no needs. 'May I accompany you, Anna?' asked Honora.

'Of course, my dear Honora.'

Mr Andre said, 'As my services are no longer required here, may I be so forward as to ask whether I may escort yourself and Miss Honora.'

Anna was amused by his very open and friendly manner. He was clearly very popular with the older ladies, so she nodded her head in agreement.

As they walked around the shops he was most attentive to both Anna and Honora, but she did notice that whenever he had the opportunity of not being closely observed, he would watch Honora.

'I believe this shop has some of the finest lace in Buxton.'

'That is exactly what I am seeking,' replied Anna and he waited patiently outside of the shop, while they went in and made their purchase.

Anna was in no hurry to return to the hotel. He was good company. Honora, while she was very quiet, smiled a great deal and looked pleased with his presence.

'Are you a frequent visitor to Buxton?' asked Anna.

'No, Miss Seward, this is the first opportunity I have had of visiting such a fine spa. Having now gained the age for a little independent exploring, I thought I would visit here after staying with some friends of my family. I shall then return to my home, in London, to assist my father in his business.'

They chatted amiably as they walked slowly around the surrounding pathways. Mr Andre did his best to include Honora in the conversation, and while she answered politely and with due deference, she said very little. So it was left to Anna to talk with him.

Having exhausted all possible paths near the spa, Anna and Honora took their leave. He pressed them earnestly to take the air with him again tomorrow providing the weather was not too inclement. Anna thought him a fine escort and after asking Honora, they agreed to meet the next day.

Anna and Honora then went to the early evening service in the church and returned to the Assembly rooms for the evening entertainment, where Anna was surprised at the absence of Mr Andre.

That evening as the dancing was not to their taste, and as her knee hurt, Anna and Honora retired to their room early. Anna could see that Honora's face was tinged with excitement. She nodded that the maid was still present. They waited patiently while the maid completed her tasks and then left the room.

As soon as the door was closed, Honora said, 'That was a wonderful day, Anna.'

She smiled at her younger friend, 'Was the day wonderful, because there was a Mr Andre involved?'

'Oh, Anna. What must you think of me.'

'This is just between us Honora. Of course we can share secrets and say to each other what we have enjoyed. I found him a very pleasant young man, with extremely good manners and an endearing smile.'

Encouraged by Anna's openness Honora said, 'I thought him one of the most handsome men I have ever met. He was so kind to me, by asking me many questions.' She stopped, looked directly at Anna and said, 'I do hope that I did not let you down with my answers.'

'Of course not, my dear Honora. Your answers were excellent and you conducted yourself as a perfect lady.'

'Is it permissible for him to escort us again tomorrow?'

'Yes, it is. At the spas there is a little more informality than in normal society, so his presence will be most welcome.'

'I shall like walking out with him again. What age do you think he is? For I cannot be sure.'

Anna smiled, 'He may be a year or so older than you, but no more which makes him a lot younger than me.' Honora wasn't sure how to take the remark, but Anna laughed and then Honora looked content.

Honora said, 'I like coming to the spa with you, because we share a bedroom and then we can talk much more.'

'Yes, it is good. Of course, it is cheaper too, but I enjoy your presence when you are close by. I wanted to talk to you Honora about a matter, that I think you are now old enough to understand.'

'Whatever you wish.' Anna moved across the room, having finished brushing her hair, but grimaced. 'Dear Anna, are you in pain? May I help?' said Honora as she jumped up from her seat and caught Anna's arm to steady her.

'Thank you, Honora, my knee is troubling me a little today. It will be good to take the waters tomorrow morning, but for now I might feel more comfortable if I lie down.'

Honora helped Anna to the bed and to get comfortable, 'Thank you dear, Honora.'

Anna noticed that that her young friend was shivering, 'Are you cold? The fire is fully alight.'

'Yes, a little, I shall get a shawl.'

Anna was always concerned whenever there was the slightest

ailment with Honora. Her pale, but beautiful face so reminded her of Sarah.

'Honora. Come and lay next to me. I am warm, it will be the easiest way. And I want to make sure you do not catch a chill.'

Honora gave a gentle smile and laid next to her on the bed.

'Now dear, Honora, let me put my arm around you like this. There is that comfortable?'

'It is very comfortable, Anna and I am beginning to feel your warmth already.'

Anna closed her eyes, and said quietly to Honora, 'Now is the time to talk about men.'

Chapter Sixteen

Anna left her house and turned along the tree-lined walk. She was on her own. Cathedral Close was well enclosed from the outside world, and she was now at the age that she considered it acceptable to walk anywhere in the close without escort. Her father did not raise any objections, but she could tell he did not approve by his manner.

She was only going as far as the Doctor's house at the other end of the close. The servant saw her coming, opened the door and showed her into the drawing room.

Within minutes, the doctor's wife Polly came into the room. Polly was of medium height, only a few years older than Anna, but about ten years younger than her husband. She had a square face, that was often a little drawn, but she was the mother of three fine boys, who were boisterous and growing rapidly.

They had met frequently after the open invitation that the doctor had given when they had met in Buxton. Today Anna had arrived to take dinner with them as they had a new guest. After the normal brief greeting between Anna and Polly, they were interrupted by the doctor who came into the room.

'Ah, my dear Anna, I am so very pleased that you accepted my invitation for today, as we have an interesting guest.'

'Might I ask who he is?'

'Even better, I hear a carriage, I shall introduce you to him.'

They waited patiently and before long, a tall, very elegant man entered the room. In the manner of a gentleman he bowed to the two ladies. His clothes were of the highest quality and his wig was neat and well powdered. Anna placed his age slightly older than herself.

The doctor said, 'May I introduce my good friend, Mr Richard Edgeworth.'

'This is Miss Anna Seward, who is one of our exalted neighbours.'

Anna's gave a delightful smile to greet the man that she had not seen before. They soon moved through to the dining room for dinner.

Anna said, 'Mr Edgeworth, I notice a hint of an Irish accent.'

'You are perfectly correct, Miss Seward, I am from Ireland. At the present time, I spend a great deal of the year in England, although I do often go to France. My Irish estate, while it could keep me well occupied, I find a little dull and mundane.'

The doctor said, 'Mr Edgeworth is an inventor.'

'How fascinating, Mr Edgeworth, may I ask if a poor female mind could understand your inventions.'

This brought a hearty peal of laughter from the doctor who said, 'Do not be deceived by such modesty Mr Edgeworth. Miss Seward has a very clear and analytical mind, although coming from a Canon's house, tends to favour poetry and reading to practical matters.'

She received a gracious smile from Mr Edgeworth who said, 'If I might be privileged to listen to some of your poetry on a future occasion, I am sure it will give me great pleasure.'

'I would be delighted to read you a little to see whether it fits with your style and enjoyment, but before the doctor's kind compliments, I was asking about your inventions.'

'My current work concerns carriages and trying to make them safer, and less likely to topple on our rough roads.'

'Then such work would have my wholehearted support, as they are the most dangerous of things. At times they can easily become out of control and even cause death.'

'You are right, Miss Seward. As you know of the doctor, he is a keen man for practical matters and has a wide reputation, which is why I have been to consult with him before.'

'And so you have returned to see him again.'

'It goes beyond that Miss Seward. I have decided to move into the area for a period, so I may talk to the doctor more often.'

The smile on Anna's face showed that she fully approved of such a move. 'Have you a residence yet?'

'Yes and very close to here, I am taking Stowe House for a period.'

'Then we shall be neighbours within sight of each other, for from the veranda I can see across Stowe Pool to the house.'

'In that case, when I am fully settled in I would like you to be my first guest for dinner.'

Polly had been listening to the conversation, but had chosen to stay quiet. She looked at Anna, but said to Mr Edgeworth, 'Will your wife be joining you at Stowe House?'

'No, Mrs Darwin, too much travelling for my wife tends to excite her nerves. So she prefers the home comforts of Edgeworth Town in Ireland.'

The conversation continued over dinner in a general manner. Then the two gentleman spent some time discussing their inventions in the doctor's study, while Anna and Polly exchanged views on the news in Lichfield.

Mr Edgeworth came to take his leave about the same time as Anna was preparing to leave, and so offered to escort her home. Anna accepted with a smile. They walked slowly while Anna explained about Cathedral Close and the people who lived there. He said that he had not yet had the opportunity to visit the Cathedral. When he had stayed in Lichfield before he had resided at an inn, and had attended a service in the town.

'Then let me press you to walk with me into this fine House of God, so that I may show you some of its wonderful features.' Anna was pointing out the nave of the cathedral when she saw her father and Honora approaching.

'Mr Edgeworth, my father approaches, may I introduce you.'

'It would be an honour.'

Mr Seward greeted him civilly, but as Anna explained about the estate in Ireland, the Canon took a decided greater interest in the man. Anna was feeling a little uncomfortable now that her father had arrived in case there was a difference on religion between the two men, but there seemed only good friendship on a first acquaintance. Canon Seward extended an invitation to Mr Edgeworth to call on him at his convenience.

Her father said, 'I was just about to escort Honora back to the house, but perhaps I can leave her in your care as I have not finished my cathedral business yet.'

'Of course, father.'

Throughout the conversation Honora had been quietly and politely standing and waiting to be introduced. Anna's father left that task to his daughter.

As she knew that Honora would have heard the conversation so far, she said, 'This is Honora Sneyd, the ward of my parents, and my very good friend.'

Honora smiled at Mr Edgeworth and gave a low voiced greeting, but Anna noticed the radiant sparkle in her eyes.

Anna transferred her eyes to Mr Edgeworth's face, and saw the most generous of smiles and the flash of his eyes. He bowed low and said, 'It is indeed an honour, Miss Sneyd and I sincerely hope that when Miss Seward accepts my invitation to dinner at Stowe House you will also join her.'

'Thank you kind sir for your invitation, I would be delighted to join you, subject, of course, to the approval of my guardians.'

Mr Edgeworth then escorted them home and then took the path past the cathedral and along the banks of Stowe Pool to his new house.

Chapter Seventeen

When Anna and Honora entered their house, the butler passed Anna a letter that had arrived during the afternoon.

' I can recognise the writing from the many letters that he has written. Come Honora let's retire to my drawing room, where we shall open this letter from Mr Andre.' The excitement in Honora's face was clear to see. They were soon settled into the drawing room.

Anna began to read it out loud. He tended his kind regards to both of them. Anna knew that as she read it, the letter was really for Honora. He was being a gentleman and, as he treated Anna as the guardian, he was writing to her. This was one of several letters that they had received from him over the past month, and each one got longer and the contents were more detailed.

Honora's excitement was greatly increased when he suggested that it would perhaps not be long before he would be able to return to the north of England. He would like permission to call at Lichfield to give them his good regards in person.

Having gone through the letter several times they decided to think about it overnight. In the morning they would write a reply. Anna particularly liked Mr Andre, even though he was several years younger than her, but she also knew that he only had eyes for Honora. They parted in the sweetest frame of mind each planning what to write in the morning.

There was a surprise at breakfast the next morning when Anna father's said that he had received an early morning message from Colonel Sneyd. He was already on his journey to Lichfield to meet his daughter and expected to arrive about midday. Canon Seward suggested that they prepare themselves to greet the Colonel. Therefore they postponed their letter writing until later in the day.

Honora was nervous all morning, because it had been nearly two years since she had last seen her father. His letters were regular, but showed little in the way of favour or disfavour to his daughter. Anna had explained to Honora that he was a strong man and defiant soldier. Such men are used to writing in a very factual way. Honora just hoped that she had not done anything to offend him, but Anna assured her that all would be fine.

He was a tall and very distinguished man, but was not wearing his army uniform when he arrived. In the courteous manner of an officer he greeted his daughter and Anna, but then immediately went to talk to Canon Seward in his office. Anna and Honora made themselves busy with their needlecraft while they waited.

After nearly an hour, the Colonel entered the drawing room on his own. He smiled, but he was a man with a naturally stern face and Anna felt sympathy for Honora as he looked at her.

'I have come to speak to my daughter.'

Anna curtsied and said, 'I will therefore take my leave to allow you to be with your daughter.'

'Miss Seward, you have been a devoted friend and mentor of my daughter. In that role I fully appreciate your worth. So may I beg of you to stay. I must speak with Honora about a serious matter. I feel she may benefit from your advice later.'

Anna returned to her seat, but the Colonel remained standing.

'I have received letters from Canon Seward, which inform me that there is correspondence with a young man called Andre. Is that true Miss Seward?'

'It is sir. We met Mr Andre at the Buxton Spa. I explained to my father and subsequently Mr Andre wrote to him asking for agreement to write to us.'

'It strikes me as a little to lax in formality. As the Canon is my daughter's guardian, I would have expected that all letters would go through him.'

Anna acknowledged his remark with a slight nod of the head and said, 'My sincere apologies sir, if my conduct in this matter displeases you.'

The Colonel ignored Anna's remark and said, 'As I have a number of friends in London I was able to seek out some information about Mr Andre. I have the gravest doubts why a young man of my daughter's age would be free and on his own at a Spa. He does not appear to me to be a man of substance and he could be far worse.'

Anna said, 'He behaved like a gentleman, sir.'

'There is many a scoundrel, who poses as one,' said the Colonel, with a severe look at Anna.

Anna was used to such views from her own father, but she managed to remain calm for the sake of Honora and said, 'Sir, may I ask what your enquiries in London yielded. Did you confirm your supposition that Mr Andre is a scoundrel?'

'I did not say that!' snapped the Colonel, 'please do not offend me by putting words into my mouth. I merely told you of a conclusion that could be drawn from such a behaviour, without any clear evidence to the contrary.'

Anna was not going to be defeated and asked, 'Did you find what you required, sir?'

'There is no evidence that he is a scoundrel.' At this Anna could see a brightening in Honora's face. 'He comes from a family that is not particularly well connected, but my friends tell me they are open and honest.'

Anna did her best to hide her smile.

'There is then the question of whether this correspondence should be allowed to continue. I have discussed the matter with the Canon. We are both of the opinion that no further contact should be made with Mr Andre.'

Anna heard the involuntary gasp come from Honora. The Colonel snapped at her, 'I will make the decision as to whom you will marry. It is getting near that time. As you are, but one of my many daughters, your dowry will not be large. But I shall not permit you to marry anyone of whom I disapprove.'

'Yes, sir,' came a very controlled reply from Honora.

'I shall send a letter to Mr Andre in London, through my friend, who will ensure it is delivered to his hand personally. In that way there can be no confusions or misunderstandings.'

He looked at his daughter, 'Honora look at me.' She duly did as she was instructed. 'You will entirely forget about this man. As far as you are concerned he does not exists anymore.'

Anna was going red with anger at the way in which the Colonel was treating his daughter, and she said, 'Sir, might I ask you to reconsider the severity of what you have just advised.'

'No, Miss Seward. You may not.' He paused and then stared at Anna with a very stern stare. 'As my daughter is forced by circumstance to be a guest in this house, I have no right to instruct you in any manner. It does however concern me that you do not seem to be a good influence on my daughter.'

'I would protest in the strongest possible way, sir.'

'Yes, I am sure you would. At present I have chosen not to tell your father of my concerns, but unless I see some changes in attitude, then I will remove my daughter from this house.'

Chapter Eighteen

'You do look very flushed, Polly,' said Anna as she greeted her friend in the drawing room of Doctor Darwin's house.

'It has been a very busy morning and with three young boys up to mischief, I am tired out.'

'Then leave your children to Mary, who is their governess, and fetch your bonnet. As it is a very pleasant day I would suggest a cooling walk around Stowe Pool.'

'It does sound as though it will do me good, but at the moment I seem to have a number of problems, which seem to relate to my poor sleeping. I can lay awake all night, but when it is morning, then I'm tired out before I start the day.'

Anna said, with concern in her voice, 'Is the doctor finding time to treat your maladies?'

'Anna please do not even suggest a failing on my husband's part. His conduct is the opposite of what I can read in your face. He is the most devoted husband that a woman could possibly have. He always listens to my little grumbles and treats whatever I mention to him. He is a wonderful man.'

Anna said, 'That is so good to hear, especially when one hears rumours of the lack of care and ill treatment of wives in some households.'

Polly collected her bonnet and the two ladies walked slowly down Cathedral Close and past the south door to join the path around Stowe Pool.

'I haven't seen Honora for sometime. Has she gone away?'

'Yes, Polly, she has. It has been so difficult for her.'

'She has not misbehaved has she?'

'No, of course not. She is totally angelic, but she took a fancy to a young man of about her age, who we met at Buxton. He seemed to me an excellent man, polite and very kind to many of the old ladies that were there.'

'Did your father disapprove?' Anna noticed there was something resigned in her voice as her father was mentioned. She thought through the contact between her family and the Darwins. It was clear that neither the doctor or Polly had any time for her father, but were too polite to say anything.

'No, it was not my father this time, although I would guess he tried to influence the decision. I haven't told you before, but her father visited.'

'I've never met him. What type of man is he?'

'I'm afraid he is a strict army man and has difficulty in knowing what is best for his daughter. In many ways he reminded me of my father.'

'So what happened?' asked Polly as they took the narrow path along the side of the pool and watched the mill workers on the far side.

'I tried to reason with him, but he was adamant that Honora should have no further contact with John Andre at all. It was a shock for me, so it must have been even bigger for poor Honora. She'd set her hopes at least on being able to walk out with him or to be able to write.'

'She must have been inconsolable. Her father came back to her and was only the bearer of bad news.' They walked a little further before Polly said, 'Surely her father realises that Honora has such a delicate constitution that he should nurture her. He should not just treat her like one of his troopers.'

'I'm afraid he is a hardened soldier and just views the whole of life in those terms.'

'Poor girl. Her father's attitude is such a pity, because she is such a pretty young lady, and with impeccable manners.'

Anna nodded her agreement and said, 'My father's house is not an easy place to lift the spirits, so I have sent her away to a house where two of her sisters live. It is a young household with many children, and much laughter, so I hope it will relieve Honora of some of her distressed thoughts.'

'So you are alone with your mother and father?'

'Yes, these days the number of visitors we have to stay is very limited and even then they tend to be of an older generation.'

'You must find it difficult without any company.'

'I have written to a dear friend, who I have not seen for long time and invited her to stay.'

'Will she come?'

'She prefers to stay at home, so whenever I invite her, she declines, but invites me to her. If she does the same this time I shall accept.'

Polly looked on ahead and said, 'Look! Mr Edgeworth and another gentleman are waiting for us.' So they walked to join them.

Mr Edgeworth was very elegantly dressed in a long outdoor coat with a modern style gentleman's hat. The other gentleman was remarkably different in his appearance. He wore a long riding cape, although there were no horses to be seen, and no hat. His black curly hair, which seemed extremely long to Anna, was unrestricted and was blowing in the wind, which whipped across the pool.

They were greeted by Mr Edgeworth in his usual manner of a gentleman.

'May I present my good friend, Mr Thomas Day. This is Mrs Darwin, the doctor's wife and Miss Seward.' Now Anna was close, she could look in detail at him. His dress was very unconventional.

'Good day, Mrs Darwin and Miss Seward.' He bowed with a considerable flourish of his hand. It wasn't the type of gesture that Anna liked, it was far too demonstrative for her tastes.

It surprised Anna, that Mr Day opened the conversation, 'We have been for a fine walk around this lovely city, and have just returned. We are going to take a dish of tea. Would you be so kind as to join us?'

Anna was confused. He had invited them into Mr Edgeworth's house to take tea. She quickly glanced at Mr Edgeworth, who only smiled at his friend. It was all very confusing for Anna. They were not far from his residence so it was only a few minutes before they reached there. Anna kept glancing at Mr Day. His clothes were very unconventional, but he definitely had the voice of a gentleman.

They entered the tall red brick house through the central front door. 'It is many years since I have been in here,' Anna said as they walked into the hall.'

'Were you born in Lichfield, Miss Seward?' asked Mr Day.

'No. I come from a small village in the Derbyshire Hills, but have lived in Lichfield since I was a young girl.'

Anna admired the taste of Mr Edgeworth. The decorations and furniture were all new. It was one of the most delightful houses she had ever been in. She noticed that Polly was looking around with admiration and approval. Anna wondered how a man had managed to create such a wonderful home when his wife was still in Ireland.

'Are the doctor's experiments with carriages going well. I have not had the chance to talk to him recently,' asked Mr Edgeworth.

'Mr Edgeworth. He is always enthusiastic about his inventions, but I really have no idea whether they work or not?' This brought laughter from both of the men, but it was kind and all four of them smiled.

While Mr Edgeworth and Polly had been talking it gave Anna another opportunity to discreetly watch Mr Day. Now that he had removed his outdoor coat, she was even more perplexed about him. He wore a jacket, that was more in keeping with one worn by gentlemen in the privacy of their own home. Most gentlemen would choose black as a colour, but Mr Day had chosen a bright green.

His hair had been blown by the wind and was dishevelled, but he had made no attempt to comb or smooth it. He wore riding breeches and large riding boots even though he hadn't been riding. The most surprising aspect of his appearance was that he neither wore a cravat or a scarf, but allowed his shirt to be open at the neck.

Anna estimated his age to be a little younger than her, but not as young as Honora. He seemed very relaxed and comfortable with Mr Edgeworth. Mr Day was quite tall, and had a handsome slightly long face, but there was an evenness and pleasantness about his features, that Anna liked.

Mr Edgeworth said, 'Miss Seward may I leave you in the company of my good friend Mr Day. I am keen to give some drawings of a new carriage mechanism to the doctor and Mrs Darwin has agreed to take them for me. So I shall take Mrs Darwin and give her the package.'

Both Anna and Mr Day nodded their acceptance and they were soon alone in the room. He did not delay in starting the conversation. Anna could see he was relaxed and looked very much at home even though it wasn't his house.

'Mr Edgeworth tells me that you write poetry.'

Anna blushed a little at the unexpected question, and replied, 'Yes, a little. Overall, I prefer to read the work of the English masters.'

'Yes, yes! You cannot go far wrong with them, I also enjoy their works,' he said enthusiastically.

'Do you write yourself, Mr Day?'

'I certainly do, but I would be very uncertain of the reception it would receive, if I chose to make any of it public.'

'I'm sure you do yourself down unnecessarily. If you have read the work of the masters, then we all hope a little of their skills will flow through to our own lines.'

'Yes, that is very true, but much of my poetry is not along the lines of traditional subjects, which makes the influence less noticeable.'

'May I be bold and ask what subjects you choose for your poetry.'

Anna was aware that any casualness in his approach had gone and that he was intently looking at her. While she found it a little unnerving, he had a facial expression that she could take no offence to.

'I write most of my poetry about injustice.'

Anna was completely taken by surprise, but was also intrigued by the man who was sitting opposite her. 'Is there a particular form of injustice that prompts your verse?'

His reply was quite fervent, but Anna had accepted that he was a passionate man. It could be seen in his eyes, at the mention of the word, injustice. 'Any form of injustice is bad in my eyes, Miss Seward. However there is one form that raises its head above all others, and that is the slave trade. If I do nothing more in my life than dedicate myself to the abolition of such a filthy trade, then I will feel satisfied, when I stand before my Maker.'

Anna was rather taken aback at the intensity with which he spoke and the way in which he condemned the trade.

He relaxed back and smiled, 'I'm so sorry for my outburst Miss Seward, especially as I hardly know you, but it is a subject very close to my heart.'

Anna said, 'You do not have to apologise to me for being passionate about injustice of whatever form it takes.' They lapsed into silence for a little while.

'I trust I have not offended you, Miss Seward.'

Anna for the first time really smiled at him, 'I can sincerely assure you that you have not offended me. My mind was occupied in considering the nature of the verse that you would write on such subjects.'

'I'm glad we are on an even relationship again.' Anna liked the smile that she received.

'Mr Day, you say that your poems are not made public.'

'That is correct. I have a tendency to keep them to myself for a number of reasons.' He paused and with an intriguing look added, 'Has your poetry been published?'

Anna shook her head and could not prevent a little laugh.

Mr Day smiled and said, 'I did not perceive it was a humorous question.'

'My apologies, Mr Day, I was just thinking of my father's reaction, if I asked him if I could publish my poems.'

'Mr Edgeworth tells me he is a Canon at the cathedral.'

'That is correct, Mr Day.'

'Then I think I understand your position and that it is better to move on to safer ground. I am sure he is a devout man in his position, and does not see his beautiful daughter as a writer.'

Anna dipped her head a little at the compliment. The sensitivity of his comments gave Anna an increasingly good opinion of the man, who was sat opposite.

'Miss Seward, if I remember correctly, Mr Edgeworth said that he was looking forward to hearing your poems.'

Anna relaxed with a gentle smile, 'In Lichfield we do not have the extensive sites for entertainment that exist in London. So a number of the families in this town, arrange small evening functions. It is at such events, that on many occasions, I have been asked to recite my poetry.'

'Then we will have no delays. I am certain that Mr Edgeworth would be fully in favour of arranging one here at Stowe House, if we were to have the pleasure of your poetry.'

But Anna immediately saw a problem. Her father would want to enquire about the nature of any new evening function arrangement. Stowe House might be best avoided, until Mr Edgeworth had established himself in the neighbourhood.

'My mother does enjoy a social evening and we haven't had one for some time due to a little illness. So the time might be right to introduce another one at our house.' In that way she would be able ensure Mr Day's presence, because he would come as a guest. She thought of her father and knew that as soon as he saw Mr Day he would never invite him again.

'So be it,' said Mr Day. 'If that is the way to achieve my objective, then we will make it happen. But the whole purpose from my point of view is to hear your poems.'

Anna wanted to steer the conversation away from her poetry so she said, 'Perhaps, not at that evening, but may I listen or read your verse? It particularly interests me as being different.'

'I am sure you rate it far too highly, it is but mere jottings.'

'Come now, Mr Day, we are all a little apprehensive about our work. I can assure you I am not a harsh critic.'

'I can easily believe that Miss Seward. You are very much a gentlewoman of the highest order.'

Anna became a little embarrassed by yet another compliment. Although she listened there was no sound of Mr Edgeworth and Polly returning, so she decided to change the tack of the conversation and asked, 'Is London your home?'

'Miss Seward I can assure you it is not. I abhor the place. Please do not misunderstand me. I bear no ill feeling to those who wish to partake of the extravagances of that city, but it is not for me.'

Anna was wondering if she should ask further, but decided it might intrude, and she was a little wary of setting off another of his passions, because she was sure that he had many.

'I have perplexed you, my dear Miss Seward. Yet again, I need to apologise. It is far from my intention to be evasive or not to answer any question that you would care to put to me.'

Anna now had very little idea how to respond.

He gave her a gracious nod of his head, and said, 'Let me explain to you in a different manner my opposition to London.'

Anna was somewhat relieved as she didn't have to ask a direct question so she politely said, 'Please do.'

'Fashion to me seems a complete waste of time. It costs an inordinate amount of money and yet what does it achieve?' This took her by surprise, but he had summarised her feelings succinctly although she had never looked at the matter with that type of consideration.

He paused and she was willing to be studied by his eyes, so she looked directly at him. 'May I be the most impertinent man on earth.'

'I would find that very difficult to conceive,' she replied with a smile.

'May I make a very personal comment.'

Anna surprised herself as she instantly responded, 'Provided it is not a compliment.'

'Only an indirect one.'

'Then I'm a little reluctant for you to proceed.'

He laughed. 'We get along very well Miss Seward so I shall be bold and adventurous.' This was accompanied by a wild wave of his hand that made Anna smile.

'I have noticed that you wear you hair about your shoulders. The leading fashions and mantua makers would have ladies pile their hair higher and higher, with a veritable garden installed.'

From this description Anna could do nothing but laugh. She replied, 'It is my choice as far as I see.'

'Exactly, Miss Seward, Exactly!' he said, slapping his hand against his thigh. 'It is an individual's choice. The government does not mind how we wear our hair, so we must decide.'

'I have only been to London for one period, and I would agree with you that it is driven by fashion.'

'Which is why I detest the place.'

Anna was feeling confident with this man. He was charming, made her laugh and was clearly a gentleman. But what of his other side. The passion and the strong views about matters that most people did not have a view about at all. She thought it best to return to less sensitive topics, but she was confident of asking a direct question, 'If it is not London, where do you come from as your accent give me no clues?'

'Nowhere and everywhere!'he said emphatically.

By now Anna was getting used to his manner, so she smiled back at him, put her head a little on one side and waited.

'You defeat me. I cannot tease you anymore. In all honesty Miss Seward. My parents both died when I was a baby and then I was moved around between relatives and my parents' friends for all of my formative years.'

'Was it a difficult experience?' asked Anna quietly.

'Absolutely dire at times, but sometimes the opposite, totally exhilarating.'

'I was being serious with my question.'

'Yes, I know you were my dear Miss Seward. But I decided long ago, that I didn't want sympathy. I have carved out for myself the man that I am. I know I am different to many you will have encountered, but sympathy for a cosseted life is not how I want people to think of me.'

It wasn't long before Anna and Polly were walking back along the path by Stowe Pool. They declined the offer of the men to escort them, mainly because they wanted to talk about them.

As soon as they were away from the house Polly said, 'What a house! Can you believe that a man did that on his own. I know he has an estate in Ireland, but one is never sure what that means.'

'It is in the best possible taste. Mr Edgeworth is one of the finest gentlemen, that we have ever had in this town. He would make so much difference if he stayed.'

'He told me that he much prefers England and that now he has met the doctor and his friends he will reside here for a long time.'

'But what about his wife?'

'That is a bit of a mystery. His only comment is that her nerves become distressed if she has to travel far from Edgeworthtown.'

'Polly he must be a man of great importance in his home country. Not only does he have an estate, but the town is named after his family.'

'Yes, I do see what you mean. He is a charming man. I can see that you like him, but what about his wife. It makes me doubt him.'

Anna said, 'I would like to be sure of him, so perhaps we can find out a little more to quell our suspicions.' Polly raised her eyebrows at Anna's suggestion.

They had only walked a little further when Polly said, 'Anna Seward, you are keeping your opinion to yourself, and I want to know what you are thinking.'

'I don't know what you mean,' said Anna with a smile.

'Yes, you do! I'm talking about Thomas Day. The way you were looking at him when I came back into the room. "Well, I never!" I thought to myself. Anna Seward likes that man and I would never have put the two of them together.'

'It's nothing like that at all.'

'Tell me what you think then.'

'He's very unconventional in his dress.'

'Yes, I can't disagree with you there. But he is a handsome man.'

'Yes he is. Talking to him is very interesting. He has views about society that are not common. He certainly is an individual man,' said Anna.

'Is he married?' asked Polly.

'I don't know. He didn't mention a wife.'

'Neither did Richard Edgeworth. It might be convenient not to mention that they are married, if their wives are back in Ireland.'

'I don't think Mr Day comes from Ireland. He hasn't got an Irish accent the same as Mr Edgeworth.'

'So what did you talk about?'

'Poetry,' replied Anna.

'Oh, Anna, not every man in the world likes poetry. I know it is a passion of yours, but you should really try to choose a wider range of subjects.' Anna laughed. 'Why are you laughing?

What's funny about what I said?'

'Polly Darwin, I do believe you are trying to find me a husband.'

A smile came across Polly's face, 'Maybe or maybe not. I think I could make a much better choice for you than your father.' Anna didn't reply. 'Now don't get upset with me Anna. You don't have to defend your father to me. I've known him far too long for that. He is a good man, there is no doubt, but the ways of the world have passed him by.'

Chapter Nineteen

Anna walked down the stairs slowly. She had finishing writing to Emma about Mr Edgeworth and Mr Day, and decided to go to practice her music, as John Savile would be coming later to give her another lesson.

As she reached the hall, so her father's study door opened. She looked around expecting to see her father emerge and was somewhat surprised to see Mr Edgeworth and Mr Day come out. They closed the door behind them.

Mr Edgeworth was smartly dressed as usual, with the latest style jacket and trousers. Mr Day was even more unconventional than when she had first met him. Again his shirt was open at the neck, but it was red in colour and, whether by design or accident, matched his red riding boots. His trousers were not normal day wear for a gentleman. They had a multitude of pockets. The only time that Anna had remembered seeing such trousers, they were worn by the workmen in the cathedral.

Mr Day spotted her first, 'Good morning, Miss Seward, this is a pleasure.'

'Gentlemen,' she replied with a brief curtsey.

Mr Day continued, 'We have just met with your father. What a charming man!' Anna nodded in acknowledgement. 'We are very glad that we have now met you, as we can say that a social evening has been planned for tomorrow at Stowe House.'

'You promised that you would arrange one.'

'Your father has accepted our invitation.' Anna tried not to let the surprise show on her face. 'We asked him specifically to extend our invitation to you, as we wished to hear your poetry.'

'And what was his reply?' asked Anna full of curiosity.

'Your father said that he would put the invitation to you, but expected that you would accept. He added that you have read your poetry many times at such events.'

'I will certainly accept. Thank you, gentleman, but please do not expect too much from my lines.'

Mr Edgeworth said, 'It is all settled then, and we will see you and your parents tomorrow evening.'

Anna replied, 'I shall look forward to it.' With that the two gentleman left the house with the intent of walking into town. She was surprised that her father had agreed to such an event, because he rarely attended them. Normally it was only with very old family friends.

She tapped gently on the door of her father's study. He was sitting in one of the chairs by the fire reading. He beckoned her to join him.'

'I have just seen Mr Day and Mr Edgeworth leave.'

'Yes, they called on me to pay their respects and to introduce Mr Day, who I had never met before.'

'I did not see them arrive.'

'No, I think it must have been when you were out earlier for they have been here for nearly an hour.'

'You must have had a lot to talk about.'

Her father considered her question for a short time and replied, 'They are fine gentleman. Mr Day is rather unconventional in his dress, but has high principles, which I admire. And Mr Edgeworth is clearly a man of the highest order.'

'They tell me that you will attend their social evening tomorrow.'

'Yes, I told them that you would be there. They wish you to read some of your poetry. Also your mother is currently feeling a little better at the moment and she does enjoy such evenings.'

'Then I shall be glad to recite my verse. Do you ascertain whether they were staying in the area for very long?'

'Mr Edgeworth is an inventor and meets with the doctor on a regular basis. Mr Day will either stay at Stowe House or take a another house nearby, but intends staying in the area, as he likes Lichfield.'

'That is good news, they will make fine neighbours.'

'Yes, I agree with you, Anna.'

Anna regretted the interruption by William, the butler, to say that Mr Savile had arrived. As she went to her music lesson her mind was buzzing with the thoughts of the two men being close neighbours. It gave a little lift to her stride as she walked into the room.

'Good morning, John.'

'Good morning, Anna,' but she could detect a strain in his voice.

'You sound very weary, John. Are you ill?'

'No, Anna, a little tired, but I'm not ill.' With that he turned to pick up the morning's music. The lesson had not started long and Anna made several mistakes, but he didn't correct them. She stopped playing and he looked at her with surprise.

'John you are very distracted this morning.'

'I'm sorry Anna, but I'm finding it difficult to concentrate.'

'Would you prefer to stop for today?'

'No, no. I must carry on as normal.'

Anna refolded the music and turned to look at him, 'We have known each other for a long time, John. If you no longer want to teach me music, I will understand. It would not break my regard for you.'

'That's not what I want at all.'

'I would understand.'

'Anna, I really enjoy coming to teach you music. There is something that I probably should not say, but I will be very honest with you.'

'Go on,' replied Anna gently.

'Coming to see you is the best part of the week for me. I cannot say what the cause of my distress is, because it would be disloyal. But what I will say is, that I am pleased to leave my own house and come here. You are always most charming and I enjoy your company.'

'John, we all have difficulties at sometime in our lives. You have always supported me, so now I can repay a little of that. I won't burden you with questions, but if you wish to talk then I will listen. Of course, it would be just between us.'

'Thank you, Anna. It will be good for me not having to be on my guard about what I say. You have made me more content, and I am ready to carry on now.'

After Anna had finished her music lesson she was keen to go and share the news about the social evening with Polly. She left the house and had soon walked the length of Cathedral Close. It was some time before the door opened and then it was Mary, the children's governess and not the butler.

Mary was seventeen years old, a very pretty girl with blonde hair. She was looking flushed, but guessed what Anna was going to ask, so she said, 'The butler has been taken ill, and the two footman are out with the doctor, please come in Miss Seward. Mrs Darwin is in the drawing room.'

Anna walked through the hall and immediately heard the young boys, who were making a noise. It got louder as she opened the door. Two of the boys were scrabbling around on the floor and the eldest was pretending to do a speech. He was practically shouting. Polly was sat in a chair look pale and ill.

'Boys! Boys!' said Anna. They were normally polite and quiet in company, but at the present time they were not expecting anyone to come in. They immediately went quiet. Anna said, 'There is too much noise. Can you not see your poor mother is not well.'

They turned and looked at their mother, 'Sorry, mother.'

Polly looked very tired, but said, 'Miss Seward, how good of you to call.'

Anna decided that she needed to do something to help Polly, so she turned to Mary and said, 'Now, Miss Parker, I am sure these boys must have some lessons to do.'

'They have, Miss Seward.'

'Then we will let Mrs Darwin go and lie down in the other room in some peace and quiet.' She turned to face the boys who were now all standing quietly next each other. 'The boys will start their learning now, do you understand me.' She looked at each of them in turn.

'Yes, Miss Seward.'

'I'm going to settle your mother, but I shall be back.'

Anna helped Polly into the next room, and made her comfortable. She then returned to check on the lessons. It wasn't long before she was sat on a chair next to Polly.

'They are all working well.'

Polly sighed, 'Mary is so young to try and control the boys, and I am very tired.'

'I shall leave you to rest, Polly.'

'No, please don't go.'

Anna made herself comfortable, 'It is not for me to interfere Polly, but Mary is very young for a governess and she doesn't seem to be able to control the boys.'

'I know, but the doctor says that we must give her time. She is an intelligent young lady and just needs some help in getting started.'

'It must be difficult for you, as you are not feeling very well.'

'The house is so different when he is here. The boys do not even have to be reminded to do their lessons. The problem comes when he is out. But I've made up my mind, that I will speak to him about Mary tonight.'

Anna looked at her friend with concern, but Polly said, 'I already feel a little better without the noise. I have some news that might interest you.' It was said with a smile, and then Polly added, 'It's about Mr Day.'

Anna had to smile, and she replied, 'What is it?'

'Mr Edgeworth and Mr Day were here last night. After they had gone I asked the doctor about Mr Day.'

'What did he say? Is he married?'

'No Anna he is not. But he did admit that he was thinking of taking a wife soon.' Polly smiled at Anna.

'I don't think so, Polly,' she said shaking her head. But the comments of her father about Mr Day had been very different to what she had expected.

'But there is more, and its very interesting. When we talked before we said that Mr Edgeworth must be a rich man, because of his large estate in Ireland.'

'Yes, I remember.'

'Well, Mr Day is a very rich man, and has more wealth than Mr Edgeworth.'

'So where is Mr Day's estate.'

'That what makes it more fascinating. He hasn't got one.'

Anna said, 'It's hard to believe that a man of great wealth would not have an estate.'

'That's what I thought as well, but the doctor said that because he inherited his wealth when he was only one year old, the estate was sold and the money kept for him.'

'Surely he would now want one.'

'He wants an estate and a wife. So what do you think, Anna?'

She replied, 'He will attract a richer lady than me.'

'He told the doctor he has enough money. A lady could become his wife whether she had a fortune or had nothing. It would make no difference to him.'

After a little further talking about the social evening, Anna checked on the boy's lessons, and then walked back to her house. She was thinking about Thomas Day.

There was a polite round of applause. Anna breathed a sigh of relief. While she enjoyed reading her poetry, she still got nervous at having to stand in front of so many people.

'That was excellent, Miss Seward,' said Mr Edgeworth as he approached her. 'Your poetry is first class and I would feel that it deserves a far wider audience than the people in this room.'

'You are very kind, Mr Edgeworth.'

'Let me add my congratulations to Richard's,' said Mr Day as he appeared next to her.

'Everyone is very generous,' said Anna, who tended to get embarrassed quite easily whenever she was praised.

'It is a little warm in here and you are looking a little flushed, Miss Seward,' said Mr Day and then he added, 'May I propose we take a walk in the cool of the evening in the garden, there are many guests already out there.'

Anna nodded her agreement and they walked through to the garden, and met the doctor, who was with Polly.

'Now don't they look a fine pair together,' said the doctor in a loud voice to his wife.

Polly scolded him and said, 'Doctor you will embarrass poor Anna,' but he just grinned at them, which made Anna flush.

He then said much more formally, 'Good evening Thomas and Anna.'

Anna said quietly, 'Good evening doctor. Hello Polly.'

Mr Day then added, 'I see you are in lively form tonight doctor, but I expect all the residences in Lichfield are used to your humour.' Anna wondered whether Mr Day was going to object to the doctors comments, but he said, 'There was a man near the front door enquiring about you. I'm afraid I don't know his name.'

'Thank you, Thomas, I shall go and see him.'

They took their leave of Polly and walked down the garden. Anna didn't know whether to speak what she was thinking, but as Mr Day had been very direct yesterday she said, 'I do not remember a man at the front door.'

He laughed and whispered, 'Of course, there wasn't. I didn't want to offend the doctor, or allow you any further embarrassment. So it was the easiest way to remove the difficult situation. There are no further jokes at your expense and the doctor thinks his humour successful.'

They walked a little and then he said, 'As the doctor greeted us by our first names, would it be appropriate to use them between us when we speak.'

'Of course, Thomas. It will allow for a more relaxed conversation.'

'Anna, I want to say something to you about my poetry.'

'I will listen with enjoyment.'

'Oh no you won't I'm sure.'

'Why not?'

'After hearing your poetry, which I greatly admire, mine is so feeble in comparison. I shall never let it see the light of day.'

Anna replied, 'But you said if you heard my verse, then you would let me read yours.'

'Anna! You are trying to twist my words. I never said that!'

Anna just smiled and said, 'I might have exaggerated a little.'

Thomas laughed, 'Do you know we are going to get along very well. I'm looking forward to staying here for a long period.'

'It will be good for the whole neighbourhood, Thomas,' but Anna's mind was beginning to drift to other possibilities.

'Now as we walk, may I ask you some questions about your poetry?'

'Of course.'

They walked for a long time discussing poetry and Anna was very pleasantly surprised at his extensive knowledge of English writers. Although he had assured her that his education dealt with Greek and Roman classics.

It was a splendid evening and Anna was pleased to see that Mr Edgeworth had invited a number of young people. Some of the girls, who were about fourteen and fifteen, were enjoying themselves by racing across the grass. Anna and Thomas were walking near the edge of the garden. There was no one else around them.

Thomas said quietly to her, 'Anna, may I draw your attention to a very large man, with a shambling gait. He is making strange noises and I believe he is coming in this direction. Shall I go forward and deflect him.'

'No, he is coming to see me.'

'You know him?' he said with surprise in his voice.

'Thomas, be prepared for someone far worst with his wit that Doctor Darwin. This gentleman always manages to embarrass.'

'Well...'

Anna put her hand on his arm. 'Please do not to send him away. He is a very fine and generous man, who I have known all my life. But at times he drives me to distraction.'

He turned and smiled at Anna, 'That is some introduction. Here he comes.'

'Young, Anna, I'm pleased to see you again it has been a long time.'

'I have been in Lichfield, Sam. Whenever you come here you know I always wish to see you.' He gradually sidled up to them.

'Please let me introduce, Mr Thomas Day.'

Sam Johnson bowed, 'Samuel Johnson at your service, sir.'

Anna could see Thomas examining Sam very closely, so she said, 'Mr Day is staying here at Stowe House, with Mr Edgeworth.'

Samuel Johnson looked around, nodded at the house, and mumbled, 'I've been here many times, when different people have lived here.'

She was still aware of Thomas's close concentration on

Samuel. Finally he said, 'Excuse me, sir, but are you The Samuel Johnson?'

Sam lifted his head to look Thomas in the face. 'That sir would imply there is only one Samuel Johnson, but there are many scattered through our fair land, so I am 'A' Samuel Johnson.'

Anna smiled and Thomas laughed, 'Sir, with such precision in the use of language you must be the author of the famous English dictionary.'

Sam bowed his head.

'It is a great honour to meet you, and may I be of any service to you?'

'That is very kind of you, Mr Day. You are looking after the fair Anna, and that is a service you perform for me very well.'

'Did you hear Miss Seward's excellent rendition of her poems earlier?'

A smile crossed Sam's face as he glanced towards Anna, but she spoke first, 'Samuel Johnson, do not say a word. Not one word.'

Sam laughed and said, 'Mr Day, I say to you, what must you think. I get to my venerable age and then I am censored by a wisp of a young lady.'

Anna was relieved when neither of the men decided to mention her poem again. They were soon interrupted by a young girl, who had won the last race across the lawn. She came rushing up and wanted to speak to Sam. She was polite and waited.

'You ran really well, young lady,' said Sam.

'I thought I would come to tell you that I am the fastest of all. I won every race.'

Sam smiled, winked at Anna and Thomas and said, 'You are the fastest in your group, but not the fastest in the garden.'

'Well ladies and gentlemen do not race, so I must be the fastest.'

'But I know of a gentleman, who does race and he is faster than you.'

'Sam, you're teasing me.'

'No, I'm not. I am that gentleman. I do race, and I'm quicker than you.'

The girl laughed, 'Don't be silly, Sam. You can't race.'

Sam turned to Mr Day and said, 'She doesn't think I can race.'

Thomas laughed and said, 'I can see why she might have come to that conclusion.'

'Anna what do you say in my support?'

Anna smiled, 'I shall say absolutely nothing.'

'Very well,' replied Sam, 'Young lady, I shall just have to race you. Come, let's go to the starting line.'

Thomas said, 'Go steady, sir. Take my advice, do not try too hard. Let the young lady win.'

'Definitely not. I would never hear the last of it.'

The young girl skipped around the large bulk of Samuel Johnson as he made his shambling way to the starting line.

Thomas turned to Anna, 'He won't really race her will he?'

Anna smiled back at him, 'Yes, he will.'

The race drew the attention of all those in the garden and it took a little time to clear a good space and to get the two racers to the starting line.

'Well, I'm astounded, he really is going to race.'

The garden went quiet and a young man shouted, 'Go!'

The girl was much quicker at staring and she was getting a long way ahead, but then Sam kicked off his slippers and increased his speed considerably.

'Well, I've never seen anything like it!' said Thomas, 'he has won the race quite easily.'

Anna said, 'He is a remarkable man.'

Thomas turned to her, 'You knew he would race and win, didn't you.'

'Yes,' she replied, 'as long as I've known him he has always been prepared to run. And never take a swimming challenge from him.'

'A swimmer as well.'

'Yes, he learned to swim in the pool outside the front of this house and will swim in the sea, if he visits the coast.'

'He continually astounds me,' said a quiet voice just behind Anna. She recognised the soft Scottish accent and turned immediately, 'Mr Boswell, how wonderful to see you.'

He bowed low, 'It is my pleasure, Miss Seward.'

Anna completed the necessary introductions between Mr Boswell and Mr Day. Richard them came across to them and asked Thomas to come with him as there was someone he wanted to introduce to him. It left Anna and James Boswell walking together in the garden.

'Any more embarrassing moments with our mutual friend?' he asked looking in the direction of Samuel Johnson.

Anna smiled, 'He has always embarrassed me, but I am sure he does the same to many. I do very much value seeing him, he is a wonderful man.'

'Yes, I am honoured to call him a close friend. I come from Scotland, whenever my legal duties permit, to be with him. But such is his knowledge that he can help with a number of legal issues as well.'

'I know that he is a very knowledgeable man, but I didn't know that he was an expert in law, like yourself.'

James said, 'I do believe he is the expert not me. I have never understood why he was not called to the bar. He lives in the poorest of conditions, but will not permit his rich friends to help. If he was a counsel he could earn substantial fees for the advice he offers for free.'

'I doubt there is anyone outside of the church who dedicates so much to others,' said Anna. James nodded, and she smiled broadly and added, 'This conversation while very true in its content would not be permitted if Sam were here, he will never accept praise.'

'You are right Anna.'

They walked through the garden in the gathering twilight, when James said, 'When I decided I was going to meet Sam at Ashbourne and then come here, I was hoping to meet you again.' Anna nodded. 'There are many questions I would like to ask you about Sam one day, but not now. I would much rather talk about you, and the poetry that you like.'

'Sam does not like my poetry.'

'He is extremely critical of a great deal of writing, especially poetry. I can assure you that your name figures in a very prominent list of some of the nation's favourites writers for whom he has little time. But I would like to hear more of your poetry. Your rendition this evening could not have been better.'

'I didn't realise you were there.'

'We only arrived just as it started and I stayed outside so as not to disturb you, but I could hear quite clearly from the hall.' He paused and then added, 'May I hear some more of your poetry and read some of it?'

'There are no more evenings planned at the moment.'

'Then please let me call on you. We could then sit in the garden and you could read while I listen.'

Anna didn't have to hesitate, 'Yes, I would like that, and I would enjoy your company.'

Chapter Twenty

A few days later, Anna was sitting quietly in her room reading after breakfast. She had thought of confiding her thoughts of the past week to Emma, but found that she could not write them down. She couldn't be clear what she felt about Thomas Day and he gave no signs of what he thought about her. Sometimes he seemed very close and friendly. At others times he was another well mannered gentleman, who remained distanced from what was going on around him.

He had walked her into town on two occasions since the social evening at Stowe House, but from her window she had noticed that he was always out walking. It didn't matter what time of day, he walked. As he was a gentleman, he knew the times that ladies liked to take their constitutional walks and he presented himself to see whether he could be of any service.

Anna sighed and decided to engross herself in some poetry. Her friend in the poetic ventures, the doctor, was completely occupied with designing and building models of carriage steering mechanisms and so couldn't make any time for her.

William, the butler, knocked and after being answered came into the room.

'Miss Anna, Mr Edgeworth is downstairs and has asked if he may see you.'

'You do mean Mr Edgeworth, it is not Mr Day is it?'

'Oh, no Miss Anna it is definitely Mr Edgeworth, he gave me his card.' He handed it to her.

'Thank you, William, I will come down, please show him into the drawing room.'

'That is not possible Miss Anna, your father has a number of guests in there.'

Anna looked around the room, normally the only man that came into it was John Savile, but she could think of no reason why she should not receive Mr Edgeworth.

'Very well, please show him to this room.' She glanced at William, but he had been their butler for far too long to even allow the slightest change in face at what he was asked to do.

Anna knew she would be the talk of the servants' quarters this evening, as visiting men were not normally received in her private drawing room. Within minutes William had opened the door and announced Mr Edgeworth.

'This is a surprise, Mr Edgeworth.'

'I do apologise for putting you to inconvenience.'

'There is no problem I can assure you. It is raining and I am sitting here reading so a visit is most timely and welcome.' He was a little reluctant to be seated, but Anna insisted.

Anna said, 'I can tell by your face that an important matter concerns you, Mr Edgeworth.'

He looked at her closely, 'It is, and I do apologise for being so mysterious, but it is also very delicate.'

Anna took a breath, as she had no idea what he wanted.

He relaxed, just a little in his chair and said, 'Thomas very much enjoyed his discussion with you about poetry the other night.' Anna just nodded her head, as she wasn't sure where this conversation was going. 'During the relating of his enjoyment of the evening he let pass that you are on more friendly terms.' Anna drew in another breath, 'and you have permitted him to call you Anna.'

'Yes, it is often much easier in long conversations, Mr Edgeworth.'

'I wonder if I might be afforded the same favour.'

'Of course.'

He said very formally, 'I would appreciate if you would call me Richard.'

Anna nodded because she was intrigued to know what was the purpose of his visit. It certainly wasn't to decide which names to call each other.

'My reason for coming is very delicate, but I hope to be able to resolve a long standing problem in the town. Last night, I was a guest at the Levitt household.'

'Ah, I see,' said Anna very quietly.

'Please do not get me wrong. I have no wish to resurrect old disputes. As I was in the Levitt household, I received a version of what had happened in the past. Mr Levitt confided it to me in confidence and I would stress that I have only heard his side of the dispute. Although, since I have arrived in Lichfield and have known him, he has been a man of the utmost honesty and I do not believe he has attempted to mislead me in any way.'

Anna replied, 'I can assure you Richard, that I hold Mr Levitt in high regard. It was an unfortunate chain of circumstances that led to the division between my father and Mr Levitt. Even after all of these years they still will not be in the same house as each other.'

'Yes, that is what I understood. However, my purpose in being here is not to try to resolve the dispute between the two men.'

Anna was now confused, 'But you must have a reason for raising such a difficult matter.'

He shifted a little uneasily in his chair, but Anna could only sympathise. Richard was a man who was trying to bring about the resolution of a difficult situation. He was new to the town and could easily have avoided involvement in an old dispute. Anna thought him a fine man for becoming involved.

He looked at Anna carefully, and said, 'A consequence of the rift between the two men has meant that two very good friends, yourself and Miss Abigail Levitt have had their lifelong relationship severed.'

Anna said, 'It is very regrettable, as Abigail was a very true and dear friend. But each of us knew that we had to support our fathers, although it has been difficult. So since that time we have been forced to be apart.'

'The social gathering last night at the Levitt house was to announce the forthcoming marriage of Miss Abigail.'

Anna raised her eyebrows, 'As I know little about the Levitt household, I was unaware Abigail was planning to marry.'

'Miss Abigail told me that you would be unlikely to know her future husband as she met him in London and that is where he lives.'

Anna nodded.

'Mr Levitt told me quite clearly that he would not condone the resolution of the dispute with your father unless fulsome apology was forthcoming.'

Anna said in a serious tone, 'It is what I would expect.'

Richard continued, 'However, it saddens Mr Levitt that you would not be able to offer his daughter your good wishes for her wedding.'

'I would not go against my father's wishes and that, of course, would include sending a letter to the Levitt's.'

'Yes, I can understand that. But I have to agree with Mr Levitt. It is unfair to you both as you have been such good friends.'

'It is regrettable, but it must be,' said Anna.

He rubbed his hands together in a thoughtful mood and peered out of the window towards the cathedral. Then he said, 'I greatly admire your resolution. You are a sincere daughter, loyal to your family, but I can tell from your discussion with me that you hold no personal animosity towards the Levitts.'

'I do not, sir. Now I am not sure why you have raised this matter. I am afraid I shall have to ask you to leave the circumstances as they are. Its resurrection by you is causing me some considerable anxiety.'

'Anna, my dear lady, that is the last thing on earth that I would want to do. It is only my greatest respect for you that has led to my involvement.'

Anna nodded, but said, 'I feel that the matter must be concluded between us, although I do appreciate your attempt.'

Richard had a fixed face of concentration and had been shifting in his seat for a little while, which was unlike him. Anna had noticed that like his friend, Thomas Day, he was a very relaxed man. He stood up and went to the window, and peered out over the desk towards the cathedral.

He turned and said, 'As you know I own a very large estate in Ireland. It has many villages, as well as a great many farmers and other workers. As the lord of the manor I often become involved in resolving disputes, and it is one reason why I have been appointed as a local magistrate.'

'I am sure you dispense justice in an honourable manner,' said Anna, who initially had welcomed Richard's presence, but now wished he would leave her in peace and quiet.

Richard seemed to suddenly come to a resolution, the frown

on his face cleared and was replaced by his usual smile. 'I shall see your father, with the express intention of allowing you to meet with Abigail to offer your good wishes for her future. Would that suit you?'

It took Anna by surprise, but she remained calm and unhurried as she said, 'I doubt that my father's view will be changed and therefore I shall give it no further thought.'

She expected him to say that he would leave the dispute untouched, but he said, 'Is your father in?'

'I believe I have heard his guests leaving, so I would expect him to be in his study.'

'Then I shall ask if he will see me.'

Anna would have normally taken him down to her father, but Richard had revived old thoughts and difficulties. She wasn't feeling well disposed to him, so she said, 'I will ring for William, he will show you to my father.'

Richard stood and said, 'Thank you, Anna,' and with that William arrived and took him down to see her father.

Anna sat for sometime in thought. She wondered whether she had been a little harsh on him. He was a kind and generous man, but why did he want to get involved in such a business. She couldn't be sure.

She glanced out of the window and as it was still raining decided to carry on with her poetry. Anna became involved in some of her writing and did not notice the passage of time. Finally she put her books away and looked out through the window. The rain had cleared and the sun was shining brightly. At that point William reappeared to say that her father wanted to see her.

'You wished to see me father?' said Anna as she went into his study.

'Come and sit.' They moved to the chairs on either side of the fire.

'I believe you know the purpose of the visit I have had from Mr Edgeworth.'

'Yes, father. I would assure you that the meeting was not at my instigation.'

'Have a care, sir. Please remember that you are a married man.'

He thought about the matter for a moment and then went and looked out of the window. 'Anna, we have only known each other a short time, but I feel there is a link in thoughts between us. You refer to my marriage.'

'Yes, sir, I do.'

'The customs in Ireland with respect to marriage are even more embedded than in this country. My wife was selected for me by arrangements between my father and another nearby estate. From the age of about ten years old, I knew what would happen.' He paused and sighed, 'I did not choose my wife, and she did not choose me. We are loyal to each other and to our families. But my wife prefers to be in Ireland while I am in England.'

'I think it is time that I left.'

'I shall walk you home.'

'Thank you, but no. It is only a short distance. I would prefer my own thoughts for company.'

Chapter Twenty-One

'You do not look well, Polly. Come take a seat.'

'I have been confined to my bed for several days, but the doctor has treated me. As I was feeling a little flushed, but generally better, I decided to walk along the Close to see you. Would you like to go for a walk?'

'I'm afraid my knee is giving me pain at the moment, but I am happy to sit and talk. How are the boys?'

'Much calmer. Mary has improved considerably. The doctor has talked to her a lot about how to manage them and it seems to be working, which gives me great relief.'

'I am glad,' said Anna.

'How goes it with Mr Day?' said Polly with a smile.

Anna laughed, 'That is the only reason you have come to see me.'

'Well, over the past few months since he has arrived everyone has noticed how you have been out walking with him a lot. At some of the social evenings you are often talking to him.'

'That is because he does not dance.'

Polly said, 'He is a very difficult man to understand. He is unquestionably a gentleman. But I have never known one that dresses as he does and will not dance.'

'It is not only that. He told me he has always refused to learn to dance and sees no reason to change his mind now.'

'But you are getting on with him well?' asked Polly with a quizzical look.

'Yes, he is a fine man and good to talk too. Father likes him as well.'

'I don't think it will be very long, before...'

'Do not tease me so, Polly! He is charming and complimentary, but no more. I'm sure he is not really interested in me. It is just that he has no woman in his life and I have no man, so when we meet we often talk.'

'Exactly...' said Polly with a smile.

Anna walked across the room and looked out into the close as thoughts crowded into her mind. She had only written to Emma this morning about whether he might ask her one day. But she was very uncertain. She gathered her thoughts and turned back to her friend, 'Enough of this speculation, Polly. Let's talk about something else.'

'Very well, no more about Thomas Day, but you have another ardent admirer.'

'Polly!'

'Richard Edgeworth told the doctor last night how much he admires you.'

'I have reminded him on several occasions that he is a married man.'

'The doctor told me that he believes that his affection for you is genuinely held.'

Anna knew she had to change the conversation. 'How is the doctor?'

The question was never answered, because there was a brief knock on the door, it then opened and Honora walked in.

'Honora, my darling,' said Anna struggling to get to her feet with her bad knee. 'You are much earlier than expected.'

'Yes, we left really early this morning. Good day, Mrs Darwin.'

'Hello, Honora. Let me look at you.' Honora smiled graciously at Polly, who added, 'You really are a very fine young woman now and without doubt one of the prettiest in the county of Staffordshire.'

Honora blushed a little and said, 'You are very kind. Forgive me for entering during your conversation, but I have been away for many months, and I have missed Anna.'

'You look very well,' said Anna, who was surprised how bright Honora looked. Some of her paleness had changed to a more healthy complexion.

'I have been running around with the young children, where I was staying, and I think it has been good for me.'

It wasn't long before Polly took her leave. Anna said, 'Honora come and sit. Tell me all about your trip and your sisters.'

'Willingly, it was such fun...'

A knock was followed by the door opening, 'Yes, William what is it?'

'Mr Edgeworth and Mr Day are downstairs, Miss Anna, and would like to speak to you.'

'We will have to wait for our talk, Honora.'

'Yes, of course, I will return after they have gone.'

'No, please stay. I am sure they are only offering their services for a walk. I cannot manage the stairs well, so please bring them up, William.'

As they arrived Anna said, 'Good morning Richard, Thomas.' She noticed the sudden glance from Honora, who had noticed the use of first names.

Both of the men greeted Anna by name.

Anna said, 'Honora you have briefly met Richard Edgeworth before.' She curtsied and agreed they had met in the cathedral. 'This is Mr Thomas Day.'

'I'm pleased to meet you sir,'

Anna noticed that Thomas seemed transfixed by Honora. He remained motionless and did not speak, but just looked at the young woman. His face showed kindness, but he only had eyes for Honora. The delay in his response was so noticeable that Richard said, 'Are you alright, Thomas?'

This caused him to recover himself quickly and he replied, 'My apologies ladies. Honora, it is a pleasure, beyond anything I could have expected, to meet you.'

Honora, who now very regularly received complimentary comments from men, was gracious in her recognition of the attention. But she was keen to move to more normal conversation and she glanced at Anna for assistance.

Anna said, 'Please be seated, gentlemen, Honora has just returned home after many months away.'

Richard said, 'My reason for calling was to give you a very brief report of the wedding of your friend, Abigail.'

'That is kind of you.'

He took his time to describe the groom, the service and he concluded that it was a successful day for all.

'I'm very pleased it went well,' said Anna hoping to move on to another subject. During Richard's account she had been surprised as to how quiet Thomas had been. He certainly didn't look ill, but it was unusual for him to say so little.

While he was no longer staring at Honora, Anna noticed a number of times he took the opportunity to look at her. On one occasion she heard him sigh, and she turned to see that a ray of sunshine had illuminated Honora's face.

On the subject of the marriage Richard finally said, 'Abigail and her husband will live in London. His house is near Wigmore Street and so it suits all parties. They are looking forward to the fashionable scenes in London as both of them particularly like the balls and dancing.'

For the first time Thomas seemed to want to join the conversation. He sat up a little straighter and said, 'It is sad that a married couple look forward so much to fashion and dancing.'

While such a comment was no surprise for Anna it attracted Honora's attention. 'Mr Day, do you think it wrong for a married couple to enjoy such entertainment?'

He said quite vehemently, 'Yes, I do. The first and only enjoyment as far as I am concerned should be themselves and their home. Even to the extent of completely excluding social matters.'

'That is a very unusual view, Mr Day.'

'Miss Sneyd it might not be what many people do, but that does not make it wrong. There are many frivolous attractions in the world and pursuit of them as an end is a folly.' Honora looked carefully at Thomas's clothes, which were as unconventional as usual. A quizzical look came over her face, and Thomas noticed, 'I am sure you have a question for me, but as you are such a refined lady, you would not ask it.' Honora blushed slightly, 'I can assure you I will take no offence whatever it might be, so please ask.'

Honora glanced at Anna, who gave her the slightest nod. 'Are you a very religious man?'

'Ah, I see your meaning, because of my views on the start of a marriage.' He thought for a moment and then added, 'No, Miss Sneyd I am not. I respect the Lord and I regularly attend church, but I am certainly not as devout as, say, Canon Seward.'

Anna felt compelled to ask, 'Would you want to shut your wife away?'

'I think shut away is a little harsh. Withdrawn from society might be a better way of putting it.'

'I'm not sure that I see your meaning, Mr Day,' said Honora. The question surprised Anna as it was so direct, but she was pleased that her pupil and friend had gained so much more confidence in the past months.

'When I marry I would expect my wife and I to retire to our estate. There would be much to do for personal enjoyment such as we do most of the time here, such as reading, writing to friends and either walking or riding. In addition, a large estate has duties to its tenants and villages. I would expect there to be a good number of visits for benevolent reasons, which I would fully endorse.'

'But you would not hold balls or other social gatherings?' asked Anna.

'No, a few friends to visit would be perfectly acceptable, but none of these large gatherings.'

'You are a very unusual man, Thomas,' said Anna.

'Perhaps, but I will hold tightly to my principles of life, come what may.'

Richard interrupted and said, 'Time enough for such laboured discussion. I would at least wish to celebrate Miss Sneyd's return. Please may I propose that tomorrow night, at Stowe House, we have a welcoming party for Honora.'

Honora said, 'I fear it would put you to much inconvenience, but I must sincerely thank you for the thought.'

'My dear Honora, it is no inconvenience to me. It is, in fact, the opposite, as I know I shall have a most delightful evening.'

Honora glanced at Anna, who said, 'Honora you will find Richard very insistent on such matters. Every social event, that I have attended, has been magnificent. So would you like to take up the kind offer?'

'If you are sure, sir, then I'll be very pleased to accept.'

Richard nodded in acknowledgement and added with a smile, 'And despite my friend, we will have dancing.'

Thomas laughed. It was obvious to Anna that while they held divergent views on such matters, they were considerate of each other and had become very close friends.

It wasn't long before they took their leave, which left Anna and Honora together.

'I've missed you so much,' said Honora

Anna stood up and limped across to her younger friend, 'And I have missed you my sweet friend.'

They embraced for a long time, each with a few tears.

Anna said, 'As it has gone noon. All the servants will have gone by now. Mother and father are away for a few days, and so I allowed them the rest of the day off. They have left me a cold platter for dinner.'

'That will be fine,' said Honora, 'I do not need them. The coachman brought in my luggage.'

'It means that we have the remainder of the day to ourselves. You can tell me all about your visit to your sisters.'

Honora smiled and said, 'And you can tell me all about Mr Edgeworth and Mr Day. But I see you are limping badly. You must be in pain.'

'I twisted my knee awkwardly yesterday when I walked around Stowe Pool. Today it is a little painful, but will pass off in a few days.'

'You'll find it eases more quickly if you lie down.'

'Yes it does, but I want to listen to your account.'

Honora replied, 'Then let us do what we did at the hotel in Buxton. You can lie to rest your knee and I shall talk to you.'

Within a few minutes Anna was resting on the bed. Honora came into her room and sat on the bed to say, 'It is so good to be back with you. May I lie with you.'

'Of course.'

Honora laid down next Anna who put her arm around her shoulders and brought her in close. 'I like it next to you like this.'

'And so do I.'

Chapter Twenty-Two

'Richard. Come in. I wasn't expecting you. I thought that you and Thomas must be away from Lichfield, as I have not seen you for at least a week.'

'I apologise for just turning up. But I am on a very unusual mission. I'm not sure how to complete it, so I must ask for your help.'

'Very well, but you are being very mysterious.'

'Shall I start at the beginning? It will be easier.'

'Yes, do,' said Anna as she relaxed back in the chair in her drawing room.

He suddenly spoke with urgency, 'Honora is not here is she?'

'No, she has walked into town, with Mrs Darwin. I'm having more trouble with my knee, so I have not joined them. You said you were going to start at the beginning.'

'A few weeks ago Honora returned from her trip of several months and for the first time met Thomas.'

'Yes, and they have met many times since, in our company and occasionally they have spoken on their own.'

'I'm glad you have noticed that because it will make my task easier.'

'May I presume it is to do with Thomas and Honora.'

'Yes. It was just over a week ago that I noticed that Thomas was becoming more and more agitated. He said he wasn't sleeping. I was concerned for his health and so I tackled him as to what had caused the change in his behaviour and outlook.' Anna sighed as she had guessed what Richard was going to say, 'Finally he told me that he believed that he was in love with Honora.'

Anna closed her eyes. While she did not like the thought of Thomas with Honora, she could see it in his eyes, whenever he looked at her young friend.

'Is that why both of you went away last week?'

Richard nodded, 'I said he needed to think clearly about her. The only way to do that would be at a distance from Lichfield. Then he would not see her at all.' He agreed and we have spent the past week on the Yorkshire coast.

'What was the outcome of those deliberations. Is he going to propose to her?'

'Yes, that is his intention.'

Anna said, 'I'm sure he realises about Mr Sneyd.'

'Yes, Anna, he does. As you probably have realised in many aspects, he is entirely conventional. He would offer his proposal. If Honora accepted him, he would then approach both Canon Seward and Colonel Sneyd.'

Anna said, 'I cannot speak for the Colonel, as I know very little of him, but my father thinks highly of Thomas.'

'I think the Colonel would be very foolish to refuse him. Thomas is a first rate gentleman, and very rich. He currently is seeking a wife before buying an estate. I can assure you he has enough money to buy several estates in different parts of the country. He is a fair and generous man, a wife of his would lack for nothing.'

'I would agree with you, Richard. It is unlikely any man would refuse their daughter to Thomas.' Anna was finding it hard to concentrate as her mind was whirling with the information that she had just been given.

She forced herself to stand and limped to her desk, and removed an item from the drawer, that she did not want. But it allowed her to turn her face away from Richard and to be able to look out of the window. Thomas Day was not going to propose to her. That was now certain, but he was going to take her Honora away from her as well. It was all too much. She had to remain calm and carry on as normal. No one must know what she had been hoping for.

As she turned she could see that Richard was watching her with concern. She took a deep breath and said, 'Has Thomas confided in you when he is likely to make his proposal?'

'Yes, Anna, he has. That brings me to the purpose of my visit.'

'Please go on,' said Anna, hoping she could bring this conversation to a close quickly. She added, 'I am really not sure why you are telling me this.' But as she spoke the reason for Richard's visit became clear. 'You have been sent to ask me to ensure that the right situation may be achieved, so that he can make his proposal under the best of circumstances.'

Richard shook his head, 'If it were only that simple, I would be sure of your support and then it would be easy.'

'You do not look easy about your purpose.'

'No, I am not, but he is a very dear friend. He has some unusual views of society, but I never thought they would impact on me like this.'

'He talked about marriage, when he first met Honora.'

'Yes, I'm glad that you remember. Well, I have spoken to him at length about the matter. He is adamant he will not change his views from those he mentioned in this very room.'

'The withdrawal from general society.'

'Exactly!'

'I believe it would be very difficult for him to propose to a lady and at the same time explain his views.'

'Yes, I'm glad we agree Anna, because that is exactly what I said to him.'

Richard then reached into his jacket and pulled out a large envelope. It was of the highest quality parchment and was elaborately sealed.

'Surely not!' said Anna looking at the envelope.

Richard nodded, 'This is Thomas's proposition of marriage to Honora. It contains a clear view of the way in which he sees married life.'

'Well, I have never heard...' but her voice trailed off.

'I can assure you I did everything that I could to encourage him to do it differently. But the man is transfixed. I am sure you cannot believe it, but as soon as I mention Honora's name, he is incoherent for minutes afterwards.'

'If I spoke to him, would that help. I could put a lady's view to him. No woman would want to receive a proposal through the post, pardoning my phrase as you are delivering.'

'My sentiments exactly, but he is adamant this is the way to do it.'

'I do know that he is very passionate about his beliefs, but I did not know they would extend this far.' They both lapsed into silence as they tried to recover their own thoughts. 'Richard do you know the contents of the letter?'

He nodded, 'Thomas was insistent. Despite my considerable reservations, I have read it. He is an eloquent and concise man so there is no ambiguity. I must admit it was very embarrassing reading the personal aspects of the letter.'

'He has written down his personal thoughts? That is unbelievable.'

'Yes, it is. But please do not misinterpret me. It is one of the most amazing letters I have ever read. It contains many aspects of how he sees his life and there is much that would please any lady in terms of future prospects.'

Anna said, 'I hesitate to ask.'

'As he knows that a dowry is a social necessary he has made clear his view in the letter. He will accept the dowry from Honora's father, but it will be paid into Coutts Bank in London and the only person who would be able to draw on it would be his wife. The arrangement would be entirely confidential, between them and no other person shall know.'

'Why did he not come to deliver the proposal himself?'

'The man is distraught, I've never seen him like this.'

'I don't really see my role in this,' said Anna, who was still suffering from the shock and surprise of it all.

'That was more of my idea,' said Richard. 'You are a wise counsel to Honora. I do not ask what your guidance will be, but I owe it to my friend to see that his proposal is considered in measured terms.'

'It is not for me to advise,' said Anna slowly.

'I agree. Honora has to make the decision herself, but she must have someone to turn to. It would not matter if she could talk to the Canon or her father, unless it was a positive answer, but she must have decided first. So it is you, who she will wish to talk to about it. I have no doubt.'

'I fear you are right,' said Anna who was getting nervous as to the type of advice she could give Honora. Richard sat back in his seat and gave a sigh. Anna guessed that he was relieved about having completed his duty to his friend.

What advice should she give, kept running through her mind.

Why would any woman turn down Thomas Day? It would only be the conditions that he laid down. In any other circumstance the life a wife could expect would be beyond many dreams. He was rich and a kind, generous man.

If she advised Honora to say yes, then Thomas Day would pay herself no more attention. She would also lose her only close friend, Honora.

Whenever Anna's mind was alive with thought she was desperate to have a solitary early morning, when she could put her thoughts in order and write to Emma, but it would not be. It was all going to happen shortly.

They sat in a mutual silence each with their own thoughts. Finally they heard the door and some light footsteps on the stairs. A few moments later there was a gentle knock on the door and Honora entered.

'Good afternoon, Richard.'

'My dear Honora, it is good to see you again.' In Honora's gentle manner she enquired about Thomas and whether they had been away, but her eyes darted between Richard and Anna.

Anna could tell from the expression of Honora's face that she suspected that something had happened, but she said nothing. After her introductory remarks, she waited patiently for either Anna or Richard to speak.

There was a quick glance between Richard and Anna, which Honora clearly noticed. Richard took a deep breath and removed the parchment from his jacket. He had replaced it after showing it to Anna.

He said rather hesitantly, 'Honora I have promised Thomas that I would deliver this directly to your hand.'

Honora looked surprised at the size of the parchment and the elaborate seal that closed it. 'Thank you. What is it?'

Richard continued, 'I cannot deceive you. I have been made aware of the contents, but it is not for me to elaborate on them. I have also shared my knowledge with Anna. All that I ask is that you read it very carefully and take time to consider its contents.'

'If that is what you ask, Richard, then that is what I shall do. Shall I open it now?'

Honora was quite surprised by the vehemence of the same immediate reply from Anna and Richard, 'No!'

'I will wait until I am alone in that case.'

Both of them nodded. Richard took his leave immediately, in a rather hurried way, which again surprised Honora. After he had left she said, 'I will sit down and read the contents.' She went to sit in the chair opposite to Anna, who had her book by her side.

'Honora, I believe for both of us it would be better to take the letter to your room and read it in private.'

'But I have no secrets from you Anna. I know not what it contains, but there is nothing in this world of mine, that you cannot see.'

'You are a wonderful friend, Honora, but please this one time will you do as I ask. I will be here for you after you have read it, but you must make a promise to me.'

'Very well, Anna, but what promise?'

'After you have read it you may want to think for yourself before talking to me. So you must promise to take as long as you need. It might take you several days, before you wish to discuss the contents, and there is a strong chance you will not wish to talk about it even to me.'

'Anna, I will promise I will think very carefully and try to uphold all the teaching you have given me as to how I should conduct myself.'

'Thank you, my darling Honora.'

Anna sat alone in her room. The thought of Honora leaving brought tears to her eyes. She brushed it away. What would Honora decide? A life of luxury on a large estate, or an uncertain future with only a small dowry. Her mind drifted. It was only a few weeks ago that she wondered whether Thomas Day had serious intentions towards her. What would she have done if she had received such a proposal? It would have been an agonisingly difficult decision. At least Honora would have her to confide in, but she would have had no one.

She looked around the room and listened. The room was empty apart from her, and the house was silent. Was this the life she was destined to live when Honora left? A few more tears ran down her cheek. Even if she turned down this proposal, would Thomas relax his requirements? Even if he was refused then there would be others. Honora was a beautiful young woman. There would be no end of rich men willing to take her.

Anna stood up and wiped her eyes. She must be evenly balanced in her views when Honora returned, because she had to support her. Anna took a deep breath, walked to her cabinet and withdrew her writing materials. Emma must know what is going on and Anna's thoughts on the matter.

She had finished the letter to Emma, tied it neatly into the top of the pile and replaced them in the drawer. She stood looking out of the window as the gloom of a wet and rainy day covered the cathedral. How long she had stood there thinking she could not say. She was brought back to the present by the familiar gentle knock on the door.

They did not speak immediately, but Honora walked up to Anna and hugged her. Anna could see that she had been crying. Still Honora did not say one word. After several minutes of hugging she went and sat down in one of the chairs on either side of the fireplace. Anna did not want to be the first to speak, so she smiled gently at her young friend to encourage her to issue her first words.

Honora looked pensive. Neither happy or sad. It was a difficult decision, Anna could see that.

'Anna?'

'Yes, my sweet Honora.'

'I want to talk to you about the letter,' and Honora went to hand it to her.

'No, Honora, that letter is very personal. I know its purpose, and I am willing to help in anyway I can, but I would prefer not to read it. The letter was written in good faith, by a fine gentleman, and it is private between you and him.'

Honora nodded and put the letter back into her lap, and in the quietest possible voice said, 'We have talked before about love, men and marriage.' Anna smiled and encouraged her to go on. 'I remember those conversations very well.'

'And so do I,' replied Anna.

'On both occasions we lay on the bed, and I was in your arms.'

Anna gave a sigh, 'Yes, you were.'

'At such a time, I can tell you my most innermost thoughts. May we go and lie together.'

Anna led the way through to her bedroom and lay on the bed. Honora moved to the edge of the bed and without delay joined Anna who wrapped her arms around her young friend and drew her close. Anna enjoyed the long silence. She felt her friend relax into her arms and body. It was sometime before Honora spoke.

As her face was resting on Anna's shoulder she whispered in the lowest possible voice, 'If I was in love with Thomas then perhaps I would be guided by that. I would then agree to his requests, but without love I cannot tear myself away from society.'

Anna breathed deeply and drew her friend even closer.

Chapter Twenty-Three

'You wanted to see me, father?'

'Yes. I believe Mr Edgeworth and Mr Day have suddenly left Lichfield. I had been hoping to speak to them about a cathedral matter.'

'Yes, Stowe House is now closed up. I spoke to the housekeeper there yesterday and she does not expect them to come back.'

'It was very sudden. Do you know the reason? I know that you have spoken with them a great deal.'

Anna took a slight pause to make sure she chose the correct words. 'I would agree father, it is very sudden. But they didn't confide in me the reason for going.'

'It's a pity, they are two fine men. The city and the cathedral have benefited from their presence.'

Again Anna decided to choose her words carefully, 'Yes, their living in the vicinity has made a great difference in Lichfield. May I presume you have had no communication from them.'

'You are correct, Anna. It is most unusual as both men are punctilious in their correctness. Even in an emergency I would expect at least a brief note, or a message through a servant.'

'May I change the direction of the conversation, father?'

'Yes, I do not think there is anything else to say on the matter. What is it Anna, that you wish to say?'

'Do you not think that Honora looks so much better after her stay with her sisters.'

'Yes, she does. I've noticed that.'

'Well, she has another sister, who lives with a different family. She only received a letter from her today. With your agreement I might suggests she visit her as well.'

'A good idea, Anna, may I leave it to you?'

'Of course, father. Now if you will excuse me, I have a music lesson shortly.'

Just as she left the study so John Savile came in the front door. She looked at him and a pang of worry went through her. He looked pale and drawn. His eyes had lost their brightness and he seemed laboured in his movements.

She said immediately, 'John, let us talk through the music before I play this morning. Please come up to my drawing room.' He looked a little confused, but as he was carrying the music for the lesson, he followed Anna upstairs.

'You are looking worried John,' said Anna.

'I have a concert tomorrow in the cathedral and I get very nervous. Also there have been many difficulties recently, which is why I could not come to your lesson yesterday.'

'I did wonder why you wished to postpone, John, but as I was busy, I did not mind.'

'You are very tolerant of my unreliable attendance on you for your lessons, and I do appreciate it. But there are some matters, which are better not to talk about.'

'John you are making yourself ill. I can see the difficulties etched on your face. We have been good friends for a long time. I think that it is time for us to share a little more of each other's burdens between us.'

'I would find it difficult to talk openly with you.'

'That is why we have come here. Honora is away for the day. My father will go back to the cathedral soon because he is taking the next service. We enjoy each other's company and we do need to talk.'

Anna could tell that he was not assured by her words, but she was intent on helping John. She put her hand on a small case that was next to her on the seat. It contained her writing materials. She would write to Emma, and tell her all about John and what an excellent man he was.

'You need to unburden yourself. We are friends, you could talk to me.'

'It's is very difficult Anna, I do not want to be disloyal.'

'Telling me the problems that are the cause of your distress does not make you disloyal. I suspect that your difficulties arise because of a woman. Am I correct?'

John only nodded after nervously glancing around.

'I implore you to tell me John. I am a woman and might be

able to make some suggestions to help you relieve your distress.'

He sighed deeply, 'I am sure you may have already guessed Anna, but I married a very vulgar woman. It is a great shame to me that she has turned to drink. I am totally embarrassed about the language she uses at the top of her voice. What the other vicars, who live nearby, must think I do not know. I just try to avoid speaking to them.'

'It is much as I would have guessed John. It will go no further than me. It is not being disloyal.'

He just shook his head and whispered, 'I'm afraid it is.'

'Is she the same woman, in mind, attitude and spirit that you married?' Again he shook his head. 'We therefore need to get her help, to return her to her former self. It is not about being disloyal, it is about asking for help for someone, who cannot or will not ask for themselves.'

'You are very kind, Anna, but I fear nothing can be done.'

'Have you asked Doctor Darwin to speak to her?'

'No, she was ill last year and he paid a visit then to treat her, but she is certainly not ill at the moment.'

'The doctor is very good with people who drink too much.'

'If she knew he was coming, she would remain sober and dress smartly.'

'Do not tell her, just take him home.'

'I don't think, I could,' but he seemed to hesitate.

'If it's a question of his fees, then I will pay him.'

'No, Anna. The doctor is a very kind and generous man. I have never known him to charge any of the vicars. He always says next time, so our feelings are not hurt, but he will never take any money.'

Anna said, 'Yes, he is a very good man to people in need.'

'Do you think he could help to reduce her drinking?' She saw the first spark of hope in his eyes.

'I know that he has done it many times with other husbands and wives. He is practically teetotal himself, and is always trying to steer people away from alcohol. He can be very severe when he talks to women who drink, so you must just leave it to him.'

'Thank you, Anna, it is a very good idea. I will see the doctor after the concert, but I feel much easier now, that I have a way forward.'

But Anna was not convinced, that he would go through with it. 'You are a very good man, John, and do not deserve harsh people in your life.'

Anna was pleased that John had relaxed and the lesson was easy and enjoyable. She was now back in her room and her writing materials were in front of her. She wrote a few quick notes for the post to carry, and then settled with a blank sheet of paper to write to Emma.

Dear Emma

Many men are strong and heroic, and they are fine men, but be aware there are a small group of men, who are gentle and kind. It is not the fighting and spoils of war for them, but tender compassion and care light up their lives. J--- is such man. If circumstances had been different, would he have been the man for me??

She decided not to finish the sentence. As she lay in bed that night her thoughts constantly turned to John. He was a good friend to her and she wanted to help. A gradual plan began to form in her mind.

The more she thought about John, the more she realised that he would not take the matter further. He was a very nervous man. While he thought that Anna's approach would be a good idea, he would be too shy and nervous to explain the problem to the doctor.

The early afternoon concert with John singing could be heard as she left the house. A glance down the length of Cathedral Close gave her the information she wanted. The doctor's coach was there, which meant he was likely to be in. She wanted to speak to Polly as well, so she walked the length of the close. She was welcomed at the door by a very weak looking Polly, who suggested they pick a few herbs in the garden.

'They've both gone,' said Polly emphatically.

'Who? replied Anna causally.

A wide grin came over Polly's face, 'You know very well who I mean. The two men who have been chasing you.'

'That's silly,' said Anna, 'first of all Richard is married, and Thomas was just being a polite gentleman. I know that for certain.'

'You do know something.'

'Only that Stowe House is boarded up and they are not expected back.'

'It's so strange that they went so quickly.'

'Did the doctor know?'

'Only on the evening before. They came to say they would be leaving at first light the following day. The doctor pressed them on the reason for such a swift departure, but they would not yield. I was expecting you to know.'

'They did not even say goodbye to me.'

'Oh dear, that is very mysterious.'

'The last time he spoke to the doctor, Richard did say he would write, but not in the near future. He would probably wait until he had returned to Ireland.'

They talked a little longer and then Anna said she would like to speak to the doctor. Polly took her through to his study.

'My dear Anna, do come in. Have you come for a consultation?'

'No, doctor. It is a discreet visit about someone else.'

'Very well. Sit down and explain.'

'You must see John Savile frequently. I know you often speak with him.'

'I do. He is a good man.'

'Have you noticed anything about him recently?'

'I am beginning to see what you mean. He has looked very nervous and even a little shaky at times, but I do not think he has any physical illness. His skin colour is pale, but stable and there is no cough or redness around the eyes.'

Anna waited for the doctor to fully take in what she had said. He was a very intelligent man and could make many deductions for himself without being told. After a lengthy pause he directly looked at her and gave an almost imperceptible nod of his head.

Anna said, 'Do you know his wife?'

'Only when I treated her...' but his voice trailed off. He was deep in thought for a minute or two. He looked up at Anna for a second time.

'By the way doctor, I was going to ask you how your campaign to make many people drink less is going?'

He smiled, 'An uphill battle I am afraid.' He rose from his chair. 'One small benefit I try to give the vicars of the cathedral is a visit every now and then to check none are ill. With their stipends they know they cannot afford my fees and would refuse the charity. So I like to visit unannounced and then I say there cannot be a fee, because I have not been called out on a consultation.'

'John is singing in the cathedral this afternoon.'

'Is he now.'

Anna took some sheets of music from the small bag she was carrying, 'I could return some music to John.'

'Come on,' he said, 'time to find out if all the vicars are fit and healthy. Otherwise they won't have the energy to listen to one of your father's sermons.' He laughed out loud, as he led Anna through the herb garden and up to the top of the close. He turned into the grass courtyard which was surrounded by small neat cottages, and a larger building that was a dormitory for the novices.

They fulfilled the first part of the visit by walking into the main hall. The novices all greeted the doctor, who they knew well by sight. He checked a couple of them and gave one a recipe for a herb mixture, to bathe some wounds.

He took large strides across the courtyard. Anna struggled to keep up with him, he rapped loudly on the door of John Savile's cottage.

A woman's voice from inside shouted, 'Who the hell's that!' Suddenly the door swung violently back and John's wife swayed slightly as she rested against the door.

Her voice was much quieter, 'John's out, and no one here is ill. Thank you, doctor.' She went to close the door, but the doctor's large bulk had already stepped into the doorway.

He said in a low and severe voice, 'Miss Seward, the Canon's daughter, has come to return some music. Are you not going to be polite and invite us in?'

She had no option, but to walk back into the cottage. She swayed slightly as she walked. Anna wasn't sure what was going to happen next as the woman was looking very aggressive.

The doctor walked straight up to John's wife and peered right into her face. 'Your eyes are bloodshot, and you have bad breath. You will know a herb cure for the eyes, and I can deal with the bad breath.'

Before she could reply he spun round, picked up two bottles that were on the tables and smelt them. 'I will cure the bad breath.' He opened the front door went on to the grass and poured away the contents of the bottles. As he closed the door again he said sharply, 'Where is it?' She looked defiant. 'Where is it, woman?' She still did not move. 'The Bishop throws vicars out of their home if there is excessive drinking.'

'He would never know...'

'He will if I tell him, and I'm seeing him tomorrow, now where is it?'

'Under the stairs.'

The doctor opened the cupboard door. He moved back as strong air swept into the room. He swung his large boot into the cupboard. Anna jumped at the sound of the crashing glass. He kicked several times and created a lot of noise as glass shattered and wood snapped.

Finally he turned round, 'That's solved the bad breath problem. Now clear up the mess. Mrs Savile just remember that today I have not assessed your mental strength.'

'There nothing wrong with my mind,' but it was said with no vehemence.

'If I decide you shouldn't be in society, I only have to sign one piece of paper, and you know where they will put you.'

Before she had a chance to reply, the doctor said, 'I suggest that you forget all about this visit. I'll expect you will be too busy tidying up and making John his meal for when he gets home.'

They walked away from the cottage, 'It was right you came to get me. It will hopefully have saved her life.'

Anna said, 'I don't see what you mean, doctor.'

'Home-made are the worst drinks especially when they are made like that. It would kill her in a few years. Once people go down that route there is often no way of return. But she hasn't gone too far yet. I can tell by her eyes and nose, so there is hope.'

'You are a very good man, doctor,'

He stopped and turned to look at her. Anna always found his face very rugged and lop-sided when she was close by, 'Anna you are a lovely lady and so kind to very many people. I know I tease you about John Savile, but you are just trying to support a man under difficulties. I admire you for it.'

'Thank you, doctor. I was worried about doing the right thing.'

'My dear Anna, you can never do the wrong thing. If you think something should be done, then follow it through.'

'Yes, I am getting a little more confident in my actions.'

He still hadn't move, 'I do appreciate you doing your best to look after Polly. She really values you friendship.'

'She is a wonderful person.'

'One last word before we part.'

'Yes, doctor.'

'I regretfully have to accept that I am much older than you, and I have known you since you were a young girl, but now we are adults with many common views of the world. You are very friendly both with me and Polly, so I think it is time to drop doctor, and to call me Erasmus.'

'Very well, Erasmus, but it does seem very strange on the tongue.'

He chuckled away as he bid her goodbye, and they separated to go to their own houses.

Anna was thoughtful as she approached her house. Should she go and tell John Savile about the visit. She decided it was the doctor who had issued the warning to his wife, so she would not mention it.

With her mind thoughtful about John Savile she walked quietly into her own home. She glanced at William who had his outdoor coat on.

'There you are Miss Anna, I was just coming to find you. This is an urgent letter for you and has been sent this very day from Sheffield by special messenger. He has ridden from town today.'

'Are you looking after him?'

'Yes, Miss Anna. He is in the kitchen now for some broth. He will sleep in the barn with his horse.'

Anna nodded and took the note upstairs to read it with all speed.

She settled quickly at her desk and opened the outer package of the delivery. From it she took an elaborate envelope. She immediately recognised the seal, it was from Richard Edgeworth.

After breaking the wax she opened the letter inside. In many ways she expected it to be a long letter with a possible explanation of why they had left so early. Although she was sure it was due to the refusal of Honora to marry Thomas Day.

To her surprise the letter was short, it only had a few lines. It contained no information apart from an earnest pleading from Richard to meet him away from Lichfield so all could be explained.

In the letter he admonished himself for going away without speaking to her. Then he made another plea to meet him, and mentioned a coaching inn at Wirksworth.

Anna put the letter down. She was undecided. It was a day's journey and would require an overnight stay. What would Richard want to say? He would only explain about his friend, Thomas and why they moved away. It was a very long way to go to hear what she already knew.

The messenger would not leave until early morning. She would decline going to Wirksworth. Perhaps she would think of how to phrase a letter suggesting that she knew of the reasons they left. Or as she was very disappointed with Richard for not making an effort to see her when he had been in the Close with the doctor. She might just send a short note of refusal.

Her deliberations were interrupted by William who said that her father wanted to see her. Anna put down her pen.

'You wanted to see me, father?'

'Yes, my daughter. I was due to leave in the next few days for

Eyam to see to the parish finances, but cathedral business for the bishop will prevent me going. As you now have a very good head for figures and accounts, could you go in my place? You know my curate Peter Cunningham well and he is always helpful. As he was expecting me he has moved out of the Rectory, so you will be comfortable there.'

'Of course, I will set off in the morning. It is a long journey, but I will be in Eyam by nightfall.'

'Thank you, my dear daughter.'

Anna returned to her room and looked at the letter from Richard. She quickly wrote a note to say that she was prevented from meeting him due to business for her father that she must conduct in Eyam. As she sealed the envelope, the reply pleased her, as she had a reason for refusing such a journey just to meet him. Her thoughts drifted and she remembered many of the conversations she had had with him. He was a fine man, there was no doubt about that.

The journey was long and tedious the next day, but she arrived safely in Eyam, and retired to bed early. The following morning Anna was refreshed and just after breakfast prepared to get on with the parish finances. She was going to Peter's cottage and remembered fondly the conversation she'd had with him before. He was a good and worthy man.

As she walked past the church she stopped to greet a number of local people in the busy high street. All attention was suddenly transferred to the noise of horses approaching at a gallop. Normally horses walked slowly through the village.

Anna turned to look at the approaching riders. There were two leading outriders on fine horses. The riders were dressed in an elaborate livery. The noise came from a six horse coach that sped into the village. The road was cleared by all in deference to the expensive coach and the speed at which it was travelling. She looked surprised as it drew to a halt outside the Rectory. One of the footmen was quickly down from the coach to open the door for his master, who stepped out.

'Richard!' said Anna, who was only a few yards away from where the coach had stopped.

'Anna.' He bowed low, 'I have come as fast as I could because, I must speak with you.'

'Very well, let us return to the Rectory.'

As soon as they were in the drawing room Anna said, 'Please explain the urgency and why come in such a rush?'

'I presume you knew that Thomas received a letter from Honora declining his proposal.'

'Yes, she confided in me her intention. I talked to her about Thomas's proposal, but did not offer my opinion one way or the other. She is an intelligent and capable young woman, who made the decision herself.'

'Did you know of the contents of the letter?'

'No, I did not. My only persuasion in the whole matter was my advice to Honora regarding the letter. I implored her to show it to no one. It was a personal letter and should only be read by one person and that was Thomas.'

'Yes I would agree with you.'

'You still have not explained the urgency.'

'On receiving the letter Thomas was near to a state of collapse and I feared for his health.'

'Did he take it that badly?'

'Extremely. So much so that I was forced to take him to Dr Darwin for a consultation.'

'The doctor said that you told him that you were leaving the following morning.'

Richard studied her for a little while, before replying. He refused to take a seat and looked very agitated. He normally was a man of even temper and calmness, but this morning he looked unconformable and distracted.

'The doctor did say he met with you, but gave no more details.'

'I suspect that the doctor was being diplomatic. The only reason we met with him was my concern over Thomas. But it came as a great relief to me when the doctor's view was nervous exhaustion. There was nothing physically wrong with him.'

'Is that why you left the next morning?'

'I had no option. I had to remove Thomas from Lichfield. I suspected that you would probably advise Honora to go away. But that no doubt would not have been immediate, so there was a chance of them meeting. That had to be avoided because I could not be sure of the effect it would have on my friend.'

'Where did you go?'

'To friends just outside Sheffield, who have a large estate. Thomas would be able to ride each day, which would help him recover his normal balance.'

'How is he now?'

'Very thoughtful, but far less agitated.'

'As I knew of Honora's refusal of Thomas's proposal, I made the assumption that is why you left Lichfield in such a rush.'

Even though he had explained about Thomas, Richard had not settled himself. He paced backwards and forwards and then stood looking out of the window. Anna waited and finally he turned, 'I put my friend before you.'

'I am not sure what you mean, Richard.'

'Anna I have already told you on many occasions how much I admire you.' She deliberately made no reaction to his remark. 'In the whole matter of Thomas and Honora your conduct has been so admirable.' He hesitated, and turned away. Anna just waited. 'I suspect that at one time you may have thought that Thomas's attention was focused on you.'

'There were no signs to me. He is a very amiable man and pleasant company, but beyond that he showed no indication.'

'Anna, at least let me say that I thought he had affection for you, and I thought that you returned it to him.'

'Richard!'

'Anna I came to see you and decided to speak my mind. Given what I have just said...'

'Please do not repeat it!'

He nodded, 'In the whole matter you conducted yourself with great dignity and composure. Despite doing everything for others I failed you miserably by just leaving. If there was one person I should have seen before I left, it was you. I am desperately sorry to have let you down.'

'Richard...'

'No Anna please let me finish.'

'I have been distraught in the way that I have treated you. I can now see by your face that you have taken it hard. I can only offer you my most humble apologies.'

'Richard, I declined to come to meet you, not only because of my duties here, but I could make a reasonable guess as to what happened. You have been incredibly loyal to your friend and I cannot fault that.' She paused and considered whether she would say any more, but she was very displeased with him, 'However, you have drawn me into the promotion of the very unfortunate position your friend took in his marriage proposal. I think it ill-judged by Thomas and I do not believe that you come out of it with any credit for not dissuading you friend from such a course of action.'

'I...'

'No, Richard. Let me finish. I see no need for your apology. When you decided to leave Lichfield, you put the needs of your friend above all else. You have just told me the doctor said he was not ill. Therefore it would not have seemed unreasonable to me that even it you did not call on me, you could have sent an immediate note.'

Anna focused on his face, which now looked completely crestfallen. 'I now wish to completely forget about the whole unfortunate incident, and put it to the back of my mind, along with much of the conduct that went on at the time.'

Before Richard could reply, there was a gentle knock on the door.

'Come in,' said Anna sternly

Peter Cunningham, the curate, stepped tentatively in the room and said, 'Miss Seward, please continue with your guest, I will see you later when you are free.'

'Peter, my apologies for not arriving when I said I would, but I have been pressed to talk with this gentleman.' Peter nodded. 'However, as he is now leaving, I shall come with you and we will work on the parish accounts.'

She turned and said, 'Goodbye, Mr Edgeworth.'

Late one evening a week later Anna returned to her home in Lichfield. The house seemed strangely empty to her now that Honora was away again, so she sat in her room reading. Her mother was poorly again, but was sleeping well, so Anna did not need to be with her.

She completed a few letters, but her heart was not in them and so, as she was tired from the trip to Eyam, she went to bed early.

It was the loud rapping on the door that made her jolt from her sleep. She was confused at first, but within seconds had worked out that she was back at home and a maid was knocking on the door.

'Come in,' said Anna as she began to get from her bed. In that moment, she assumed it would be about her mother and she was immediately prepared to go to her.

It wasn't only the maid that came in. 'Mary! What are you doing here in the middle of the night.' Anna could see the tears streaming down Mary's face. 'What's happened, Mary?'

'Come quick, please Miss. It's Mrs Darwin. Please come quick!'

'Yes, of course,' replied Anna, 'give me a few minutes to dress.'

Anna was as quick as she could be. She was met by Mary at the bottom of the stairs, who was holding her large cape ready for her.

They rushed down the length of the close as fast as they could go, and went straight into the house. 'This way, Miss,' said Mary as she went up the stairs. Anna did not wait to remove her cape, but rushed up the stairs. 'In there, Miss,' said Mary, she cried again, and said, 'It's so terrible!'

Anna did not know what she expected to see. The room was lit by several lamps. In the middle of the bed, propped by several pillows, lay a very pale and weak looking Polly. Her eyes were closed and her breathing was very shallow. There were no signs of pain. A movement in the shadow of the lamps caught her attention. The doctor stepped forward.

Before Anna could speak a word, he shook his head, 'She

asked for you. It won't be long, please stay with her.'

'Oh, Erasmus, you poor man.'

He said in a low voice, 'Go to Polly, she wants you.'

He gently kissed his wife on her forehead and said in the same gentle voice, 'Anna is here.'

There was a momentary flicker of her eyes and she smiled at Anna, who kissed her and held her hand. Anna's eyes were on her friend, but she heard the doctor very slowly walk from the room.

Anna continued to hold her friend's hand. Polly had slipped back into sleep. The shallow rapid breathing filled Anna with fear. Anna did not move for nearly an hour. Polly was still sleeping, but suddenly she moved and her hand gripped Anna's

'I'm here for you, Polly.'

For the first time since Anna had arrived, Polly opened her eyes fully. 'Erasmus is such a good man. He has been a wonderful husband to me.'

'Rest, dear Polly.'

A smile came to Polly's face, 'You have been a wonderful friend to me. Will you do me a favour?'

'Of course, Polly, what is it?'

'Look after Erasmus for me.' Before Anna could reply, Polly closed her eyes and her breathing stopped.

Part Three

Chapter Twenty-Four

Anna walked solemnly and slowly to the altar in the Lady Chapel of the cathedral. She knelt in prayer. After a short time she was aware that someone came, kneeled next to her, and began praying. She didn't look around, but the low familiar intonation she recognised immediately. It was her father. She finished her prayer and rose to her feet. Within a few moments he also rose to his feet.

She rarely prayed alone like that, but she knew that her father would never ask, so she said in a gentle voice, 'It is a year to this day that my poor friend Polly died.'

'Ah, yes. I remember now. She was a fine woman, a good wife and kind to the poor. You miss her, don't you?'

'Yes, she was always so lively and friendly. Even when she was ill, she could still manage a smile and a genuine welcome.'

'Is the doctor well?' said her father, 'I have not seen him for some time. He rarely comes in here.'

'Yes, but he is very busy with his patients, who seem to increase in number. I see him quite often when I go visiting.'

'Yes, I am proud of you, helping so many poor women in this town.'

Anna replied, 'I am going to a particularly poor street today. Poverty has a hold there father.'

'Do you need someone to go with you? You could take William or I'm sure one of our vicars would come with you.'

'No, father. I know it gives you concerns that I go on my own now, but people in that neighbourhood treat me well. I am perfectly safe.'

'Yes, I believe you are. The local church speaks highly of you.'

'Father, I am seeing the Swift family today. Lucy has just given birth and I know they have little money.'

'Yes I know of them. There are many in the family, but they are good god-fearing people. Would you like me to send the almoner from the cathedral there?'

'Yes, please father.'

He replied, 'I will arrange it for later today. You may tell them.'

'Thank you, father. Now I shall go and see Lucy.'

Anna walked through Lichfield towards a street of very old small cottages. She had decided that if she could walk around Eyam on her own, then Lichfield was safe provided she was sensible about the time of day. Her father was hesitant, but she had only gradually extended her visits. More often than not she did have someone with her.

She arrived at a small cottage in the middle of a group of five that were packed tightly together. She knocked on the door, while keeping a careful watch about her. It was soon opened by Mrs Swift.

'Oh! Good afternoon, ma'am,' she said as she curtsied and wiped her floury hands on her apron.

'Good afternoon, Mrs Swift, I have come to see Lucy.'

'We're in a bit of mess, what with the new baby.'

'That's not a problem.' The woman led her up the tight narrow stairs of the house. In a very small bedroom only just large enough for a bed Lucy, who looked about nineteen years old, was propped up by the pillows and was feeding the baby.

'Sorry, Miss, I can't get up,' she said.

'Stay there, Lucy,' said Anna. Her mother then said she would be in the kitchen if she was wanted, and left the bedroom. Anna looked around. The area near Lucy and the baby was surprising clean. 'How do you feel Lucy?' she asked as she looked carefully at her.

'Very well. He was only born yesterday. I'm a bit tired, but will get up later.' Anna didn't take much notice as young mothers would get up as soon as they could stand. Otherwise they were a burden on the rest of the house, who had jobs to do. Anna was surprised how well she looked.

'You both look well, Lucy and its good to see it so clean around the baby.'

'Doctor said it had to be like that.'

'Doctor Darwin?'

'Yes, Miss.'

'Has he been here?'

'Yes, Miss. He has been here everyday. It was lucky because he came very early yesterday, examined me and said he would be back later. He came as the little one was coming out.'

'That's good,' said Anna, 'but who's paying him?'

'He said it didn't matter, as I used to work for him.'

'I didn't know that.'

'Yes, Miss. I started in the kitchens just after poor Mrs Darwin died and worked there until I had to stop because of the baby.'

'Now Lucy,' said Anna, but she must have guessed what Anna was going to say, because she looked down and wouldn't make contact with her eyes.

'You are not married are you?'

The reply came very quietly, 'No, Miss. I've been a bad girl. Will you forgive me Miss?'

'Lucy, it's not something within my power. Only God can forgive.'

'Yes, Miss.'

'I am more concerned about what will happen to the baby. Are you going to have to give him away to a foundling home.'

'No, Miss. I'm going to keep him.'

'Your family will not be able to afford another mouth to feed.'

'It's alright, Miss. I've been given a little bit of money to help the baby.'

'I see,' said Anna. She decided that she could do nothing else for Lucy and went to take her leave of Mrs Swift.

'Are you sure Mr Swift will take the baby in?' Anna said to Mrs Swift as she went into the little kitchen.

'Yes, Miss Seward. He says we'll look after him. Look here he comes now.' As she looked he passed the window.

The man walked boldly into his own house. He saw Anna and stopped, whipped of his cap, and nodded, 'Miss Seward.'

Anna said, 'Good afternoon, Mr Swift. Your wife tells me that you are going to keep Lucy's baby.' She watched him carefully as he replied.

'Yes, Miss Seward. Our Lucy has been a bad girl and I told her so, but we'll keep the baby.'

'Thank you, Mr Swift, that's what I wanted to know. I will bid you and your family goodbye.'

'Thank you, Miss,' he said as he nodded and opened the front door for Anna.

His wife's voice boomed from the kitchen, 'Henry Swift, I very much hope you are going to be a gentleman.'

He thought for a moment, then hurriedly said, 'I will walk you back, Miss.'

'That's very kind of you to offer, but I am content to walk on my own.'

He looked offended, 'I'm a working man, Miss, but that doesn't stop me being a gentleman.'

Anna did not want to offend him, 'Then I would be grateful if you would walk me back to my house in Cathedral Close.'

He wouldn't speak much as they walked through the town centre and answered her questions with as few words as possible. But he went away pleased that he had done a good job.

Anna went straight into see her father, and explained about her visit. He listened to her carefully, and said that he would send a note to the almoner not to call.

After he had dispatched it, he looked at his daughter and sighed, which confused Anna, and so she said, 'What is the matter, father? Have I offended you in some way?'

'No, Anna you have done nothing wrong. It is the opposite. You do everything right including the visit you made this afternoon. My concern is that before me now I do not see a young girl anymore, but an intelligent woman who is dealing with the difficulties of the world.'

'I wouldn't want to have it any other way, father.'

'It is not a criticism. With regard to the Swift family I will explain my thoughts, as I have seen this pattern many times.'

Anna nodded, but wasn't sure what her father meant.

'I am afraid that Lucy went with a gentleman and to keep it quiet, that man is making a little money available for the Swift House. That is why they are so keen to keep the baby. Did you ask her about the father?'

'No,' said Anna, 'I thought it would be difficult, but I'm sure

Lucy would not have told.'

'It was probably wise not to ask,' replied her father. 'She was probably in service at a gentleman's house and he took advantage of her. It is a very familiar pattern. So there is no scandal he's prepared to pay the family to look after the child.'

Her mind was whirling at what her father had just said, 'Thank you, father.' She then quickly made her way to her rooms, to think about her father's words. The conclusions that she was coming to made her very uncomfortable. She had no proof, and perhaps the most charitable view would be to give Dr Darwin the benefit of the doubt.

She sat at her desk and looked out at The Three Ladies. Her mind went back to the letter she had written to Emma about the three ladies of the house, herself, Sarah and Honora. It was with sadness, she now reflected there were only two of them, but Sarah would never be forgotten.

It prompted her to write a long and loving letter to Honora. As she came to the end of it, so William arrived to say that Dr Darwin was downstairs and would like to call on her.

He hadn't called in the house for many months. So to call on the day when she had been thinking about him seemed a little unusual to her. But she would not refuse him and told William to bring him up.

'Good evening, my dear Anna.'

'Good evening, Erasmus, and to what do I owe the pleasure of your visit.'

'I've been at the other end of town visiting some of the poor houses. For my last call I stopped to check on Lucy Swift and her baby. She told me you had been in to see her this afternoon.'

'Yes, I do try to visit any new mothers that I hear of in the poorer parts of town.'

'Yes, you are very kind in that respect and the people do tell me how much they appreciate it.'

'Thank you, Erasmus,' said Anna but she wasn't sure what to say next.

'I've been meaning to come and talk to you since last week.'

'Why since last week?" asked Anna who was confused.

'I met with the bishop then. He has not been a well man, but while I was with him, we prayed together for the end of the mourning for dear Polly.'

'Ah, I see,' said Anna, but was very uncertain as to what he was going to say next.

'Anna, you are a very fine woman, who I have known since you were a little girl of nine and moved to Lichfield. We have talked a lot about poetry and we still do.'

'Perhaps, now a little less than we did, because you are so busy.'

'Yes, that is true. But my thoughts do move on as my life must. You are very much the same age as Polly and you know me very well.'

'You are a fine man, Erasmus, you have been a good husband to my dear friend, and a really good father to your three sons.'

'It is early days at the moment, but I didn't know whether you would like to meet a little more often. Come to dinner more and we can talk through some of the poetry.'

Anna's immediate reaction was to say no, because of what she had concluded from this afternoon's visit, but she hesitated. If the afternoon had not happened, she would have willingly said yes. She felt very lonely in the evening and had often hoped that Erasmus would invite her, but he hadn't done so far.

'Yes, I would like that, Erasmus.'

'Good, you have made my day for me, Anna.'

Chapter Twenty-Five

'I find the waters a little tepid here, but the hotel is very pleasant and so is the company,' said Anna as she helped an old lady up some stairs in the Bath Hotel in Matlock.

'Are you here for long?' shouted the lady who was a little deaf.

Anna was never embarrassed at raising her voice to make sure she was heard, 'I think so, I find it pleasant and relaxing. At the moment there is nothing to attract me away.'

'Young woman like you must have plenty of attention.' She had to stop on her way up the stairs to turn and look, 'You are a fine and beautiful lady.'

'Thank you.'

'Don't thank me, there should be a husband. Some lucky man tomorrow will find you. Mark my words.'

Anna smiled and helped the old lady upstairs. She then went on to her own room. Honora was on another extended stay with her youngest sister and so there was no one at home to talk to on a regular basis.

Anna had visited Erasmus several times over the past weeks. He was a delight to be with, for most of the time. However he had a very embarrassing form of sarcastic humour, which she did not like at all. She tried to point this out to him, but he never relented.

So tiring a little of Erasmus's jibes she had decided to come away. Her father didn't wish a trip to Matlock, so she was content to take the waters on her own, because there were always plenty of women to talk to.

The hotel and spa were very enjoyable, but the only difficulty with Matlock were the walks. In Buxton it was easy to walk around the town, but the steep sided Derwent valley was prohibitive. The only footpaths were called Lovers Walks and she wasn't going to go there!

If it was a good day the gardens of the hotel were pleasant and there were a number of natural springs cascading down the hill, which she particularly liked.

Having finished with the spa for the morning, as it was a good day, she decided to take a turn around the gardens. There was normally someone she found to talk to. Several writers liked coming to this resort. She had met a few and exchanged some interesting poetic ideas.

Anna was making her way to the gardens through the main entrance of the hotel, when she suddenly stopped. He wasn't looking in her direction. She was too close to avoid meeting him. As soon as he turned he would see her, and that is exactly what he did. By then they were within talking distance of each other.

She saw first the surprise, and then a total look of horror on his face. She smiled and said, 'Good morning, Mr Day.'

'Oh!,' he quickly recovered himself, 'Good morning, A... Good morning, Miss Seward,' but the shock of the surprise meeting still registered on his face.

They stood facing each other without speaking. Anna quickly resolved that she would not make any opening encounters. He scratched his head in a very uncharacteristic manner and said, 'It really is a delight to see you again, after how long must it be...' Anna did not answer. And he recovered himself like the gentleman he was. 'Sorry, it was such a surprise seeing you here. May I presume you are staying and, if so, may we take tea together this afternoon?'

Anna had intended dismissing him if they had ever met again, but she found it difficult to hold to her own resolution, which she had never told anyone.

'Mr Day we parted under difficult conditions, not of my making. So I wonder whether there is a purpose in wishing to meet or not?'

He smiled for the first time, 'There is a very real purpose. I would very much like to tell you all about my current plans.'

Anna replied, 'Will I want to hear them?'

He became flustered just for a minute and said, 'Whenever we spoke in the past we were very direct with each other. I see no reason to change now, and clearly neither do you. I did not treat you well. Having met you again, I realise how foolish my conduct must have seemed to you.'

'As you say, we spoke directly to each other. From my opinion neither you nor Mr Edgeworth seemed to come out of the situation with any credit.'

'Yes, I can appreciate that.'

'So if you will permit me to ask my question again, about taking tea with you?'

'Of course, I would like to apologise,' said Thomas.

Anna held up her hand and looked him straight in the face, 'I want no apology from you. If any sort of concession to me might have been made, I would have expected to receive some form of deference within a week, or in extenuating circumstances a month. But a year and a half. You either think of me as a half-wit or a non-thinking lady. Mr Day it will not do!'

Anna had to try very hard not to reveal her thoughts. He was horror struck by her comments. But her feelings were tending to amusement at his discomfort, which she knew was wrong but...

He recovered himself, bowed low, and said, 'You are of course quite right. Richard mentioned that some time ago he met you in Eyam. I should have understood your position from his explanation of the meeting to me.'

Anna had resolved for over a year that she would not give in to any advances he made toward her in reparation. But as he stood in front of her she knew her own mind was wavering, because she liked the man. She was getting very annoyed with herself.

His face turned as serious as she had ever seen, but he was forthright, 'Are you refusing to take tea with me?'

Her reply was instant, 'No Mr Day, I am not. I would have thought my sentiments were obvious. If you have something of interest to impart to me, I will willingly listen and talk. If you wish to harp back to the past then I will not take tea with you.'

His face showed recognition of what she was saying, 'I have something very significant to say to you about the future. Nothing about the past, I agree. It's the future that is important, shall we say four o'clock.'

'That would suit me fine,' replied Anna.

He took his leave, but Anna felt a little uncomfortable and exposed. She glimpsed the same old lady that she had helped this morning coming down the stairs and rushed to help her.

'Now, that was interesting my dear,' the old lady said, as with Anna's supporting arm, she walked down the stairs.

Anna's mind was elsewhere so she gave an easy reply, 'What was interesting?'

'You talking to that man. I said you would meet someone.'

'You did, I remember.'

The lady continued, 'He would be a good husband.'

'Why do you say that?' asked Anna.

'Kindly face, never severe. I was watching. I don't know what you said to him, but he didn't like it, but there was no anger in his eyes.'

Anna helped her down the last step and assumed her duties were finished when the woman said, 'His style of dress is unconventional, but you shouldn't hold that against him.'

As the old lady wasn't going away, Anna wanted to transfer the conversation from her, 'Did you marry an unconventional man?'

She laughed loudly, 'No. He was a doctor. Nothing unconventional about him. Good man, heart of the society. I was the second one he married. I gave him ten children. A better life for me couldn't have been possible.'

***

'Thomas Day, that is the most preposterous idea I have ever heard. You cannot do it!' said Anna as the sat with him on the verandah of the hotel in the afternoon sunshine.

'Anna I have very good reasons approaching the matter this way. I believe in my principles.'

'We won't go into that now. I don't agree with some of them, but that is a matter of choice for you. I most strongly disagree when it could affect the lives of two young girls.'

'They will not be damaged by the experience.'

'I do not see how they could avoid being hurt and injured by what you are proposing. I suggest you drop the idea before it even starts.'

Thomas looked around at the other people. He was concerned because Anna's voice was getting louder and louder. He said quietly, 'Anna I have already started.'

The look on Anna's face was incredulous, 'You have selected two girls, who you are going to educate and train. Then you will pick one of them to be your wife.'

'Yes that is exactly correct.'

'How old are these girls?'

'They are now fourteen.'

'Where have they come from?'

'Please do not be concerned about their welfare. I have drawn up a legal document with the foundling home from which they came. At all times when they are with me they have a governess, who acts as a chaperone.'

Anna was very restless in her seat. She had now really wished that she had not started to talk to Thomas. The idea of a man training his future wife seemed against nature to her. Finally she said, 'I'm not sure I want to listen to anymore of your story Thomas. It is against the nature of man and God. I cannot understand what has prompted you to even consider such an evil process.'

He looked indignant, 'It is not evil, Anna. The girls will be well looked after.'

Anna snapped, 'And then one will be discarded like old clothes. No I cannot tolerate this. I thought at first it was just a ridiculous idea that you were having and had not done anything about it. Men do have such ideas from time to time. But it makes me shiver to think that you have picked two girls already.'

'Please hear me out, Anna. I would like your opinion. When we met at Lichfield you had some very clear views of your own about matters. You are an intelligent lady. I have met very few women who are your equal, and that is why I want to share my thoughts with you. And to even ask for your help.'

Another look of astonishment crossed Anna's face, 'I will not help you, or be part of any such scheme, which could injure two innocent girls.'

'You might change you mind if you were to meet the two girls. You could then ask them questions and satisfy yourself against any misgivings you have.'

'Thomas, I was of a mind not to talk to you again in my life after you left Lichfield. I look back on this morning, as very unfortunate, that I did not stay with that resolution. I am here listening to your story about training a wife, and it is making me shiver. I am so frightened for those poor girls.'

'Will you meet them? If for no other reason than to put your mind at rest.'

'I am very uncertain as to whether I am going to stay here and talk to you about the matter. Certainly I shall never see you again. It would give you the impression that I tolerate such behaviour.'

'Please, Anna, meet the girls. You will like them and then you can put your mind at rest.'

'This is our last conversation, Thomas. All the time you contemplate these ridiculous ideas, I want nothing more to do with you.'

He hung his head down. 'It would be so disappointing to lose your friendship after all that we have talked about, but that must be your decision. I'm very concerned that I at least put your mind at ease concerning the girls. May I bring them to you?'

'Thomas, you are not listening to me. This is our last meeting.'

'Yes, you said that, but will you see the girls? I will fetch them immediately.'

Anna suddenly picked up his meaning, and said very hesitantly, 'Where are they?'

'Here in the hotel, of course. They go everywhere with me. I shall also bring down their governess, who is also their chaperone.'

Anna hesitated. She didn't want to be associated with his scheme in any way, but she would feel easier if she could see the girls. If she had any doubts at all, she tried to think quickly what she could do. In her mind she decided she would tell the Bishop at Lichfield. He was a man of influence.

'Please, Anna,' asked Thomas as he saw her hesitating.

'Very well.'

'Thank you Anna, I will go and fetch them.'

Anna felt strangely nervous as she waited for him to return. She did not take her eyes from the door of the hotel. Two girls and a women in her thirties then appeared, with Thomas behind them.

He had been surprisingly quick in fetching them, and had no time to tell them who they would be meeting and what to say. The girls looked about fourteen years old, as Thomas had said. One had dark coloured hair, which was almost black, and the other was a very light blonde. They were pretty, but both in different ways. They walked correctly for young ladies, and as they approached, Anna could see they were wearing the finest clothes.

The woman, who followed the two girls, was tall with a kind face and was also neatly dressed as befitted a woman in the role of a governess. Anna stood to greet them.

Thomas came and stood next to Anna and said, 'This is Lucretia, and this is Sabrina. Miss Jenkins is their governess. Girls, Miss Jenkins, this is Miss Seward, who is a very good friend of mine. She is interested to meet you and would like to talk to you.'

Anna was just going to speak, when Lucretia curtsied, very neatly and said, 'Good afternoon, Miss Seward. It is a pleasure to meet you.' The same was repeated by Sabrina. Anna could see no resentment in the girls faces. They were polite, well mannered and under the constraints of greeting new adults they smiled well. Anna could only conclude that they were two happy girls. Miss Jenkins also curtsied to Anna.

Thomas said, 'I wish to talk to Miss Jenkins for a little time so I would like you, Sabrina and Lucretia to stay and talk to Miss Seward.'

They both replied, 'Yes, Mr Day.'

Anna began to ask some general question to find out how much the girls knew about their situation. The only part that they didn't know was that one of them would be picked as his wife.

'Lucretia, do you enjoy your life travelling around with Mr Day.'

'Oh, yes, Miss Seward, he is very kind to us. When we were in the home we had little clothes and hardly ever went out. Now we have the finest of clothes and we go to lots of places. We are learning to dance and play the piano.'

Anna continued to talk to them for a while, but neither of them showed any signs apart from being happy young girls. Thomas returned and said, 'If Miss Seward has finished talking to you, I shall leave Miss Jenkins with Miss Seward and we will walk down the road to look at the petrifying well.'

Within a few minutes the young girls had walked away with Mr Day and Miss Jenkins was sat with Anna.

Anna said, 'Were you not concerned about taking up such a post under these circumstances?'

'Yes, Miss Seward, but Mr Day took a very long time to explain how the arrangement would work. I came to him with very good references and I wanted to make sure I was not going to be in the position that could affect my future employment.'

'How do you find your position now?'

'It is an excellent job. Mr Day is very kind and generous. He always totally supports me, because as you know, girls will be a little naughty at times. He is a man of honour. The only time Mr Day will be alone with the girls is when he is in public, like now. Otherwise I am always there. I eat at his table and have freedom to go anywhere in his house that I choose.'

'He seems like an ideal employer, Miss Jenkins.'

'Yes, he is Miss Seward.'

Again Anna could find no fault in the arrangement. She took a liking to Miss Jenkins and they spent some time talking about education and Anna explained about Honora's education.

Anna then glanced up and her spirits fell again. Miss Jenkins had noticed her expression and turned to look to see what had caused it and then said, 'Oh, it's Mr Edgeworth, do you know him Miss Seward?'

'Yes, very well,' she said as she rose to her feet to greet him.

'Anna so good to see you again. I see you have met Miss Jenkins. You must now know what Thomas is planning to do.'

'Yes, and I am very uneasy about it, I can assure you.' Miss Jenkins frowned. 'Please do not misinterpret my reactions. You are doing an excellent job, and the girls are clearly very happy and well looked after. My concern is about the principle of the matter.'

'Shall I see if I can put your mind at rest, Anna,' said Richard. With that the governess took her leave to go and find Mr Day and the girls.

'It is a very nice surprise to meet you here, Anna.'

'Richard, I go to spas regularly including this one at Matlock.' He looked a little uneasy at Anna's severity of tone. 'I do not like this idea of Thomas's at all. It is unnatural.'

'It came as a very great shock to me when he said what he intended.' He hesitated and then said, 'Anna you will remember admonishing me for not doing enough to stop Thomas with his method of proposal.' Anna nodded. 'I was very conscious of your words, as he explained his plan. I attempted to be much stronger and even told him that such a scheme would put the friendship between us in jeopardy.'

'But it did not in the end,' she said severely.

'Thomas announced to me one day that he had definitely decided to go forward with the scheme and that he would commence immediately. We argued as we have never done before.'

'What happened?' asked Anna. She could see from his face that he was suffering at the memories.

'We became estranged for nearly nine months. I did not see him and refused to answer his letters.'

'Did you relent in the end.'

'Only partially. You will see when we are together that we are different to how we have been in the past. A mutual friend made every attempt to re-unite us. As we have many friends in common, to avoid Thomas would have been very difficult. I agreed that I would only speak and associate with him again if I was completely satisfied as to the legal basis for what he was doing.'

'Did you ascertain that satisfaction.'

'You know that Thomas is not secretive and is always prepared to have matters in the open. He gave me access to his solicitors and to all the legal papers and correspondence about the girls. He wrote a note that I had full permission to speak to anyone that was involved and that is what I did.'

'Who did you speak to?' asked Anna wondering whether he had been thorough.

'My first stop was the foundling home. I spoke to the woman who ran the home and the chairman of the Board of Trustees. There was no doubt of the integrity of the arrangement.'

Reluctantly Anna nodded, but asked, 'What is the future if he changes his mind and decides not to marry either of them?'

'I know you find this very hard Anna, but everything has been thought through very carefully. If one or either of them is not required by Thomas then he will pay for a full apprenticeship in a good trade for them. In addition he has set aside a good sum to act as a dowry. And Anna, this is for girls who started with nothing. The money has already been given to independent people to look after.'

'Very well I must accept that there is nothing underhand and illegal about the process, but I still do not like the principle of the matter.'

'I can understand that, Anna, and neither do I. My conscience has been wracked by the agonies of deciding about my friendship with Thomas. Now I have been so fortunate to meet you again perhaps I can ask your advice as to what I should do.'

Anna was rather taken aback at the suggestion. 'It is not for me to say.'

'I believe it is. You are one of the most intelligent and sincere women I have ever met. You see matters through different eyes to men, and I certainly could do with your view. Neither of us are content with Thomas's approach to this matter, but if you say to me that I should sever the friendship because of it, then that is what I shall do.'

Anna shivered a little at the thought of such a decision. She looked hard at Richard's face. There were undoubtedly lines of anguish there. She had to admit he wasn't a trivial man, and had always been a man of his word and honour. Was it right for her to break up a friendship that had existed for so many years?

She hesitated for sometime before she said, 'Richard, I cannot make a decision to break a long-standing friendship, only you can do that. The more I think on the matter, the clearer it is to me that Thomas does need a guiding hand to check on his behaviour. Perhaps you are in the position most likely to influence him.'

'Thank you, Anna, as always you are very wise and helpful.'

'I came to this spa for some rest and relaxation, but meeting Thomas and yourself has renewed the old matters in my mind. It has also now added new thoughts about which I am uncomfortable. I think that it would be best to avoid you and Thomas at the moment and as you are staying, I may well return home.'

Richard visibly sighed, 'Will you give me the opportunity to say one last thing before you leave.'

She studied him carefully, but it was a genuine look of concern on his face. 'Very well.'

'Anna you are the only woman, who has ever admonished me so thoroughly. I am thinking about when we met at Eyam.' Anna remembered it very well. 'I cannot think of anyone who I would have accepted that from. When I left there I was furious with you, but as I thought more and more, I realised that you were correct. Again, you are right in your concerns. I will do everything I can so that I do not lose touch with you, so may I return to Lichfield with your blessing?'

'Richard it does not need my blessing for you to return to Lichfield.'

'I know it does not. But the city would not seem the same unless I could meet you under the guise of friendship. This does not mean that I expect to return to our old way. I must earn the right once again to be a friend of yours, because I have let you down in the past. You are a wonderful woman, Anna.'

Anna could not take anymore. She rose from her seat, 'Enough, Richard. Deep down you are a good man. I know that. If you choose to return to Lichfield then I shall be content to receive you. But for now it is goodbye.'

He bowed low, 'Thank you Anna. I shall return to Lichfield at some time, and will look forward to meeting you.'

Chapter Twenty- Six

'Oh! Anna, such news I do not know how to cope with it,' said Honora with tears in her eyes.

A tear trickled down Anna's cheek, 'We knew it would happen one day, it's just that it has come a little earlier than we thought.'

'Why won't he let me stay here with you, Anna?' Anna was fighting back her emotions, but tried to show Honora a calm face.

'It matters not what we say, it is not just you. If it were so then I would feel very aggrieved, but it is all your sisters as well. Your father has now left the army and is to be married. It is right and proper that he wants his family to return to him.'

'But you are my friend, I cannot, and do not want to leave you.'

'It breaks my heart for you to have to leave this house after so long, but your father is right and deep in your heart you know that to be true.'

'Oh Anna!' cried Honora as she embraced Anna and clung to her.

'We are not parting Honora, we will still see each other regularly. When you have become established in your new home with you father and sisters then perhaps you will visit.'

'Of course I will,' she said as she continued to cling on to Anna.

'But for now we must prepare for your departure to your father's home. It should be very exciting for you to be re-united with all your sisters again.'

'Yes, it will be, but my heart lies here with you.'

Anna was finding it very difficult to control herself. Honora was being taken away from her. Mr Sneyd had been to explain. He still had his stern frown and expression, but as the Canon had explained he had been a military man for far too long to change. He doubted whether Mr Sneyd would ever lose the hold that a military career had over him.

There were no complaints or any other reason given to Anna. It was simply that he was leaving the army and setting up a new home.

'You must look at matters differently, Honora. You are a very pretty young woman, who very soon will find a husband. I am sure that one reason your father wants you at home is to begin the process of finding a man for you. If you marry you would leave me and go to your new home.'

'I still think that it is a pity that my father stopped Mr Andre communicating with us. He was such a handsome gentleman.'

Anna tried to lighten the conversation a little, 'There is a lady who lives in London, but visits Buxton Spa often and that is where I met her.'

Honora smiled to encourage Anna to go on.

'She wrote to tell me that she met Mr Andre in London a few months ago. He was in an army uniform and was about to go to America.'

'Perhaps father would have thought more of him if he had been in the army.'

'Perhaps, my dear Honora, but it is time to move on.'

Honora was thoughtful for a little while. 'It was said some time ago that you would get married soon, but that has not happened has it?' They stood close looking at each other.

'No, although either of us might, but there are no men at the moment, are there Honora?'

A smile came over Honora's face.

'Have you got your eye on someone you haven't told me about,' asked Anna in a lighter voice.

'No, I haven't. I was just thinking about you.'

'There is no one for me at the moment.'

'Oh, Anna, how can you say that!' said Honora as she giggled.

'Honora, what do you mean? And stop giggling,' said Anna smiling.

'You know.'

'No, I don't know. Who is supposed to be my man? Who do you think it is?'

'You're teasing me. You'll be married long before me,' said Honora.

'Tell me, who it is and why you think they are the man for me.'

'It's not just me, the whole of Lichfield is expecting it.'

'Don't be so ridiculous,' she laughed, 'come on Honora tell me.'

'Where are you going for dinner tonight?'

Anna's eyes opened wide, 'To Dr Darwin's,'

'Exactly,' said Honora as she kissed her friend on the cheek, skipped towards the door and said, 'Have a good time!'

'Honora!..' but the door closed and Anna could hear Honora singing as she went along the corridor.

Anna sat at her desk for a little while thinking about what Honora had said. At first she laughed to herself, but then she became more serious. Why would Honora think that Erasmus was her man? She had been to his house many times for dinner. On a few occasions he had asked her to be the hostess for a dinner party. He told her that Mary was too young, but he liked to invite both husbands and wives. Therefore, he needed someone who was familiar with the house to make things run smoothly.

She was in a very pensive mood as she walked down the close to the doctor's house. There would be no other guests for dinner. It would just be her. Would she have noticed any little hints in the direction Honora was suggesting? It was difficult for her to judge. She didn't particularly like some of his humour and he teased her a lot. Was there more than it seemed? She didn't know.

Her mind began to race, Honora said the whole of Lichfield was waiting. That was a total exaggeration, but she must have got the idea from somewhere or someone told her. As she approached the door, Polly's last words came back to her, 'Look after Erasmus.'

He was in the hall to greet her with a warm smile, 'Good evening, Anna, you look very beautiful this evening. Shall we go straight through to the dining room?'

Anna was normally very relaxed eating meals with Erasmus. She had been with him so many times and he was good company. They talked for a little while about a new poem that had been in the London Magazine, and she gradually began to relax.

The conversation lulled a little. Erasmus said, 'I need to talk to you, Anna.'

Her stomach turned and she felt a shiver run down her spine. Her voice was quiet as she said, 'Yes, of course, Erasmus.'

'We have known each other for a long time now. I enjoy your company and do appreciate the help that you give Mary and the boys.' Anna only gave the slightest of nods. 'Everything is really good from my point of view, except that you do seem to want to keep your distance from me. You seem to relax, but then your guard goes up and you consider everything you say very carefully. I think at times you seem very uncertain about me.' Anna didn't want to answer, so she delayed.'I've noticed that you are distant tonight. Have I done something to offend you?'

'No, Erasmus, you have not. As usual you have been courteous and excellent company.'

'You come practically every time I ask you, but you seem to make no assumption that you will ever be invited again. I find that is difficult between friends.'

'I would willingly invite you to our house.'

'We both know it is best to keep your father and myself apart from each other, whenever we can. Besides, he and your mother prefer eating in the afternoon, whereas I prefer the evening.' He stood up and walked across the room. He took a deep breath. 'Anna I would have asked you sometime before tonight if I thought I stood a chance of a positive answer, but I can see from your face, it would be negative. And that I do not want.'

To Anna's surprise he stopped spun round quickly and stamped his foot on the ground. 'No, it won't do! I'm sorry Anna it wasn't my intention to go down this line tonight, especially not now.'

He looked impatiently out of the window, but there was nothing to see in the garden as it was long past sunset.

Anna said very gently, 'What has happened Erasmus to make it different tonight?'

'It is not tonight. It will all be clear in a minute. You must be told there is no way around it.'

'I don't understand. You must be more clear in what you are saying.'

'I have not conducted myself well. There have been indiscretions, for which I am not proud. I could try justifying it to myself that I am not a married man, but it is not convincing.'

Anna said, 'It is not for me to judge, Erasmus.'

'I don't mean to be critical of you Anna. But you do judge people by your own very high standards. I'm afraid I am one of many of the human race that falls below them.'

Anna said, 'I find it difficult to talk in abstract terms, Erasmus, but I do not wish to pry. May I suggest the name of Lucy Swift.'

He dropped his head, 'I thought you had found out, did she tell you?'

'No, I worked it out for myself, but I promise I have told no one of my thoughts.'

'You are too good to me, Anna. I know you would never dream of repeating such information.' He continued to look at the floor, 'There is no way I can tell you.' He sighed loudly. 'Will you come with me please, Anna?'

She nodded, didn't speak and followed him, as he led her into the drawing room. 'Please wait here a moment. I will not come back to you, but please Anna don't break our friendship. I beg of you. It will take you time, but please come back to me.'

'Erasmus, I do not...' He put up his hand and walked towards the door.

Anna wondered how long she would have to wait and what was going to happen. But it wasn't long before the door opened and Mary came in. Anna was surprised, for Mary was always dressed in her long flowing skirt with a tight bodice, normally of light blue, which was very common for governesses. But tonight she was dressed very differently. She wore a light chemise that acted as her night clothes.

'Mary!'

'May I come in Miss Seward?'

'Yes, of course,' replied Anna as her mind whirled trying to see the significance of what Erasmus had said.

'I have been asked to come and speak to you. I wanted to anyway, but you are so important in this part of town, I daren't.'

'Oh, Mary, I really am not, I would willingly talk to you if you needed me.'

'I'm alright now, it's all settled and while my family do not like it...'

Anna interrupted her and said, 'Come and sit. Let us talk.' Anna was beginning to guess, but as Mary moved in her thin chemise with the background of one of the candle lights, then the shape of her body was obvious.'

'Four months?' whispered Anna.

Mary nodded.

'I don't need to ask do I. You do not have to say. Erasmus as good as told me.'

'He wanted me to tell you.'

'Yes, I can see that. Even the doctor would find that difficult.'

Anna immediately examined Mary's face, 'You look well.'

'I am very well. The doctor has told me what changes to expect. When they come, I am not alarmed.' Anna wished to say that he is a kind a considerate man, but she could not bring herself to form the words.

Anna said, 'I must ask whether he is looking after you. Is he thinking of your future.'

'Yes, miss, he is.'

'Did he say, you may tell me.'

She nodded, 'He said that I should treat you as a true friend and that there wasn't anything that couldn't be said to you.'

'Tell me then about the future,' said Anna with a very strange feeling inside her.

'I will have the baby in this house and will carry on being the governess. The baby, God bless him, will be brought up in this house. It will not be given to a foundling home.'

Anna tried to show no reaction. To bring an unmarried governess's baby up in the house, regardless of whether it was in the servant's quarters, was unusual. She knew the rumours would start as soon as people saw that Mary was pregnant. But Erasmus was different to many men. He wouldn't care and would always walk with his head high down Market Street.

The only way the rumours would affect him would be his medical practice, but it was so large with so many of the aristocracy that Anna thought he would not worry. He was a rich man, there was no doubt about that.

There was very little that Anna could do now that she knew. She talked to Mary and told her of some women that Anna would introduce to her, who knew what happened. The doctor used them regularly so she should have no worries about that.

Finally Anna said, 'You need to go to bed to rest, Mary. You have three lively boys to deal with tomorrow.'

Mary smiled, 'It is getting easier with them. I do not need the doctor now.'

'That's good. Goodnight Mary.'

'Miss, before you go.'

'Yes, Mary.'

'I have been content that I could tell you all about it. The doctor said I could. Thank you for listening, Miss Seward.' Anna's immediate reaction was one of sorrow for such a wonderful young lady, 'but may I say something that the doctor would not want me to say, but it is what I believe.'

'Yes, of course, Mary, what is it?' Anna steeled herself for another shock of the evening.

'I'm a servant girl. I've done well from a poor family. Sunday is my day of prayer and I know what I have done is wrong. I genuinely do ask for forgiveness.'

Anna said, 'I've no doubt that in your heart you are a good girl, that has been led astray...' She couldn't think of how to finish the sentence.

'It's not that, Miss.'

'What is it then?

'The doctor really likes you. He often talks about you.' Anna went to interrupt, but Mary wasn't finished, 'Please don't take any notice of what has happened with me. I was thinking about it, and many earls and lords have babies not in their marriage.'

'They do,' said Anna not sure where this line of conversation was going.

'If you were thinking of marrying him. He is good man. Please don't let me get in the way. I'd love you to be the new mistress of this house.'

Chapter Twenty-Seven

Anna walked slowly down the stairs at her home and turned into the dining room. Only her father was there.

With a heavy sigh she selected a little breakfast, and sat at the table. Her father was reading the newspaper, and unusually he put it down.

'The house seems empty without Honora,' said her father, 'I know she only left for her new home with her father yesterday, but we shall miss her.'

'We will father. I shall be quite desperate without her. I know we will meet a great deal, but it will not be the same without her close by.'

'Times move on my daughter.'

They lapsed into silence until there was a loud rapping on the front door. Within minutes William entered the dining room, and said, 'Dr Darwin is in the drawing room and has asked to speak to either you sir, or Miss Seward.'

'Very well, show him in here.'

The doctor entered. He looked a little flustered. 'I'm sorry to disturb you, but I have only just returned from a call.'

'Please take breakfast, Doctor,' said Anna's father.

'Thank you, I will.'

After filling his plate and sitting at the table he said, 'I had two reasons for coming. First, I have received a message that might interest both of you, and secondly there is a matter that concerns Anna, that I would like to discuss with you both.'

Anna went a little cold. She had not met with the doctor since that evening when Mary told her the news. She had passed him from her thoughts and had been keen to avoid him for a long time.

The doctor glanced at her, but turned his attention to the Canon.

'I have received a note from Richard Edgeworth, which says that he intends returning to Lichfield for a period.'

The Canon said, 'He went away very quickly last time, but he is a fine man, I have no problem with him returning. He is an asset to the locality.'

The doctor turned to face Anna as he added, 'In the latter part of the note, he says that he had a family tragedy and that his wife had died.'

The Canon was not watching the doctor and said, 'I shall pray for them.'

Anna's face did not change. She suspected the doctor was watching for her reaction. She didn't know whether it would make any difference to her, but quickly resolved to think about it later, long after the doctor had left.

The Canon said, 'You said there was a second matter.'

'Yes, Canon, and it is a little delicate, which is why I have come personally. My sister, who is much older than me, has come from her home to keep house for me, which she will do for as long as I require.'

Both the Canon and Anna nodded.

'My boys' governess is expecting a child in a few months, I am sure you might have seen her around the Close.'

The Canon said, 'She is not married, is she?'

'No,' replied the doctor quickly.

'What is she to do with us?' asked the Canon.

'Anna has been a frequent visitor to my house, and has admirably acted as a hostess for me. So as not to be a further burden to her, my sister can now do that role. However, Mary has enjoyed Anna's company, but now sees her far less. She would like to call on Anna, but in view of her condition, I thought it diplomatic to ask you Canon whether it would be acceptable to you.'

'You are right to ask, doctor. While I do not condone the young girl's behaviour and see no excuse for it. She is away from her family and I would not like to see her slip further into sin. Anna would be a good influence on her and so she may come to this house, if Anna wishes.'

The doctor said, 'Anna?'

'Yes, I would very much adhere to my father's view. Except for this lapse, I have found her a good hard working girl, who reads the bible regularly, so I will receive her.'

'Thank you, both.' The doctor had finished his breakfast and took his leave.

'Unmarried mothers seem to be increasing in numbers,' said the Canon with a sigh.

'Yes, father, but we cannot abandon them.'

'No you are right my child. However difficult it is, we cannot leave them to further evil.'

Anna was about to leave when her father said, 'Please stay a minute Anna. There is something that I have been thinking about and I need to talk to you.'

'Of course father.'

'Over the past few years we have talked many times about your marriage. A lack of suitable local families initially delayed the finding of a husband.' Anna was feeling very nervous that her father had suddenly decided to raise the subject again. 'You are now our only daughter. Myself and Elizabeth have to think of our old age, so I have assumed that you will stay at home, although we have never discussed it.'

'Yes father. That is what I have assumed as well.'

'But there is one thought that keeps entering my head.'

Anna was very uncertain but she said, 'Yes, father.'

He sighed, and said, 'It is the doctor.' Anna could guess where this was leading, but he added, 'He has many characteristics that make him a good man. As you know we are not the best of friends. He has a far too flippant attitude to God and the church, and that concerns me a great deal.'

'I know that you find him difficult father.'

'Putting that aside. He is a leading member of Lichfield society and is now a rich man. You have known him for a considerable number of years and there always appears to me to be a friendship between you.'

'Yes he has been good to me over the years, and for a long time now I have been pleased to call him a friend. Although like you, I do find him with blemishes on his outlook on life.'

'He is looking for wife. I am sure of that. I can find no fault with him in that respect. He has a young family and a busy home to run.'

Anna shivered as she said, 'Are you going to approach him

father about me?'

'It has been in my thoughts, but the circumstances are different to normal. Very much different to normal and so I thought I would seek your opinion. Would you like me to approach him about taking you for his wife?'

'Oh, father, what a question!'

'Yes, I know it is, my daughter, but he will find a wife soon. I have no doubt. So I would need to approach him immediately.'

Anna had to decide, she shivered again, 'No, father I do not want to marry the doctor.'

'Very well, we will say no more about it.'

Anna's mind was whirling and was grateful that her father rose from the table soon afterwards. She needed something to distract her thoughts from the doctor and marriage. She was slightly shaking as she left the house. If she had said 'yes' to her father's question, then she would be waiting to find out whether she was to be Mrs Darwin.

She knew she was right in saying no, but would that be the end of it? Both her father and the doctor were persistent men. She feared they might talk together and then both try to persuade her to the opposite decision she had just made. Her only hope was that they normally liked to avoid each other, but she knew both would seek the other out for any good reason.

It was hard to forget about thoughts of marriage, but the cathedral would offer her some solace. When in deep thought she did often go to the Lady Chapel to pray. She walked into the cathedral to say a short prayer and then she would go to visit some of the poor families of the town.

As she walked through the cathedral, she glanced into the small St Chad's chapel, which was set on the south side near the choir. A man was kneeling in prayer. Anna immediately went in and quietly knelt down next to him.

After a few minutes she sensed him rise. She finished her prayer and joined him outside, 'Peter, how very good to see you. It is a long way from Eyam.'

'My dear Anna. It is a long way, and not a journey I make

without great necessity, but your father requested I come to Lichfield to meet the bishop. Having now fulfilled their wishes and prayed to St Chad, I will make my way home.'

'Where will you stop? It is a long way to set off at this time of day.'

'Please do not fret about me, dear Anna. There is always a house or inn that will give me alms and perhaps a stable.'

'Did you come in a waggon.'

'Do not concern yourself, Anna. I have achieved my purpose of coming here and I am content to return at Godspeed.' He smiled benevolently at her. He had the manner and speech of an old man, but he was close to her age.

'What has my father said about your travelling?'

'I insisted from the beginning that he was not involved. It is by far the best way. And he has obligingly left such arrangement to me.'

Anna stared at his pock-marked face, which was lop-sided with unruly hair, but his blue eyes sparkled, and his smile was the most benevolent that she had ever seen.

'Will you walk to the door with me, Anna. I do feel a little nervous meeting with you again, but ...'

'Let us walk together, Peter.' His offer of a sanctuary in marriage that he had put to her when they were together in Eyam came back to her mind.

They reached the main door. The weather outside was blowing hard and the rain was beginning to fall. Peter only stopped momentarily. He put on a cape he was carrying and pulled it tight around his cassock, and then turned to take his farewell.

Anna's eyes were sparkling as she said, 'I am going to be distressed and worried this evening, and it will be your fault.'

His blue eyes opened in amazement. He stumbled for his words, 'My dear Anna I would never cause you any concern or worry. Tell me what to do, I would be distraught at such a notion.'

'Peter, you are a very dear friend. I would be concerned for any of my friends if they were preparing to travel in this weather. I would be worried about them in a coach and four with footmen at the ready, but to go on your own with no idea of transport.'

'Please be assured...'

'No, Peter, I will not be assured. And moreover it will not do, because I refuse to accept the situation. My father might. I do not.'

'Dearest Anna, I will speak to William, your butler, I am sure he will not mind me staying in the barn tonight. I would not like to disturb the other vicars in the dormitory as I know it is very full.'

Anna smiled, 'Come on, Peter.' She led the way. He went to take his leave to go to the back door, 'No, Peter, this way.' She led the way in through the front door.

William bowed, 'William, due to the inclement weather the Reverend Cunningham will be staying here this evening.'

With no change in facial expression William replied, 'Yes, Miss Anna. May I seek your guidance as to the most suitable place.'

Peter went to speak, but she held up her hand, 'Is the small bedroom next to the chapel ready for use?'

'It is, Miss Seward.'

'Peter, I believe that will suit you. The chapel is next to your bedroom'

Again he went to speak, but Anna said, 'Father and mother will be out, so we will use the dining room for our evening meal.'

'That was a delicious meal, Anna,' he said as he took the offered seat by the fire in the drawing room, 'You are so kind.'

They had talked about Eyam, the classics and Lichfield over a long meal. Anna enjoyed his company. Despite his appearance he was a very clever man and she discovered that he also wrote poetry. She hadn't enjoyed such an evening for a very long time.

He wasn't a man to relax easily in a large house, but sitting by the fire, Anna detected an increasing amount of unease.

'Something is troubling you, Peter.'

'I recollect the conversation I had with you in Eyam. There is no doubt in my mind I overstepped the mark. I just hope you can forgive me.' He looked relieved that he had spoken.

'You are a sweet dear man, Peter. There is nothing to forgive.

Marriage for me has been in the offing now for several years, but I am quite resolved it will not take place. You will make someone a wonderful husband one day. Neither of us are ready to take any step in that direction at the moment, but for both of us, circumstances will change.'

Chapter Twenty-Eight

Anna knew the last lines of the poem. She looked around at the audience and continued to read in her clear voice
For all the wrongs which innocent I share,
For all I've suffer'd, and for all I dare;
O lead me to that spot, that sacred shore,
Where souls are free, and men oppress no more!

She added, 'Ladies and gentleman that was a poem about the injustice of the slave trade written by Mr Thomas Day. She then closed the little booklet. There was a gentle round of applause in the drawing room of Stowe House.

Her eyes immediately went to the two young ladies, who were the wards of Mr Day. Lucretia looked bored, but was polite and sat still, but Sabrina seemed to enjoy the poem. She smiled at Anna, who went over to them.

'You read that very well, Miss Seward,' said Sabrina as she got to her feet. She then nudged Lucretia, who also stood up. But made no comment and just gave Anna a small smile, that quickly disappeared from her face.

'That was excellent,' said Richard Edgeworth as he approached Anna. 'It was far better read by you than me. You have an exquisite voice for such a poem.'

'Richard, it is the poem that captured people's attention. It is a very impressive piece of writing. The pain and agony of the condition came clearly through in the strength of the writing. That is what touched people's hearts.'

'Why not go into the garden and tell Thomas it was successful.'

'Why he would not read it himself, seems very strange to me,' replied Anna.

'Yes,' said Richard, 'and he would not even listen to it being read, which is why he is sitting in the garden.'

'He has talent as a poet. In many other aspects of his life he is very confident, but not with his poetry.'

Richard said, 'He is a complex character. I will look after my other guests. I do believe that he is hoping you will join him outside.'

As she joined him in the garden he said immediately, 'Thank you Anna. I wish my poem to help the campaign. I do not wish to have criticism or praise.'

It was the first time she had spoken to him since they were at Matlock. He had sent her the poem through the post and asked her to read it at Richard's party. At the time he stated that he did not expect to be there himself.

They walked in silence for a while, and finally he said, 'You were right, of course, about Lucretia and Sabrina. You cannot train a wife.'

'Are you abandoning your plans?'

'Yes, I am making arrangements for them to undertake the apprenticeships I promised. I have already laid down their dowries for when they do eventually marry.'

'It is good that it has gone no further.'

'I am going to seek a wife in a more normal manner.'

'Are you still going to stay with your principles of abandoning society?'

'Yes, I am Anna. It is what I believe. Perhaps I might be a little more flexible in my approach, but it remains the same.'

Anna said, 'I could never agree to marry a man who wishes to lay down such restrictions.'

'Yes, I know. That is very unfortunate.'

'Why do you say that?'

'I think with time we might well have drawn closer to each other. There is much we have in common.'

'But there are too many differences as well, Thomas.'

'I think they would evaporate over years, but it is all speculation, because we have an impasse. I will not abandon my way forward and you would not accept it.'

Anna felt anger and frustration at Thomas, but he still had that something about him, that she liked. She hoped he was not going to stay in Lichfield.

She was relieved when he said, 'I only intend staying a short while in Lichfield, I have decided it is not the place for me.'

Anna took her leave of Thomas and returned to the house with the intention of going home. Meeting Thomas again had unsettled her. She was met by Richard as she entered the house. He was talking to Honora. They both looked very serious.

Anna was feeling a little distracted by Thomas, but tried to be cheery. 'You have been here two weeks now Richard, but I've hardly seen you. Are you settling here permanently.'

Anna thought that he looked strangely nervous, 'No, I will not be staying much longer, it is my intention to return to Ireland.'

She sighed a little at the news, she had been hoping he might be living in Lichfield for some time. Richard did not look like he wanted to continue the conversation so she was just going to take her leave and had picked up her bonnet, when James Boswell appeared. She had seen him earlier, but he had always been in earnest conversation and they had only smiled at each other across the room.

'My dear Anna. Leaving so soon? I'm afraid I was engaged with some from the legal profession and such conversations can take a long time.'

'Yes, I am leaving. I feel a little tired after the reading this evening.'

'Then let me insist on escorting you back to your house.' Anna knew that it wasn't necessary as one of the footmen would walk the short distance with her, but she liked James. 'You are very kind and I would appreciate your attendance as it is now dark.'

'I can summon my carriage, if you prefer.'

'No, to walk will be fine.'

They were soon away from the house. James praised her reading of the poetry and the short conversation that followed focused on an article on verses in the Gentleman Magazine that they had both read.

As they reached the door of the house, so Anna's father arrived home in his coach. The Canon invited him into the drawing room to make the introductions. In responding to the Canon's questions, James was eloquent about his legal career and then about his estate in Scotland.

Finally Anna's father took his leave. James waited until he

had gone and they were alone in the drawing room before he said, 'I greatly regret I must travel home tomorrow at first light, so will take my leave of you now. It is to my great disappointment that I have not had the opportunity of more time spent with you.'

'Yes, I would have liked that,' said Anna. She was aware that he was closely studying her. She smiled, his look was intensive but she felt no reason to concern herself.

'I shall stay in Scotland for the foreseeable future as the legal terms start very soon.'

Anna felt disappointed, as he was a fine and handsome man, but she nodded.

'May I take a little memento to remind me of you.'

'What a strange thing to say James,' but she smiled and added, 'what did you have in mind?'

'I would like a lock of your lovely hair.' Anna went red with embarrassment. 'Poor Anna, making you red is more like our mutual friend. But it is my heart felt thought, so that I can remember you when I am in Scotland. Only a small lock,' he added with a wonderful smile.

Anna surprised herself as she went to her needlework bag, removed her scissors, looked in the mirror and cut a lock of hair.

Chapter Twenty-Nine

Anna was sitting quietly in her drawing room. Her reading concentrated her thoughts until she heard a gentle knock on the door.

'Honora!' she said with delighted surprise as her friend, dressed very elegantly, came into the room. 'It's so wonderful to see you. I've missed you. It has been very busy for you with your father and his family. I understand why you have not been able to come.'

They embraced and held each other tight for several minutes, until Honora stepped back.

'Are you unwell, you look very pale.'

'No, I feel fine, Anna. I want to speak to you.'

'I will listen, as I always will.'

'It is so difficult, but I was the one who had to tell you.' Anna could see it was very trying for her so she smiled encouragement, 'As soon as I have told you I will go, I couldn't cope with you.'

'Honora what is all this about? I don't understand.'

'Richard came back to Lichfield for one reason.'

'Yes,' said Anna warily.

'To propose marriage to me. I have accepted and so has my father. We will soon be married and move to Ireland.'

***

It was noon on the day after Anna's father had married Richard and Honora in the cathedral. They left for Ireland later that day. Anna was sat at her desk, with her writing materials in front of her.

Dear Emma

It is supposed to be the brightest part of the day, but the heavy overcast storm clouds throw a dark shadow over the cathedral. Only one spire now has some light, the second is completely subsumed in darkness. The final one is receding into the dark and will soon be lost...